THE CAPTAIN AND THE CAD

Captain William Perronet was a most honorable gentleman. He was strong, honest, handsome, uncorrupted by the fripperies and follies of fashion, and determined to make Miss Isabelle Holland his bride and to be the best of all possible husbands to her.

Adrian, the Marquess of Sutterton, was quite a different sort. His gambling and womanizing were notorious even in the fastest circles of London. And his dazzling charm and extraordinary good looks could not long mask his naked greed and heartless sensuality.

Clearly there should have been only one right choice for Miss Holland when it came to picking a mate. And just as clearly, she had made the wrong one. What wasn't at all clear, was why . . .

Miss Holland's Betrothal

Miss Holland's Betrothal

by
Norma Lee Clark

A SIGNET BOOK

NEW AMERICAN LIBRARY

NAL BOOKS ARE AVAILABLE AT QUANTITY DISCOUNTS
WHEN USED TO PROMOTE PRODUCTS OR SERVICES.
FOR INFORMATION PLEASE WRITE TO PREMIUM MARKETING DIVISION,
NEW AMERICAN LIBRARY, 1633 BROADWAY,
NEW YORK, NEW YORK 10019.

SIGNET TRADEMARK REG. U.S. PAT. OFF. AND FOREIGN COUNTRIES
REGISTERED TRADEMARK—MARCA REGISTRADA
HECHO EN CHICAGO, U.S.A.

SIGNET, SIGNET CLASSIC, MENTOR, ONYX, PLUME, MERIDIAN AND NAL BOOKS
are published by New American Library,
1633 Broadway, New York, New York 10019

First Printing, August, 1986

1   2   3   4   5   6   7   8   9

PRINTED IN THE UNITED STATES OF AMERICA

One

As he lunged toward her, the girl skipped back and swung herself lithely, skirts and cloak belling, around the corner of the desk and, without pause for thought, picked up the ink pot and flung it straight into his face.

Her sudden movement gave him no time for deflecting the pot or even for thought to do so, and the heavy crystal, brass-trimmed object caught him squarely between the eyes, gouting its contents in a blue-black film down his face before dropping to the carpet and rolling away. Stunned, he back-stepped rapidly and then sat down quite suddenly.

It had all taken no more than two or three seconds in time and the girl was almost as much surprised by the suddenness of her victory as was he by his defeat. Brilliant color flamed her cheeks, and her eyes flashed with indignation and triumph which served to enhance her looks, for her small, neat oval face was usually pale and her gray eyes cool and distancing. She was a pretty girl with a pretty figure, thick, shining ash-blond hair, and delicate features, but maturity would no doubt bring her to greater beauty.

"Is there any way I can be of assistance to you, Miss Holland?"

She started and turned to find the ship's captain in the doorway. Had it been her father she might have flung herself into his arms and indulged in a brief, but restoring, bout of tears. However, she could never do such a thing with a man like Captain Perronet. She therefore pulled herself together and tried to answer calmly despite her rapid pulses and the sorry state of her nerves.

"I believe the situation is now under control, sir. I fear Señor Hernandez must be suffering under some misapprehension regarding me, though it is difficult to correct it when we do not speak a common language."

"*Ai de mi,*" groaned the man on the floor, feeling gingerly around the small knob rising between his eyebrows. He was a stout young man of dark complexion and great, liquid brown eyes. He began rather groggily to climb to his feet and the captain crossed the room to help him up.

"Perhaps you will care to explain to me the reason for this regrettable occurrence," said Captain Perronet sternly to him in Spanish.

At this the man broke into a spate of Spanish, hands waving and eyes rolling expressively. The captain listened without interruption, then turned to translate.

"He says he meant no disrespect. He was only trying to tell you how much he loves you and asking for your hand in marriage."

"My hand! Why the man tried to—tried to—embrace me!"

Eyes lit with amusement, the captain turned to repeat this indignant speech to Señor Hernandez, who again broke into agitated Spanish.

"He says that in his country an embrace between an affianced couple is permitted. He thought when he proposed and you smiled and nodded, you were accepting his offer. He goes to England to open an eating establishment. He is an excellent cook, he says, and though he would expect you to help out in the beginning, he feels sure that within a few years he could set you up as a fine lady with a satin gown and a carriage."

"An eating establishment—help him . . ." Miss Holland said faintly, too astounded to be indignant.

"Yes, and a handsome offer, too. Will you like me to give him your answer now, or would you like some time to think the matter over first?"

She stiffened and glared at him. "I am sure I am happy to know that I have been able to afford you some entertainment to lighten the dreariness of this voyage, Captain Perronet. I myself do not find it in the least amusing, however." She pulled her cloak about her and stalked around the desk and up to Señor Hernandez. "Sir, I did not understand your proposal. I thank you for it, but I cannot accept. I am sorry I threw the ink pot at you and hope I did not hurt you too badly. The captain, I am sure, will translate my words for you."

Without a glance at the captain, she raised her chin haughtily and sailed out of the cabin. Behind her, she heard the captain begin to translate her speech to Señor Hernandez. She hurried up to the deck where she marched determinedly up and down taking deep breaths in case the captain should follow her. Really, the man was beyond bearing, she thought furiously, and if only she had not been so astonished by his impudence in suggesting that she might want to think over such a proposal, she would have been able to give him a much more resounding set-down than she had.

Her father emerged from the companionway and strolled along to meet her. He pulled her arm through his own and said, "You are looking uncommon agitated, my dear. What is wrong?"

"Nothing important, Papa. Let us not speak of it. There, I have forgotten it already."

He smiled and did not persist. He was an elegantly tall, handsome gentleman in his mid-fifties, whose serenity of countenance might have puzzled those who knew of his life and nothing of his character. As the cadet son of a minor baronet, he had had little to look forward to in the way of inheritance, his chance at the title and estates depending on the demise of three robustly healthy older brothers. Naturally, he would have been provided for in some way by his father but for two things: He had refused the army career designated for him and the bride chosen for him as well. His father might have forgiven one, but not both of these denials, and was in a great taking when young Mr. Holland further exacerbated the situation by eloping with the local parson's daughter, a sweetly pretty young woman of extremely shy disposition. When Sir Walter Holland was presented with this *fait accompli*, he sent, through his agent, the sum of a thousand pounds and a message that nothing further could now or in the future be expected from him. Nothing could have better pleased Peregrine Holland. His only natural talent and inclination was for gambling, and he at once booked passage for the Continent and set forth with his young bride to roam the capitals of Europe, a totally contented man.

Their peripatetic life was filled with ups and downs depending upon Mr. Holland's luck at the tables, and there were times when Mrs. Holland was installed in a grand suite in a superior hotel, but more frequently they lived in out-of-the-way lodgings with few amenities. Through it all, Mrs. Holland remained adoring and uncomplaining, even when the birth of a daughter further stretched their funds. When Isabelle was five, poor Mrs. Holland expired with as little trouble to anyone in her dying as she had caused in her living, and thenceforth Mr. Holland and Isabelle traveled on without the comfort so loving a mother and wife had given to their precarious life.

Mr. Holland was by nature amiable and optimistic, but vague regarding the hard facts of existence, so it became Isabelle's duty at an unnaturally early age to take into her own hands such basics as finding lodgings and securing funds from her father's winnings for rent and food, and for dressing and educating herself. As a result, she grew into a highly independent young woman of decided opinions and no backwardness at all about expressing them.

Their presence on Captain Perronet's ship had come about through Isabelle's decision that the time had come to take some steps regarding her own future. It was all very well for her father to diddle along happily from one gaming table to the next, but for a girl just attaining her seventeenth birthday the prospects of reaching the quiet haven of settled respectability seemed dim indeed if she continued in her present mode of existence. Her yearning for a settled life had been built up over years of traveling. She wanted one home and she wanted the walls about her to be her own, as well as every room they enclosed. The furnishings of those rooms would, of course, be of her own choosing and their disposal at her whim. She had had enough of furnished rooms under the jealous eyes of possessive landladies. She wanted to know any footstep that sounded in the corridor and never to fear that stepping out of her room might subject her to an unpleasant encounter, a problem that had become paramount in the last few years. She wanted, in fact, to go to England, her own country, never seen by her, but which held the promise in her mind of all the peace and safety she longed for.

Her decision to speak to her father about it coincided with a particularly long streak of luck for Mr. Holland at the gaming tables of Paris. When the run seemed on the point of changing, she held in her hands the sum in francs equal to seventy-five hundred English pounds and adamantly refused to relinquish any of it for further gambling.

"Oh Papa, please do not go on or you may lose it all again and I do so long for—I want to . . ." She hesitated, uncertain of how to explain what she wanted without hurting her father.

"What is it you want, my dear," he encouraged her indulgently. "Why, you may have it, you know. Of course, you may have just whatever you like."

"May I, Papa? But perhaps you will not like it."

"Well, we can't know until you tell me, can we? Now, what is it, a new gown or some trinket you have set your heart on?"

"Nothing so simple. I want to return to London."

"But why, Belle? You won't like it above half, I'll wager. Dull place, London, 'pon my word it is."

"I will not mind that. I am quite used to dullness."

"How can you say such a thing? Why, you have traveled the world—"

"And done what? I have seen the insides of innumerable drab lodging houses and inns, and had exciting conversations with innumerable landlords and their suspicious wives." Mr. Holland looked so crestfallen at this retort that she relented. "Forgive me, Papa. I should not have said that to you, for you have always been so good to me. But it is not any sort of a life for a girl my age. What is to become of me if we just go on this way? I should like to be settled someplace, a house of my own, and for that I shall need a husband, and I shall not find a husband trailing about after you all over Europe."

"But you are only a child yet. You—"

"I am seventeen, Papa."

"Good lord, can it be so? Well, well, I suppose you are right, but you need not leave the Continent to marry."

"I want a good English husband—like you, dearest Papa. And a good English house. I dream of that house—solid, centuries old, with some bit of garden about it perhaps. Once there, I shall never leave it, even for a London Season. I never will travel anywhere again, except to my nearest neighbor for a dinner party."

All this was said with such a passion of longing that Mr. Holland came to take her hands and press them. "I—I am truly sorry, my dear. I had not realized that our life must appear differently to a young girl than it has done to me. I came from such a house as you described and all I ever longed for was to get away from it. I should have thought—"

"No, no, why should you have done so when you were happy as you were. But I have had a great deal of time for thinking and I have made a plan. With this money we go back to England and I will be presented as a marriageable girl with a dowry of five thousand pounds. The rest of the money we will use to pay our passage, fit ourselves out with new clothes, and set ourselves up in London. If all goes as I hope, I will be married inside a year to a gentleman of enough substance to enable me to return some or all of your money to you. Now, if this does not agree with you, I have an alternative plan. We will divide the money and I will go alone to England and throw myself on the mercy of one of your relatives, find a husband, and we will be quits as far as money is concerned.''

"Certainly not! Do you suggest I could so far forget what is owing my daughter as to allow her to travel unaccompanied and to let her arrive in London before my family as one abandoned by her own father?'' replied Mr. Holland unhesitatingly and somewhat indignantly.

They spent some ten days in shopping and settling their affairs in Paris, then packed their belongings and set off for Le Havre, the nearest port. Once there, Mr. Holland was directed to *The Silver Falcon,* a merchant ship bound via Calais for Dover. Captain Perronet was also the owner of the vessel and was returning from a third highly successful trading venture to the East Indies and Africa, but was not averse to making use of the two empty passenger cabins to add to his fortunes. He at once sized up Mr. Holland for what he was by the extreme pallor of his face, the long, white finicky fingers, and the studied blankness of his expression as they negotiated the price of passage to Dover for two. A gambler, thought Captain Perronet, but a gentleman born for sure. There is no mistaking that fine-boned aristocratic face and the manner of speaking.

He had nodded gravely at Mr. Holland's explanation that he and his daughter were returning to England after an extended tour of the Continent, but privately, and rather cynically, he assumed that the "daughter" was no doubt Mr. Holland's bit o' muslin. He did not change his mind when he saw her ascending the gang plank ahead of Mr. Holland, in a dark blue merino cloak and a red velvet bonnet with several rather too dashing looking white plumes. It was the only article of clothing she had ever purchased by herself and its vivid jauntiness had drawn her like a magnet. Her papa had always picked out her clothes, dressing her in extremely simple gowns of white or the palest colors, and the red bonnet had seemed to embody in itself all her longings for color and sophistication. Mr. Holland had not liked the bonnet, but had not been able to bring himself to deflate her bubbling enthusiasm for it when she had showed him her purchase. He had made sure after that always to accompany her on shopping expeditions to guide her, and felt sure that as her own taste was formed she would see for herself that the bonnet was unsuitable for her years.

Captain Perronet, looking down upon the gaily waving white plumes, felt confirmed in his suspicions, and his mouth turned down at the corners in a sneer.

Isabelle looked up in time to observe his look of contempt and knew at once, as though he had spoken, what he thought her to be. The blood mounted into her face and she stumbled slightly. How dare that horrid old man look at me in such a way, she fumed silently.

Captain Perronet, his complexion darkened by years of exposure to sun and rough weather, was a stern-faced man, with heavy black brows nearly meeting over a strong, hawklike nose. There was nothing soft about his face nor in his expression, and at this distance he did indeed look a much older man than was actually true.

As Isabelle and Mr. Holland stepped onto the deck he moved away from the railing and doffed his hat. "Good day to you, sir, and to you, Miss—ah . . ." He paused, as though waiting for an introduction.

"My daughter, captain," Mr. Holland reminded him hastily.

"Ah, of course," the captain replied, too blandly and without a trace of repentance. "Here, Scroggs," he called to a seaman standing behind him, "show Mr. Holland and his daughter to their quarters. We will be weighing anchor immediately, Mr. Holland."

"Thank you, captain. Come, my dear." Mr. Holland took Isabelle's arm and led her away after Scroggs, glancing uneasily at his daughter and noting the angry patches of color in her cheeks. He had witnessed the captain's sneer and known as well as Isabelle what the man thought. He blamed the bonnet, which he had known was unsuitable. Of course, one could not blame the man for thinking as he had, but he need not have shown it so clearly. Now Isabelle was in a temper and it looked like being a stormy voyage. Mr. Holland sighed. He liked things to be comfortable.

His prediction proved true, for though Isabelle was as sweet and compliant to himself as she always had been, she resolutely snubbed the captain at every meeting. Meals, which were all taken in the captain's small dining room, were stiff and frozen affairs, chilled so thoroughly by Isabelle's coldly withdrawn air that all attempts at conversation on the part of Mr. Holland and the captain withered after a few words. The only other passenger, Señor Hernandez, knew no English so rarely spoke except to exchange a few words with the captain, who spoke Spanish. He showed his admiration clearly for Isabelle, however, by rolling his eyes expressively in her direction from to time and sighing breathily. Though she kept her eyes upon her plate for the most part, when she did happen to look at him he broke into an engagingly gape-toothed grin that she could not prevent herself from returning. He was so clearly harmless, so comically good-natured, she felt it would have been gratuitously uncivil to snub him.

She had no such reservations about the captain, however, returning only monosyllables to any polite remark he addressed to her and never raising her eyes to his face lest he should glimpse the anger she could not conceal. She felt it was beneath her dignity to allow him to know that anything he might think of her was of any importance whatsoever to her, though she still trembled with rage at the memory of his contemptuous look as she boarded his ship and at his pretence that he hadn't known who she was.

Captain Perronet, on his part, had begun to realize that he had been overhasty in his assumptions and that he owed Miss Holland an apology. The words for such a speech, however, simply would not form themselves in his mind. He was not a man accustomed to making apologies, nor, indeed, accustomed to making mistakes for which he must apologize.

He was the son of solid English yeoman stock, people who had farmed their own land prosperously for hundreds of years. His father had hoped to send him to Oxford and make a gentleman of him, but William Perronet had accepted his uncle's invitation to go to sea at the age of seventeen. Uncle Percival, his mother's brother, was the captain of his own trading ship, but had made sure his nephew was shown no favoritism because of their relationship. As a consequence, William had served a rough apprenticeship, learning in the process all there was to know about treacherous waters, unpredictable weather, ships, and the men who sailed them. By the time he had reached one and twenty he was his uncle's second in command, a tall, dark-visaged youth, forged by necessity into a man of firm character and rapid decisions far beyond his years.

When he was four and twenty his uncle had died, leaving him the ship, which he had captained now on three trading voyages over as many years, and though he had carried passengers as a rule, this was his first experience with a lady passenger. In fact, he had had little contact at all with women, other than with his sisters and mother on rare visits home. He had eschewed social calls and parties in the homes of gentle folk at their various ports of call where he might have been exposed to the softening effect of women of breeding. His meetings with the other sorts of women would have to be discounted for they were not meetings where the social graces were observed, or even encouraged.

He was well aware of his social inadequacies, indeed he rather gloried in them, for he had lived too fully and adventurously these past seven years for such fol-de-rols, as he contemptuously called them. But lack of fine manners did not preclude fair-mindedness, and he was aware that in jumping to conclusions about Miss Holland he had behaved in a way that his mother and sisters would have disapproved had they known of it.

His own observations of Isabelle with her father as well as the reports of his crew had shown him the error of his thinking and her steadfast enmity had gradually changed his initial feelings of animosity into a grudging admiration. He recognized backbone and approved of it, but having no inclination for soft words, he had no way of telling her of his change of attitude. His feeble attempts at conversation with her at mealtimes were met invariably with a stony silence or the barest civility. He rarely saw her except at mealtimes with her father and it was unthinkable that he should attempt an apology in front of Mr. Holland, but he could think of no way to contrive an accidental encounter with her where he might be able to mumble out appropriate words to relieve his conscience.

He was given the opportunity one day as the ship beat its way up the coast of France, but he managed it so awkwardly he only made matters worse. He had returned to his cabin for a map from his case and upon leaving had come face to face with Miss Holland in the passageway, caped and bonneted, on her way for a walk on deck. Before he could speak the ship tilted deeply and she fell against him. His arms came up to catch her and he held her for the few seconds it took for the ship to right itself. He then set her gently away.

"Rough seas in patches today, I fear, and you haven't your sea legs yet."

She had blushed furiously, her eyes lowered. "I—I—beg your pardon."

"A pleasure, Miss Holland," he had replied with a smile.

She nodded and, still without looking at him, hurried away. He stared after her in bewilderment. What had he done to offend her now? Should he not have caught her? Though he could hardly be faulted in that since he had not caused the ship to roll, and had he not been in that exact spot at the time she might have injured herself. Should he not have mentioned "legs"? Still, she could hardly expect him to say "sea limbs," could she, no matter how starchily proper she was?

Then she had begged his pardon, her longest speech to him to date, and he had said—was that it? Had she thought he was being impertinent? She had not looked up so she could not have seen his smile, but he supposed it could be heard in his voice and she had thought him to be insinuating something. Oh, lord, women! he groaned. He was not cut out for drawing-room fandangos, and no mistake. Settling his hat more firmly on his head, he stalked off purposefully to his own domain on the bridge, vowing to make no further effort at amends, even for Mr. Holland's sake or that of his own conscience.

After that, they had reached Calais, unloaded and loaded again, and set off on the last leg of their voyage. Sticking to his resolve, he had avoided Miss Holland as much as possible and echoed her own cold nod when they did meet, never vouchsafing so much as a greeting in words. This state of affairs had continued up until this very morning when he had returned to his cabin to find Miss Holland defending her virtue against the advances of the impetuous Señor Hernandez. That situation also, he had handled unwisely, for he had been unable to conceal his amusement, nor had he even tried to do so. Even now he was unable to suppress a chuckle when he remembered the scene, causing his helmsman to turn to him inquiringly. Captain Perronet drew his brows together in a frown. The man turned away hastily.

Ah well, what's the odds, thought the captain. Tomorrow, thank God, we land in Dover and I'll see them no more. She'll sail past me with one of her stiff-necked little nods and I'll raise my cap to her back and that will be an end of it. I'll have no more women on any ship of mine for sure, he swore fervently.

Having given the captain the expected cold nod, Isabelle went unassisted down the ramp at Dover while her father lingered to take his farewell. She breathed a sigh of relief as she felt an oppressive weight lifting from her shoulders at the thought of no longer having the dour, disapproving presence of such a man to spoil her pleasure and excitement at what she knew was the most important step in her life. The beginning of her adventure had not been promising, but that was no longer of any importance now that she had reached England. The real adventure would now begin.

Two

The relative to whom Mr. Holland had applied to further Isabelle's plans was the brother closest to him in age, Sir Walter Holland's third son, Nathaniel Holland, who had married a great heiress. That her fortune was derived from her father's prosperous career as a brewer was sneered at by the female Holland relatives, but the marriage had endeared Nathaniel to his father, who was happy to have one dependent less to provide for out of his own estate.

Mrs. Nathaniel Holland was an attractive, round little woman who had been a fetching girl, but there could be no doubt that she was slightly vulgar. Prosperity had come too late in her life to affect her education, so that she had not attained the enamel of refinement that even brewers' daughters may acquire with the money to pay for it, and that might have made her low birth more acceptable to society. Still, she had a vast fund of good nature and generosity that stood her in good stead with those to whom such things were more important than a high polish, especially when accompanied by a vast fortune and marriage to the son of a baronet of an old established family. One of these was the Countess of Bromley, whose family came from the same village as that of Mrs. Holland. They had not been bosom bows as girls, moving as they had in entirely different circles, but they had been life-long acquaintances. So it happened that when Mrs. Holland had raised her status by marrying Mr. Holland, the countess had condescended to call upon her and in some measure to take

her up, to the astonishment of the countess's friends. Not
that Mrs. Holland was thus embarked on a round of gaiety
in the upper strata of society, but over the years she had
entertained and been entertained by the countess several
times a year and had even on one occasion had the gratifi-
cation of helping the countess in the small matter of a
gambling debt when the countess was unwilling to apply to
her husband for the sum to repay it. Not that he was a
stern man in most things, but he heartily disapproved of
gambling.

When Mrs. Holland read her brother-in-law's letter she
was delighted, for she was generally snubbed by the rest of
her husband's family. She immediately ordered rooms prepared and began to think of whom she could invite to meet
them. Mr. Holland urged her to curb her enthusiasm until
she had at least met the visitors, for she might find she did
not want to present them to her friends.

"Why, Mr. Holland, I am surprised at you. Ain't he
your own brother, and a gentleman bred as surely as
yourself?"

"Well, yes, but still a black sheep. Done nothing but
gamble since he came down from Oxford, eloped with a
parson's daughter, and left the country. Oh, he was a good
enough fellow, as I remember him, but the Lord knows
what he's like now, after the way he's lived. As for the
daughter, raised as she's been, with no mother to guide her
for over ten years, I can hardly think she will be present-
able at all."

"Hard words for your own kinfolk, Mr. Holland," she
rebuked. "I, for one, will welcome the poor things with
open arms."

And so she did, embracing them both enthusiastically
and bestowing many kisses on the elegantly turned-out
Isabelle, whom she declared to be "just as pretty as she
could stare."

Isabelle was more than gratified by this reception and
returned her aunt's embrace fervently before turning to her
uncle's more restrained welcome. She liked them both at
once; a good omen, she felt, for all she hoped would follow.

In the privacy of the connubial chamber that night, Mr. Holland was constrained to admit that his relatives were not so entirely disreputable as he had feared.

"Why, they are fine folk. I wouldn't be ashamed to introduce them to the countess!" Needless to say, no higher accolade could be made on Mrs. Holland's part.

The following morning after breakfast, Mr. Holland took his brother off to his club and his wife took Isabelle into the back drawing room where they settled down for a cozy chat.

"A charming morning gown, my dear. Paris, I feel sure," remarked Mrs. Holland approvingly.

"Yes, ma'am. I had a few things made up there before Papa and I left."

"Very clever of you, for you'll find nothing so elegant here, to my way of thinking, though you spend ever so much. I suppose you will be looking to go about a bit with all them fine feathers?"

"That would certainly be pleasant, Aunt," admitted Isabelle. "Have you a—ah—large acquaintance in London?"

Mrs. Holland laughed heartily. "Bless you child, not so large, to be sure, being as I am, but still I think I can contrive to be of some use to you." She paused and after a moment cleared her throat and said, "You mustn't mind if I'm plain-spoken, my dear, for I mean no harm by it, but I think you must have come home to catch a husband, eh now?"

Isabelle replied to this question with the honesty it deserved. "Yes, I have."

"And very sensible of you it is," said her aunt approvingly. "Being dragged all over them foreign parts is no way to find a respectable husband, and a girl your age has to start thinking of such things. I ain't saying as how it might not be somewhat on the tricky side, but then you've got your looks, though you may have no portion."

"No portion? But I have a dowry of five thousand pounds," declared Isabelle proudly.

Mrs. Nathaniel expressed her astonishment, for it had not occurred to her that after so ramshackle a life as

Isabelle's father had led these many years he could have provided a dowry for his daughter. Though she herself had brought sixty thousand pounds to her marriage, she had been poor too many years to sneeze at five thousand pounds. Besides, the girl had the Holland blood, a quality Mrs. Holland knew the value of very well, and then of course she was such a pretty young thing, and had such nice manners that she would be bound to take very well. Mrs. Holland began to speak of her friends whom she was eager for Isabelle to know, especially Mrs. Doctor Richmond, the doctor's wife, for she had two daughters just about Isabelle's age who would be good company for her, and then there were Mrs. Wilde and Mrs. Thorne.

"Yes, of course I shall be happy to meet your friends, Aunt. I imagine you are all very gay during the Season," she queried hopefully.

"Oh, dearie me, the Season is it?" laughed Mrs. Holland merrily. "I fear we don't think so much about being gay only during the Season, though we do manage to be very jolly on occasion. Mrs. Thorne gave a dinner party only last month and afterward had four couples stand up to dance. She's got this spinster aunt living with her who plays the pianoforte a treat, so Mrs. Thorne always has dancing at her parties."

"Do you attend many balls, Aunt?"

Now Mrs. Holland had never attended a ball in her life, but she was loath to admit it. "Not so many," she equivocated, "but naturally we must see that you get to some. Never you fear, my dear, I've a string to my bow I haven't mentioned as of yet. I speak of the Countess of Bromley."

"The Countess of Bromley," repeated Isabelle, suitably impressed. "Is she a friend of yours?"

"Indeed she is," replied Mrs. Holland proudly, "and has been here to call more than once. We grew up together, you see. At least, we lived in the same village and have known each other since we was girls. She has been very kind to me, indeed she has, and has had me to meet her friends many a time and once to dine. Oh, it was ever so grand, but you'll find there's no side to her at all. Very condescending she is, to be sure."

"I shall certainly look forward to meeting her." avowed Isabelle fervently.

Mrs. Holland at once assured her she would do so and began to plan in her mind how she could suggest to the countess that she help out in this matter of balls for Isabelle. Mrs. Holland had never mentioned the matter of her little loan to the countess and never meant to do so. She didn't feel that she had bought the countess's friendship by the loan, for it had not been required until they had been exchanging calls for over a year; however, she did feel the countess was somewhat in her debt and would be aware enough of it herself to be open to a plea for help in launching Isabelle into society.

Accordingly, several days later when Isabelle was to be taken to the Botanical Gardens by her father, Mrs. Holland donned her newest bonnet and ordered around her carriage. Presently she was deposited on the countess's doorstep and sent in her name. In a moment, she was bid to step upstairs to the drawing room where the countess, Lady Bromley, held out her hand and greeted her guest warmly.

"How kind of you to come today. I was feeling lazy and had meant to spend the day upon a sofa with my book, but I have already wearied of it." Lady Bromley sank back upon the cushions of the sofa. She was Mrs. Holland's age, but wore her years much more gracefully. She had a dark, slender beauty and had spent lavishly on the preservation of it.

"Then I'm glad I came. I've had no time for anything for some days now, what with my niece and her father in the house and all."

"Your niece? I thought you were an only child, Mrs. Holland."

"Oh, so I am. 'Tis Holland's niece, his youngest brother's girl."

"Oh, I see," replied Lady Bromley, carefully not allowing her relief to show, for the Hollands were gentry and one need not be anxious about receiving them.

"I was hoping you would let me introduce her to you."

"Why, I should be delighted," said Lady Bromley graciously. "Let me see, the youngest son. I believe I have heard he has been out of England for many years."

"Oh, dearie me, yes, ever so long. Poor child, to be dragged around like that with no mother neither to see she was proper taken care of an' all. I can't think what the man was thinking about, indeed I can't. Still, she seems to have come out all right, for she could never be mistook for else than quality. I make no doubt she will take very well when she gets around some."

Ah, thought the countess with good-natured amusement, now we are coming to it. I can only hope the girl is not an antidote. "Does she mean to make her come-out this Season then, Mrs. Holland?"

"Yes, lord love us. She means to find a husband, so she does, and who can blame her after the life she's had all these years."

"Very sensible, I am sure. Is she—ah—attractive?"

"Pretty as a picture, your ladyship," replied Mrs. Holland promptly. "Oh, she'll make them sit up and take notice, you may be sure. And she's a tidy bit of dowry to go with the looks as well."

"Has she indeed," said the countess with rather more interest than she had felt before, for she knew what a "tidy bit" Mrs. Holland had brought to her own marriage, close to a hundred thousand pounds one heard. What could the girl have to cause Mrs. Holland to name it a "tidy bit"? Twenty thousand, perhaps? Or even more possibly? She wondered if she could persuade her scapegrace nephew to leave the gaming tables and his horses long enough to engage the interest of this girl. Lord knew, he must marry money. "You must bring her to visit me, dear Mrs. Holland," she said warmly, for of course she must see the girl for herself. Lady Bromley was not the woman to buy a pig in a poke.

"Thank you, Lady Bromley, that I shall, and very kind

it is of you, to be sure. You see, I know so few young men that would be suitable for such a girl as Isabelle, and I don't go to the grand sort of balls where she could meet them and I thought—''

"I understand, my dear Mrs. Holland. We must see what can be done.''

Mrs. Holland went her way well-satisfied with her morning's work. Lady Bromley would not fail her, she knew.

In the meantime, Mrs. Holland's lesser friends lost no time in calling to meet Isabelle, being too overcome by curiosity to wait for a summons. The first to be announced were Mrs. Doctor Richmond and her daughters, Miss Horatia Richmond and Miss Victoria Richmond.

The two girls, dressed in the very latest London fashion, fluttered and chirped enthusiastically, but Mrs. Richmond was inclined to be more upon her dignity. She had been a Miss Terwhitt, of *the* Terwhitts, a family spread over most of England with roots sunk deep in antiquity. Mrs. Richmond was a large, imposing woman of exceedingly plain aspect, who had certainly married beneath her when she became allied to a lowly doctor, but her portion had been sizable, enabling her to live in a style suitable to her blood, which made up for everything, to her mind. Certainly she had no intention of being intimidated by the granddaughter of a comparatively obscure baronet.

For all her stiffness the visit was considered successful and soon the two Misses Richmond were calling every day, declaring they could hardly bear to be parted from their dearest Isabelle.

Their mother, while always cordial, was somewhat less enthusiastic, for her daughters were certainly thrown into the shade when Miss Holland was in their company. Though the Misses Richmond could not be called antidotes, there was no denying that they were on the plain side. They had very early in life recognized this fact themselves and had developed great vivacity as a substitute. They could become enthusiastic on almost any topic a young gentleman should care to broach and would fill awkward conversational pauses with much teasing and rallying of one another on the subject of beaux.

"Ah, I hope you will forgive my sister, Mr. Griggs," Miss Victoria would say to a tongue-tied young man. "I suspect she is pensive because of certain words spoken last night at Mrs. Courtney's dansant by a gentleman who shall be nameless."

Miss Horatia would lower her eyes modestly and attempt a blush before protesting in laughing confusion that her sister had read too much into what amounted to only two dances, after all.

"And supper and a tête-à-tête later in the evening. Oh yes, sister, I saw it all," Miss Victoria would reply, shaking an admonitory finger at Miss Horatia.

The object of the charade, of course, would be to raise a spark of interest in Mr. Grigg's breast toward Miss Horatia, who would return the favor to her sister when an occasion arose.

Though their mother was rather dampening in regard to Isabelle, the girls saw matters somewhat differently. Isabelle, they saw clearly, was sure to attract a great many young men with her beauty, not to speak of the fact that she was an heiress, which made it even more of a certainty. Had not Mrs. Richmond been told by Mrs. Holland and then reported rather sourly to them that the girl must be worth ten thousand at the very least, since Mrs. Holland had revealed it as a "tidy sum" with such evident satisfaction?

The Richmond girls were too intelligent not to be aware by this time, having been "out" for four unsuccessful Seasons, that their own drawing power was not great, and they were determined to be Isabelle's best friends in order to benefit from the horde of young men they anticipated would soon descend upon Mrs. Holland's drawing room. To catch a husband one must be where potential husbands congregate, and such opportunities had been very rare in their experience so far.

Thus, Isabelle found her first days in London filled with engagements, nearly all including the Misses Richmond.

She had never had female friends of her own age, and quite enjoyed it. She did not condemn their single-minded pursuit of a husband apiece, for what else was there for young women to do, and was she not engaged upon the same pursuit herself? Or at least she meant to be when the proper opportunity arose.

Mrs. Holland's other friends, Mrs. Wilde and Mrs. Thorne, were not tardy in calling either, and since all of these people were delighted to have an excuse to entertain, Mr. Holland and Isabelle found themselves dining out on nearly every night that Mrs. Holland herself was not entertaining.

At Mrs. Thorne's the obliging spinster aunt was always easily persuaded to play for the impromptu dancing that inevitably followed Mrs. Thorne's dinner parties. Isabelle was introduced to a great many men, for everyone seemed to have a younger brother, nephew, or protégé in need of a wife with a dowry, and as word of Isabelle's had spread the amount had grown. The dowry drew them, no doubt, but Isabelle herself kept them there. The younger men were for the most part callow and tongue-tied, making their first appearances in society just as Isabelle was doing. The men of five and twenty or more, generally civil servants or lawyers' clerks, while more polished in manner, seemed more dusty in some way to her. She was not drawn to any of them, but was enjoying immensely the novelty of popularity. Also the loving kindness of her aunt had given her a security she had never known. As a result, she sparkled with confidence in herself and felt no need to hide behind the cool exterior she had adopted as a protection over the past few years as she grew from little girl to young woman.

She had succumbed almost at once to Mrs. Holland's motherly cosseting, the first she had experienced since the now only dimly remembered first few years of her life. Her uncle was always kind and courtly to her, but like her papa, more restrained in manner. He carried his brother off nearly every day to White's, where Mr. Peregrine Holland occasionally indulged in a sedate game of whist, refusing all deep play, to Mr. Nathaniel Holland's great relief. He found this brother he had not seen for so many years, and who had come to seem a family black sheep in his mind, still the amiable, sweet-natured brother he had known as a boy. They spoke of their parents, and of the installation of their eldest brother as Sir George Holland of Holland Hall. Sir George had married, Nathaniel Holland said, an heiress very high in the instep and of an appalling plainness, and had become, himself, something more pompous than was pleasing. Their second brother had the living in George's gift and had also married, though not so prosperously, and the two couples lived in one another's pockets, lording it over the neighborhood and producing uncountable nephews and nieces. Nathaniel Holland had had but one son, now at Oxford, of whom he was inordinately fond despite the offhand way he spoke of him.

Mr. Peregrine Holland was enjoying himself much more than he had thought possible when Isabelle had first proposed this return. He had resolved to put gambling behind him until his daughter's objective had safely been reached, and part of his contentment with his present lot was in seeing the happiness in his daughter's face.

"Well, my dear, and how is your quest proceeding?" he asked one evening as they stood before Mrs. Holland's drawing room fire waiting for her dinner guests to arrive.

She laughed lightly. "Not exactly at a gallop, I suppose, Papa, but I am enjoying myself so much I had nearly forgotten my original objective."

"That is as it should be, my love. Believe me, it is much better to forget it and let events fall as they may. There is something unbeautiful in the obvious pursuit. Those Richmond girls, for an example—I could not bear for you to have such a look in your eye."

Isabelle shuddered. She herself could not bear the thought of becoming so desperate as they for marriage, but then they had been searching so much longer. Dear heaven, she thought suddenly, is it possible that I too will be so long seeking a husband that—no! I shall never allow it. I will do as Papa says and forget the quest and wait for what providence has in store for me. At least I am here and have friends and darling Aunt Nathaniel. Surely only good things can happen.

Three

Mrs. Holland decided that Isabelle's wardrobe, Paris gowns notwithstanding, was inadequate for the busy social life in which she was now engaged.

"You will allow me to make you some little welcoming present, my dear, of a gown or two. I have been puzzling as to what it should be and I think that would be the most practical thing."

"But Papa bought me so many gowns in Paris—"

"Yes, yes, and very fine, too, but you have only two suitable for evening parties, apart from your ball gown. Naturally, you could not have known there would be need for more, nor that you would be meeting the same people night after night."

"But I cannot allow you to—"

"There now, missy. Cannot allow, indeed! I'm your auntie and may give you a gown if I choose, I hope," returned Mrs. Holland huffily. "Mercy on us, such a fuss, I do declare. Now fetch your bonnet and let me hear no more of such airy-fairy nonsense."

Meekly, Isabelle went to do as she was bid and some quarter of an hour later was bowling along in Mrs. Holland's carriage, bound for the silk warehouse. After a highly satisfactory hour spent amid billowing silks and gauzes and figured dimities, they followed the clerk, staggering under the burden of their purchases, out to the carriage.

"Good heavens, Mrs. Holland, what a great deal of

dressmaking you seem to have in store," they heard, the remark accompanied by an amused laugh.

Mrs. Holland turned to find Lady Bromley just being handed out of her own carriage. Mrs. Holland hurried forward to take her outstretched hand. " 'Tis you, dear Countess! Yes, we've done a deal of picking and choosing, you may be sure. For my niece, you see. She's"—she turned to Isabelle—"come along, love, and make your curtsy to Lady Bromley."

Isabelle, her mind still whirling with visions of peach-blossom silk and primrose gauze, continued for some seconds to stare bemusedly and unheeding into the distance. Then, as the words penetrated and made sense, she blushed with embarrassment as she came up to drop a curtsy to the older woman. What a grand impression I must have made, she thought, standing at gaze like a country bumpkin with the straw still in my hair.

"How do you do, Miss Holland." Lady Bromley turned to smile at Mrs. Holland approvingly, and then said, "I hope you do not find London intolerably dull and provincial after your years on the Continent."

"No, indeed, Lady Bromley. I assure you I had nothing like so exciting a time there as these last weeks in London have been." She forced herself to respond coherently, not wanting to embarrass dear Aunt Nathaniel before this grand friend of whom she was so proud.

"You are being kind to us, I think," laughed Lady Bromley. "Still, if those packages are a sign, you must be tolerably entertained, I suppose."

"More than tolerably, Lady Bromley, quite royally," said Isabelle, eager to defend her aunt's provisions for her entertainment.

"Indeed, Countess, not a free moment since she arrived," contributed Mrs. Holland proudly.

"Oh dear, I see I have been behindhand with an invitation. I hope you will still be able to find time for me," said Lady Bromley with mock ruefulness.

"I'm sure Isabelle would be happy to visit you at any time you like to say, dear Countess."

"Then perhaps you will give me the pleasure of seeing you Tuesday week. Just a small dinner party. I will send a note to remind you."

She made her farewells then and turned to the silk warehouse entrance, where the owner was awaiting her in smiling deference.

"There now, nothing could have turned out better," sighed Mrs. Holland as she climbed into her carriage and sank back against the blue velvet squabs. "All informal like, better really than a morning call."

The note, when it arrived the next day, proved to be an invitation not only to Isabelle and her aunt but also included the two Mr. Hollands. Isabelle's father seemed pleased to be included, but her uncle groaned in protest.

"Now, you'll stop that, if you please," said his wife firmly. " 'Tis an honor she does you, to be sure. Not just everyone is invited to take a meal with Lady Bromley, you know."

"No," he replied morosely, "just a gaggle of the prosiest old bores in town, all jealous that someone else will take precedence over them when we go in to dinner."

"Pay him no mind, Isabelle. He carries on so at the very mention of a dinner party, no matter who gives it. Prefers his club where the prosy old bores sit about swilling brandy and asphyxiating themselves on tobacco smoke."

"I prefer to take my mutton at my own table, thank you. At least there I can choose my company," replied Mr. Holland, getting in the last word.

There not being time to have a gown made up from the newly purchased materials, it was decided that the grander of the two Paris gowns would do very well "since no one at Lady Bromley's will have seen it," as Mrs. Holland said. The grander was of sea-foam-green silk trimmed in blond lace which, Mrs. Holland declared, suited Isabelle a treat.

Mrs. Holland herself wore a purple lustring and a silver tissue turban sporting a small lilac plume pinned to the side with an amethyst the size of a dove's egg, set in diamonds. This grandeur sat somewhat incongruously atop her round, genial face, but seemed to give her immense self-confidence, for she sailed regally past Lady Bromley's manservant on the appointed night with all the aplomb of a duchess.

At her side, Isabelle felt her own self-confidence slipping somewhat as she glanced about, for the hall of the Bromley townhouse was of awe-inspiring dimension and decoration. She had become used to the mansion of her aunt and uncle, and even to the luxurious comfort it provided for its guests, but this house could be sensed at once as visible evidence of centuries of wealth and cultivated taste.

She and her aunt followed a footman up one side of a sweeping divided stairway to lay aside their cloaks. This interval before being taken into the drawing room gave her time to take command of herself again. They are only people, she rationalized, like Mrs. Doctor Richmond or Mrs. Thorne, and if they are very grand and have titles, they are still only people. A Holland need not be intimidated by such as these. Then, coming down somewhat from such high-flown sentiments, she remembered facing up to the hardest-faced, meanest-spirited landlady of her experience in Brussels and putting the woman in her place with a few well-chosen words. After that, she thought with a little gurgle of laughter, I should fear nothing.

After rallying herself thus, she was able to follow her aunt and uncle, her own arm securely in that of her father, into Lady Bromley's drawing room with her chin up and a small smile to indicate her pleasant expectations. These were surprisingly fulfilled, for as she was taken about and introduced to the guests who had arrived before them, she found herself being smiled warmly upon and assured of how much pleasure her acquaintance was giving them. How very kind English people are, she thought, unlike the French, for instance, who always seemed to look upon one in so superior a way. She was not to know that Lady Bromley had dropped a discreet hint into the ear of her dear friend Lady Maggs-Brown, who had less discreetly passed it on, that Miss Holland had a respectable portion.

The sum had increased a few thousand pounds with each telling.

Isabelle made her curtsy to an exceedingly fat lady who glittered with various bits and pieces of jewelry scattered over her arms, earlobes, fingers, and immense bosom. This was Mrs. Fairbrother and she greeted Isabelle in a breathless wheeze. Peeping from around a vast arm, much as a chick shelters under the wing of a fat mother hen, was a painfully thin young girl in pale blue gauze cut low enough at the neck to reveal her prominent collar bones.

"M'daughter, Miss Holland. Stand up, Gwendoline, and greet Miss Holland properly." Miss Fairbrother obeyed with a shy smile and a furious blush to the roots of her pale blond hair. "Here, Brimsley." Mrs. Fairbrother raised a pudgy hand flashing with diamonds in imperious summons and a young man detached himself from a group of gentlemen and strolled up to them. "Miss Holland, allow me to present my son to you. Bring a chair for her, Brimsley."

Mr. Fairbrother bowed over Isabelle's hand, smiled warmly into her eyes, and turned to draw up a nearby chair. "Sit you down, Miss Holland," said his mother. "Gwendoline, do you mean to stand there gawking all evening?"

Isabelle sank somewhat resignedly into the chair placed squarely before Mrs. Fairbrother, Gwendoline tucked herself back under her mother's arm, and Mr. Fairbrother stood beside the sofa. He was a personable young man with a fresh complexion, honest blue eyes, and light brown hair, with no sign of his mother's girth or his sister's painful thinness. Isabelle could see little resemblance between any of them and wondered what Mr. Fairbrother's father looked like.

For a time she was forced to submit to Mrs. Fairbrother's searching catechism on her life to date, questions which became increasingly embarrassing to Isabelle. Evidently Mr. Fairbrother became aware of her discomfort, for in a moment he smoothly took over the conversation and changed its direction from the very particular to the more general, and in another five minutes said their hostess was looking their way, no doubt wishing to introduce Isabelle to the guest of honor, the Dowager Duchess of Duffty, and asked to be allowed to escort Isabelle across the room.

Isabelle gratefully rose at once and was led away. Mrs. Fairbrother gazed after them calculatingly. Brimsley, of course, had no need to find an heiress, she thought, his own fortune being considerable, but money should go to money. Her greatest fear was that her son might fall into the clutches of a fortune hunter of low breeding. She had seen many a sensible man's head turned by a pretty face.

After curtsying to the duchess, Isabelle was led aside by Mr. Fairbrother and held in pleasant conversation until dinner was announced, when she was not in the least displeased to find that Lady Bromley had assigned him to take her in. Lady Bromley watched them in animated conversation during dinner and smiled indulgently. The girl would do very well, she thought. She was pleasant in company without being pert, and while clearly enjoying herself with the attractive Brimsley Fairbrother, there was nothing at all flirtatious in her behavior.

Yes, she would do very well for Adrian if the hoped-for alliance with Lady Caroline Bray did not materialize. Lady Caroline was preferable, of course. She was not so pretty as Isabelle Holland, but her portion was larger and the amount well known, not a matter of speculation as was Miss Holland's, and her family connections were powerful and influential. Lady Bromley sighed contentedly at the thought of having two heiresses lined up for her darling nephew, who so desperately needed a wealthy wife.

Adrian, the Marquess of Sutterton, was her sister's son, and the very apple of the childless Lady Bromley's eye despite his many faults. He had run through the fortune left him by his father and blithely continued to pile up staggering debts through deep play at the gaming tables, keeping up a string of hunters, and setting up one mistress after another in luxurious apartments and lavishing presents upon them. Meanwhile, his family estate in Northumberland crumbled away. He could only save himself from complete ruin, perhaps even debtors' prison, by marriage, as soon as possible, with money. Even the announcement of his betrothal to Lady Caroline Bray would stave off his most pressing creditors. He would be here next week and she must do everything in her power to bring them together as much as possible. If Adrian dug in his heels and positively refused to offer for Caroline Bray, she had the Holland girl to fall back upon.

She began to go through her acquaintances mentally, planning her guest list for a dinner party for him, but at last, having assembled a tableful of people, all of the greatest consequence naturally, she became dissatisfied with it. They would bore darling Adrian into fits, she decided. She must have more young, interesting people or he would simply slip away at the first opportunity and refuse further invitations.

She glanced down the table and saw that the liveliest pair at her table were Miss Holland and Mr. Fairbrother. She would have them to meet Adrian to begin with, she decided. It might not be the wisest course to take, to introduce both girls to him at the same time, but after all, what real difference could it make. He would make his own choice no matter what she might think wisest. No one had ever yet succeeded in forcing Adrian against his inclination.

Mrs. Holland had no idea of Lady Bromley's plans for her niece, but she felt assured that Isabelle had made a favorable impression and that the coveted ball invitation would not be long in coming. Isabelle, of course, was also unaware of the role she might possibly be cast in by the countess, and was not unduly preoccupied by thoughts of a ball, though any girl in possession of a Paris ball gown would be unnatural not to think of it from time to time. At the moment, however, she was much more engrossed in thoughts of Brimsley Fairbrother. He was such an attractive young man to meet at one's first important dinner party, certainly in a totally different class than any of the young men she had met so far. Apart from this was his obvious interest in herself. There could be no mistaking the looks he bent upon her all through the dinner and afterward in the drawing room, when he never left her side. She was gratified by such assiduous attentions, but also somewhat embarrassed by them, for it seemed to her they were the object of interest for most of the other guests. But then she comforted herself by thinking how much more uncomfortable she would have been had he, the only man at the party near her own age, ignored her completely.

On the whole, when she could forget the many eyes observing them, she enjoyed her conversation with him very much. He was well-read, much better educated than she, and keenly interested in a great variety of things. He spoke knowledgeably on all of them, but not in a condescending way, assuming her own interest and listening carefully to any comments she made. At the end of the evening he asked Mrs. Holland if he might call upon them one morning and Isabelle was quite looking forward to seeing him again.

He did not come the morning after the dinner party, for which Isabelle was grateful, for Victoria and Horatia Richmond were shown in promptly at ten, agog to hear all the details of Lady Bromley's party. They would have been even more agog had Mr. Fairbrother been announced, and Isabelle was filled with uneasy anticipation all through their visit that he might appear. She mentioned him only casually as Mrs. Fairbrother's son in reciting to them the list of guests and then went on quickly to a description of the gowns worn by the women. She knew that inevitably they must meet him if he continued to show his interest in her, but just at present she was not ready for their arch looks or teasing questions.

She was spared any anxiety regarding the following morning when they regretfully announced upon departure that they would not be able to see her for two days as they were being taken by their mama to pay a visit to an ailing Terwhitt aunt in the country. Thus, she was able to greet Mr. Fairbrother calmly the next day. She and her aunt received him alone and he sat talking pleasantly, dividing his remarks courteously between them. His eyes, however, were pronouncedly warmer when he turned to Isabelle. After a correct half hour he rose to take his leave.

"Perhaps I could persuade you to ride with me tomorrow," he said, pressing the hand Isabelle extended to him.

"I regret that I do not ride, sir," she said.

"Ah, a drive in the Park then. Now the weather is so fine it will be very pleasant, and you are sure to see nearly everyone you know there."

Isabelle was quite sure she would not, for she did not number among her acquaintances so far any who included a drive through the Park in their daily pleasures, but she thought that she would enjoy it nonetheless, so she turned inquiringly to her aunt.

"Oh yes, my dear, of course you must go. Betsy will go with you," she added, so that Mr. Fairbrother would understand that she knew very well what was proper, though she thought privately that it was all nonsense to suppose two young people could not go out in an open carriage together in a park full of people without the attendance of a chaperone to make sure they behaved themselves. How were young people to get to know one another with a third person always in attendance?

"Oh, I need not take your maid away from her duties, madam," said Mr. Fairbrother easily. "I shall bring my sister. She will be delighted to improve her acquaintance with Miss Holland. She was quite taken with her."

Isabelle found this a little difficult to credit, since the girl had not spoken to her at all after her first shy greeting, but she certainly would prefer her to Aunt Nathaniel's abigail, Betsy, a dour woman guaranteed to blight any occasion in which she participated. They settled it that he would call for her at eleven the following morning and he went away.

"What a very nice young gentleman," said Mrs. Holland, carefully noncommittal.

"Oh, yes, very nice indeed," said Isabelle enthusiastically.

Mrs. Holland was somewhat taken aback by this strong

assertion after so brief an acquaintance. After all, there were a great many more men in London, perhaps more eligible than Mr. Fairbrother, whom Isabelle had not even met. Why, she hadn't even attended a ball yet! No girl should be firmly attached before she had been to her first ball.

"I hope you have not—you must forgive me, my dear, if I speak very frankly—but I do hope you have not allowed yourself to—to—form an attachment for Mr. Fairbrother so soon."

Isabelle laughed. "No, darling aunt, of course I have not. He is attractive and conducts himself so well that I enjoy his company, but I hope I have more sense than to be swept off my feet by the first attractive man I meet. I shall look about me very carefully, you may be sure."

"That is very sensible, of course, but sometimes we have little to say when the heart speaks. My papa had intended me for the son of his partner, practically betrothed us in our cribs, but I knew the moment I first saw Mr. Holland there could be no one else for me."

"Oh, falling in love," said Isabelle dismissively. "I doubt that I shall ever do so. I do not think it at all necessary, or even wise, in marriage. It clouds one's senses and one is unable to make a wise choice."

Mrs. Holland was made speechless by this sweeping statement, and held her peace. Useless to point out that her own marriage had turned out entirely successful even though she and Nathaniel might have had their judgment clouded by love when they chose one another, or that had her own father and mother not fallen in love she, Isabelle, would not be sitting here at this moment. Ah well, the girl was sensible, for which one must be grateful.

Dressed in a pea-green muslin pelisse opening over a white flounced muslin walking dress, green kid Spanish slippers, and a plaited straw beehive bonnet tied with green ribbands, Isabelle greeted Miss Fairbrother confidently as she was handed into the open landau by Mr. Fairbrother the next morning. She knew she was looking as fine as five pence in her Paris clothes and they would have no occasion to be ashamed of her company. Besides this, it was the sort of fine, warm, early summer day that always made her want to sing, and this morning Aunt Nathaniel had received another note from Lady Bromley, inviting her and her niece to dinner next week, which proved that Lady Bromley had found Isabelle a guest worthy of her table, according to Aunt Nathaniel.

"For 'tisn't me she's honoring, you know, for well she knows I'm not up to the sort she has at her table. 'Tis proper of her to include me, of course, being as you're my guest. Thank goodness your uncle was not asked this time, for I doubt I could get him to go again so soon."

Isabelle was glad that she had found favor with such a diamond of the first water as Lady Bromley, but was happy she would be going with her aunt, who was so comfortable to be with wherever she found herself.

"Good morning, Miss Holland," said Miss Fairbrother shyly as Isabelle seated herself and Mr. Fairbrother sat down facing them, his back to the driver.

"How good of you and your brother to allow me to accompany you, Miss Fairbrother."

"Oh no—I mean—it is I who must be grateful to be— that is Brimsley . . ." she faltered to a halt, blushing furiously and glancing apprehensively at her brother.

"Well, Mouse, what about me?" laughed Mr. Fairbrother.

"I only meant that you would not be taking me for a drive in the ordinary way," she replied with a bit more spirit.

"Possibly not," he agreed equably. "One does not care to go about too often with one's own sister. Besides, you go nearly every day with Mama if the weather is good."

"Yes," replied Miss Fairbrother in so doleful a tone that her brother laughed outright and even Isabelle had all she could do to keep from joining in.

"My sister, Miss Holland, is a fraud, for she is not in the least afraid of our mama, but twists her about her little finger whenever it suits her."

"Miss Holland," said Miss Fairbrother, ignoring him

and determinedly changing the subject, "I believe you will be attending Lady Bromley's dinner next week."

"Why yes," said Isabelle in amazement. "Her invitation only just arrived before we came away this morning."

"I know of it because she has invited Brimsley and mentioned in her note to him that she hoped you would be there also."

"I hope you will be there as well, Miss Fairbrother."

"Oh no, I am not at all the sort of guest she would invite for this occasion."

"Really? What sort of occasion is it to be?"

"It is for her nephew, the Marquess of Sutterton, so Mama says. Mama would not allow me to go, in any case," she added sadly.

"Whyever not?"

"Oh, he is a famous rake-hell!" replied Miss Fairbrother, her eyes wide.

Her brother looked sternly at her. "And what would you know of rake-hells, young woman?" he asked repressively.

"Nothing really, but that is what I heard Mama say to Lady Maggs-Brown, and from the way she said it, I knew it was not in the least nice. Besides, it is such a——a—— devilish-sounding thing to call someone. I wish I might meet a rake-hell."

"Never you mind about rake-hells, young lady. I should own myself astonished if you enjoyed the experience in the least. Now, Miss Holland," Mr. Fairbrother said, firmly taking the conversation back into his own hands, "tell me how you like driving in the Park."

His sister retired into her corner of the carriage and studied the scenery while her brother and Miss Holland discoursed at great length about carriages, horses, hunting, racing, and all such boring things, in Miss Fairbrother's opinion. The paths were crowded with carriages and riders and after a time Miss Fairbrother raised her hand to wave. In a moment one of the riders picked his way cautiously through the traffic to her side.

"Well, Mouse, you are looking very fine this morning," he said, doffing his hat. He was an exceedingly tall, thin young man with a jutting nose and receding chin, but twinkling blue eyes and an infectious grin offset the initial impression of rather startling homeliness.

"Well, well, Swinburn, sent down to rusticate again I take it?" said Mr. Fairbrother.

"Now, now, Brim, you know I graduated with honors five years ago," replied his cousin, his eyes riveted upon Isabelle. He turned an inquiring glance upon Mr. Fairbrother.

"Miss Holland, you will allow me to present my cousin Swinburn Tuberville to you," said Mr. Fairbrother resignedly.

"A very great pleasure, Miss Holland," said Mr. Tuberville with as sweeping a bow as was possible from the back of a horse. Isabelle smiled and nodded.

"Oh, Swin," said Miss Fairbrother, "are you here for a long stay? Have you seen Mama? Will you come for dinner tonight?"

"Yes, no, yes, to take each question in order. And I shall also give myself the pleasure of a call upon Miss Holland, if she will be so obliging as to allow it."

Mr. Fairbrother frowned at this impudence, but Isabelle said she and her aunt would be happy to welcome any cousin of the Fairbrothers, and perhaps Miss Fairbrother would also honor them with a call.

"Oh, wonderful, Miss Holland. Thank you! Swin shall bring me tomorrow morning," exclaimed Miss Fairbrother happily.

"A chance to get from under Aunt Amelia's thumb, eh, Mouse?" said Mr. Tuberville with a wide grin. "Well, I must bid you all good day. Promised to meet old Edgeworth at Watier's."

"Setting up for a dandy are you, Swin?"

"Heavens, can you picture it? No, no, Cousin, Beau Brummel doesn't own Watier's you know." With another grin all around, he bowed and turned away.

"How fortunate for you to have such a nice cousin," said Isabelle agreeably.

"Oh, he is my favorite, Miss Holland. Always so goodnatured and kind to one," enthused Miss Fairbrother.

"Enough of Swinburn," said Mr. Fairbrother, with a pointed stare at his sister before turning to reengage Isabelle in their previous conversation. Gwendoline retreated into her corner again. She was anxious to please her brother so that he would include her the next time he wanted to drive out with Miss Holland. It was glorious to get away from Mama. One was not afraid of Mama, of course, who was always so good to one, but it could not be denied that one felt oppressed just the least little bit in her presence.

Isabelle was very pleased with her morning and reported to her aunt that they would be favored with a morning call from Miss Fairbrother and her cousin, Mr. Tuberville, the next day. There now, thought Mrs. Holland, another young man of the *ton*. Didn't I know she'd make them all set up and take notice?

Four

Miss Fairbrother arrived for the promised call the following morning accompanied by Mr. Tuberville and, of course, by Brimsley Fairbrother. Not ten minutes after them came the Misses Richmond. They halted abruptly in the door of the drawing room, wide-eyed at the sight of the guests already there.

Isabelle rose at once to greet them and bring them into the room for introductions. The two girls were more subdued than was their usual wont before these rather grand guests, for which Isabelle was grateful. Both gentlemen had risen upon their entrance and after responding courteously to the introduction continued to stand during a very brief pause that ensued while the two girls looked about in some confusion, uncertain of where it would be politic to seat themselves. They had noted at once that Isabelle had been seated upon a sofa with Mr. Fairbrother, while his sister and Mrs. Holland sat facing each other in arm chairs before the fire. Mr. Tuberville still stood before the sofa where he had been sitting alone. Now he turned away, fetched another chair into the circle, and with a small bow indicated to the two girls to seat themselves upon the sofa.

Miss Victoria, with a second's hesitation, sat herself upon the chair, an act of unselfishness unappreciated by anyone in the room but her sister. Miss Horatia sat down demurely upon the sofa and Mr. Tuberville sat down beside her. For a time the conversation was general among them all, but gradually Mrs. Holland and Miss Fairbrother began speaking about bonnets and Mr. Fairbrother took the opportunity to begin a private conversation with Isabelle. Miss Victoria leaned toward the bonnet discussion and presently joined in with great interest, leaving her sister to Mr. Tubervulle.

Miss Horatia was, of course, an accomplished conversationalist when the need arose, but was intelligent enough to know when other measures might be more successful. Mr. Tuberville's easy smile and manner caused her to lower her eyes demurely to her hands and allow herself to be cajoled out of her shyness.

Mr. Tuberville, having received enough hints regarding his cousin's interest on the way this morning, knew he had been warned off beginning any flirtation with Miss Holland, and therefore he cheerfully turned his charm upon Miss Richmond. In no time at all he had her giggling delightedly and responding more openly to his teasing. He began to feel himself no end of a fellow for having thawed out such a demure miss and Horatia slowly put aside her assumed airs of missishness and responded to him in a natural way totally unnatural to her.

Isabelle, watching covertly, was amazed. Why, she thought, Horatia is very nearly pretty, with her eyes bright like that and the color coming and going in her cheeks! She watched Mr. Tuberville lean forward to speak and Horatia laugh in a spontaneous way without simpering at all. Mr. Tuberville watched her with evident satisfaction. Well, well, thought Isabelle, is it possible Horatia has made a conquest? She slid a glance around to Victoria and found her leaning forward to speak earnestly and at length to Miss Fairbrother. It even looked as though she had brought her chair nearer to them and farther away from the sofa where her sister sat than it had been before.

Mr. Fairbrother recalled Isabelle's wandering attention by asking if he might have the pleasure of taking her for a drive again on the following morning. She assented readily.

"And my mother asked if I could persuade you to come take a dish of tea with her afterward," he added.

"Well, of course I should be delighted. How very kind

of her," said Isabelle, her heart sinking at the thought of Mrs. Fairbrother's appraising eyes and delving questions. Still, there was no way she could refuse the invitation.

Every day for the remainder of the week she accompanied Mr. Fairbrother and his sister on excursions about London. They drove in the Park; they witnessed a balloon ascension; they went to Astley's Amphitheater to view the panorama of The Battle of Waterloo, which thrilled the spectators with cavalry advances, bugle calls, and cannon fire; they visited Mrs. Salmon's Waxworks. Isabelle enjoyed all of it thoroughly, even the visit to the formidable Mrs. Fairbrother, who had spoken to her in a most kindly way and had not subjected her to interrogation.

"Well, my dear," said her father as they walked together to church on Sunday morning, "I suppose I may expect a visit from Mr. Fairbrother any day now."

"Why should you suppose such a thing?" Isabelle said, laughing.

"Now, now, my girl, no missishness if you please. It is clear to all of us what his intentions must be."

"Well, whatever his intentions may be, I must tell you that he has not made the least push to attach my affections."

"Clearly a very cautious young man, and clever also."

"Why clever?"

"To have seen that the spark did not light."

"Good gracious, Papa, whatever can you mean?"

"That happens, you know. It did for me with your mama and fortunately for me it happened for her at the same time. Now Mr. Fairbrother's spark was lit at once, we could all see that, but your own was not. So he has courted you patiently and very slowly, hoping that familiarity and propinquity will accomplish it for him in the end."

"You are very romantic, Papa," she said wryly, "and I have never suspected it of you in all these years."

"Did you not, my dear?" he said sadly. "I must take the blame for the lack of romance in your life. You had to grow up too soon I think, had to face the hard practicalities of living at too young an age to give you time to dream."

"Pooh, nonsense," she protested vigorously. "I never felt in the least deprived, and if I am more practical-minded than most girls, it is all to the good, I think."

"No, my dear, I am afraid it is not. That should come with experience and years, as the result of the trials and errors of the youthful romantic impulses. You are turned around and I very much fear you have it all still to go through."

She laughed with genuine merriment. "No fear, darling Papa, I shall not be so silly. Romance is not in my nature, thank goodness!"

He shook his head and said no more. For a time they proceeded in silence. Just as they were approaching the entrance to the church, he stopped and turned to her.

"Then you have made up your mind to accept young Fairbrother?"

"He has not asked me, Papa."

"But he will, as you know very well."

"And will you object?"

"Not if you send him to me, of course."

"Then we will both just have to wait and see what comes of his slow and patient courting, if that is what it is. I cannot imagine any sparks being lit, but propinquity, as you say, may well do the trick. He is a good companion and I have enjoyed his company until now. That, I think, is a very good basis for marriage. Much more reliable in the long run than being swept off one's feet by romance."

Mr. Holland's only response to this speech was a heavy sigh. Isabelle pressed his arm lovingly and said no more. She was aware that she had disappointed him, but could not think of any way to help it. I cannot change my nature, after all, she thought.

Isabelle had not spent a great deal of time on introspection about her lot in life, but it had always seemed to her to be proven that a prosaic outlook was of more utility than a romantic one. Thinking of it now, she wondered how she and her father would have fared all these years had she been the sort of feather-headed girl given to novel reading, daydreaming, and swooning at the least shock to her sensibilities. She was not aware, any more than was her father, that her nature was not only the result of the life she had led, but was also due to Mr. Holland himself. He was an intrinsically kind and invariably courteous man, but never the man to indulge in demonstrations of his affection. His own mother had died while he was still a small child, and as the youngest of four brothers in the charge of an irascible father, he had grown up in an atmosphere in which it was impossible for the tenderer emotions to have any chance of expression. He was certainly not as rough in his behavior to his daughter as his father and brothers had been to him, but kisses and caresses were not his way either, and as a consequence, Isabelle, whose memory of her mother's tenderness was but a dim one, had had no experience with them to temper her outlook. She had coped with day-to-day living, calculating the spending of every penny that came her way, and had become as cool and withdrawn as her father in the process.

She was sincere when she scoffed at romance as a necessary ingredient in choosing a husband. She looked upon the role of wife as an extension of the one she had played so far in life. She was not interested in wealth or a title, but in roots and a comfortable security with someone as kind and courteous as her father.

As for Mr. Fairbrother, she was not anywhere near making up her mind about him as yet. She accepted his invitations and his company with a clear conscience, for she had never by so much as a coy word or languishing look encouraged him to show her his feelings. Though she was aware of his interest, she did not want him to express it yet. She did not discount his chances as hopeless, but felt there was plenty of time as she had only been in London a month.

They met the Richmonds in the church porch when the service was over, Horatia wearing a sedate, almost seraphic smile, while Victoria hovered solicitously at her elbow as though lady-in-waiting to royalty. Mrs. Doctor Richmond's manner was less frosty than usual when she greeted Isabelle and her father, and presently they all began to walk away together.

Victoria and Isabelle walked somewhat ahead. "It must be quite a week since we have seen you, dear Miss Holland. I do not mean that in the least reproachfully, of course. We are so very happy that you are being so well entertained by your friends the Fairbrothers."

"Yes, they have been very kind."

"Oh, Miss Holland," Victoria burst out after a short silence, "I simply must tell you our news. We have been honored by two morning visits from Mr. Tuberville! It is early days yet, of course, and Horatia will not be persuaded to admit it, but I am convinced he shows a pronounced interest in her. Is not that the happiest news?"

"It is indeed, Miss Richmond, if your sister welcomes it."

"Oh, I think she likes him very well. He has asked us to ride with him tomorrow, which is the most fortunate thing, for Horatia has a new costume that becomes her enormously, and I must say she looks her best on horseback. She has a beautiful seat, you know."

Isabelle was much struck by the unselfishness of Victoria's remarks, for it seemed that nothing could be dearer to her heart than her sister's good fortune. Isabelle remembered now how quickly she had assumed the chair, leaving her sister to sit with Mr. Tuberville the day they had first met him in Mrs. Holland's drawing room, and how determinedly she had disassociated herself from their conversation, leaving the field free for Horatia. No doubt Horatia would do the same for Victoria when the occasion arose, thought Isabelle. What very good-hearted girls they are, after all, despite their desperation to find husbands. I shall never allow myself to think disparagingly of them again. I wish I might have had a sister to be such a good friend to me.

On the next morning while driving with Mr. Fairbrother and Gwendoline, she saw the Richmond girls again, on horseback, accompanied by Mr. Tuberville. The two parties converged and engaged in a lengthy light-hearted exchange before the riders went on their way. Victoria was right, thought Isabelle, Horatia does indeed show to advantage in riding dress. She looks quite splendid, actually, and sits her horse with so much ease.

A round of calls with her aunt prevented Isabelle from seeing Mr. Fairbrother the next day, though she would, of course, see him in the evening at Lady Bromley's. Isabelle was looking forward with some excitement to the evening, for like Miss Fairbrother, she longed to see a verified rake-hell, though also like Miss Fairbrother, she had very little real knowledge of what that term actually meant. Her imagination projected a dark, satanic-like man, cloven hooves discreetly hidden in black kid evening pumps.

Her eyes raked Lady Bromley's drawing room somewhat fearfully as she entered, but no such apparition presented itself to her eyes. Mr. Fairbrother was there, however, and quickly came forward to claim her attention. When she asked, he informed her that Lady Bromley's nephew had not yet put in an appearance. There was something stiff and disapproving in his voice that caused her to change the subject.

More guests were arriving all the time and as the room filled she noticed that the preponderance of them were younger than those she had seen at the last visit. Many more pretty young women strolled about in soft-hued gowns, fluttering fans and eyelashes at the young men. The older women were clearly only there as chaperones for the young women.

There was an air of electric suspense growing in the room. Eyes turned eagerly to the door at every new arrival, causing a tiny moment of silence before conversations were resumed. It was plain to Isabelle that they were all—at least the women—as impatient for the arrival of the notorious nephew as she was. She noticed that even Lady Bromley's usual serenity was marred by a small, worried crease between her brows as she hovered watchfully at the door. Then, when the atmosphere in the room had become almost hectic with expectancy, the butler announced "The Countess of Boll and Lady Caroline Bray."

Standing in the doorway was a shimmering vision in a gown of rich figured white French gauze over white satin. She stood there a moment in the silence she had created, smiling with a radiant impartiality upon the assembly before turning to greet Lady Bromley, who was speaking to the Countess of Boll.

As Isabelle covertly studied Lady Caroline, she came to realize that the girl was not truly beautiful. Her complexion was almost startlingly white, but even from this distance a sprinkling of freckles was discernible. Her hair was a blazing red aureole about her face, but its texture was that extremity of curliness that could only be termed frizzy. Her hazel eyes were well spaced and brilliant, but her features were thin and sharp. She was, however, acclaimed in London as an accredited beauty, according to all the gossip Isabelle had heard, and she thought this reputation must rest on the fact that she carried herself with all the supreme self-confidence and poise of a beauty, and Isabelle was forced to admit there was certainly something compelling about the girl that caused the other girls to fade in her presence.

Isabelle, heretofore perfectly confident in her blossom-pink gauze Paris gown of deceptively simple cut, felt positively dowdy in comparison and imagined every other women in the room was experiencing the same feeling. Eventually, Lady Bromley brought her forward to where Lady Caroline and her mother were holding court on a sofa. Isabelle made her curtsy and felt two pairs of sharp eyes rake over her.

"Miss Holland, what a delicious gown. Paris-made, of course. I noticed it the moment I entered the room," said Lady Caroline pleasantly.

It was a pretty compliment and Isabelle thought a sincere one. She also believed Lady Caroline when she said she had noticed it on entering the room. Those sharp eyes missed nothing, and Isabelle felt sure she had made a note of every other gown in the room as well.

Mrs. Holland was brought up to be introduced and then she and Isabelle moved aside to make way for other guests eager to greet Lady Caroline. Isabelle realized that in the excitement of the moment she had forgotten about the rake-hell nephew. She glanced about and saw the butler approach the door again, receive a slight shake of the head from Lady Bromley, and fade back into the hall. This happened once more a few minutes later and Isabelle thought the man must be awaiting orders to announce dinner and Lady Bromley was delaying this as long as possible. It could only be because her nephew had not yet arrived. Isabelle was relieved, for she had supposed she must have missed his entrance.

Lady Bromley's frown had deepened and the butler had appeared yet again when a tall, lean gentleman in an exquisitely cut black evening coat sauntered past the man into the room unannounced. There was nothing satanic about him, for he was fair-haired, his expression casual in the extreme, but Isabelle knew instantly that this was the notorious Marquess of Sutterton. His thin, bony face was pale with pronounced black smudges beneath his eyes, eyes that Isabelle thought must be blue, and his mouth was full and sensuous-looking and more red than was usual in a man.

"Adrian, you naughty creature! Can you never contrive to be on time. My cook is in hysterics!" cried Lady Bromley happily, the frown now erased as he bent over her hand. She took his arm and led him at once to the sofa where he bowed first to the countess and then to the daughter, who extended her hand. He kissed it lingeringly and Isabelle saw the girl flush as she stared, mesmerized, up into his face, her hazel eyes glittering.

There was not time for him to go around the room as the butler had again appeared and Lady Bromley nodded for him to announce dinner. Isabelle was taken in by Mr. Fairbrother, the two of them following the long line of guests in strict precedence, behind the Countess of Boll escorted by Lord Bromley. Lady Caroline, to no one's surprise, was taken in by the Marquess of Sutterton, and Isabelle found herself seated directly across the table from him. She and Mr. Fairbrother chatted comfortably together, and from time to time she allowed herself to glance across the table at him and Lady Caroline. They were certainly the most striking couple at the table, and she noticed other guests openly staring at them. They seemed oblivious to this attention, as though too accustomed to it to notice it anymore, and appeared absorbed with one another. Isabelle saw that Lady Caroline did not flirt or behave missishly, but seemed much at her ease despite the fact that she was engaged in a conversation with a rake-hell. Isabelle hoped she could manage as well when the time came for her own introduction to the man, though, she reassured herself, he certainly seemed harmless enough.

At that moment Lady Caroline turned away to respond to something said to her by Lord Bromley on her right and the marquess looked up squarely into Isabelle's eyes, as though he knew she was looking at him. His mouth curled into a slight smile of acknowledgment, his look seeming to imply familiarity, as though they two shared an intimacy. His eyes did not question, but seemed to assume her awareness of it. She felt herself to be impaled by his look and could not have forced her eyes away, even had she been inclined to do so. They are green, she thought helplessly, dark green. It was her only coherent thought. When Lady Caroline turned back and spoke to him, he smiled ruefully and withdrew his gaze.

Isabelle felt strangely breathless and disoriented. She was glad Mr. Fairbrother had been turned away to his other partner and had not noticed the encounter. It could only have lasted a brief moment, yet she felt hours must have gone by since she had last been aware of the rest of the room.

The remainder of the evening, with the exception of a few brief moments quite a bit later, remained forever unclear in her memory. The ladies retired to the drawing room while the gentlemen had their port. She sat with her aunt, who chattered along comfortably while Isabelle stared into space. Eventually the gentlemen rejoined them and Lady Bromley persuaded various of the young ladies to play or sing for the company. Notable among those who allowed themselves to be so persuaded was Lady Caroline, who accompanied herself at the pianoforte as she sang, charmingly, several songs to the great appreciation of her audience, particularly the marquess, who stood beside her devotedly turning the music pages for her. After a single glance at the handsome pair glowing in the candlelight, Isabelle concentrated her attention upon her folded hands in her lap.

The few moments of the evening when her faculties sharpened into focus were when Lady Bromley led her across the room to be introduced to the marquess. He stood in conversation still with Lady Caroline and her mother, but turned courteously as his aunt touched his arm.

"Adrian, you have not yet met a very particular friend of mine, Miss Holland."

"My lord," murmured Isabelle, curtsying.

He took her hand. "Miss Holland, a very great pleasure indeed," he said, bending to brush his lips lightly against her knuckles, then rising to give her again his lancing look. Mercifully, this time it was only for an instant, as Lady Caroline spoke, too commandingly to be ignored.

"Ah, Miss Holland, I understand you have just come from the Continent."

"Yes, I—"

"You will find us all too boring for words, I suppose, after Paris."

"Oh, no, not in the least. I—"

"Do you go to the Haworthys' ball tomorrow?"

"No, I am not acquainted with them," said Isabelle firmly, determined to finish at least one sentence. Did the girl do it deliberately to make her look stupid?

"Of course you will be going, Isabelle," said Lady Bromley. "There has been no time to tell you that Lady Haworthy begged me to bring you. I will take you up in my carriage about ten o'clock."

"That is very kind of you," said Isabelle.

"And I shall request that you save a set for me, Miss Holland," said the marquess.

"Ah, I see the tea tray is being brought in," said Lady Caroline, "and I am simply perishing of thirst. Will you give me your arm, sir?"

The marquess bowed to the other ladies and led Lady Caroline across the room, and for Isabelle the evening sank back into obscurity.

"A ball at the Haworthy's!" exclaimed Mrs. Holland, her voice rich with satisfaction as she and Isabelle drove home some time later. "I knew the countess would remember. She is so very kind, is she not, to take you?"

"Yes, very kind."

"Nothing could be better, for as her protégée you will meet every eligible gentleman there, you may be sure, and have every dance taken. Oh dear, how excited you must be."

"Yes, Aunt."

"Are you all right, my dear?" said Mrs. Holland, peering anxiously at her in the dark carriage.

"Something tired, I think."

"Tired? After only sitting about all evening. I hope you are not coming down with a fever."

"No, no, I am quite well, I assure you. Only—only—so many new people to meet. My mind is reeling with names."

"You shall drink a glass of port when we get home. Very strengthening, port is. Tomorrow you will stay in your bed all morning and have a tray. You must have all your energy for the ball. Such a grand place to go for your first ball. The Haworthys are the very top of the trees, you know."

She carried on happily in this vein all the way home, allowing Isabelle to sink back into mindlessness. She dutifully drank a thimbleful of port on their arrival and went gratefully to bed. Strangely enough, she slept instantly, and so deeply that in the morning she had no memory of disturbing dreams, but woke thoroughly refreshed and clear-headed, all last evening's cloudiness swept away entirely. She sat up against her pillows and accepted the cup of chocolate the maid handed to her.

She could not actually recall most of the evening, but

she remembered those dark green eyes and their enigmatic message. Pooh, she thought, disgusted with herself. It was all my imagination. What a pea goose I am. I had built up this fairy-tale of an evil ogre and was only waiting for him to live up to my expectations and—and—cast a spell over me. I can only hope I did not make too much of a spectacle of myself, but at least now I know it is all foolishness and shall not be so susceptible again. She set aside her chocolate and threw back the bed coverlet.

"What are you doing?" cried Mrs. Holland, rushing into the room. She drew the coverlet back over Isabelle's legs. "I absolutely forbid you to leave this bed before midday."

"But I feel wonderful, Aunt Nathaniel!"

"Never you mind. You gave me quite a fright last night when we came in and I saw you in the light. White, you were, as that pillow sham. You'll rest today, my lady, if I have anything to say about it, as I do, being in place of a mother to you and you barely out of the schoolroom."

"I was never in the schoolroom, Aunt," laughed Isabelle.

"Sauce! Now drink up your chocolate. Betsy has ironed all the creases out of your ball gown and it looks a treat, so you have nothing to concern yourself with all day. I have brought you a novel by that Miss Austen. I read very little myself, but I'm told she's all the crack these days. I sent Betsy out for it first thing this morning."

"You are so very good to me, Aunt Nathaniel. What a fortunate girl I am to have you to take care of me."

Mrs. Holland flushed up with pleasure and became very busy smoothing out the coverlet and tucking it in. " 'Tis a blessing for me, never having had a daughter to do things for and young Jack away to Oxford and all. But then, it's never the same with boys, in any case, they being so independent-like from the time they're out of leading strings. There now, you rest. By and by I'll send up a tray and you're to eat every bite. You need your strength tonight for the dancing."

She hurried away and Isabelle sank back into her pillows with a sigh and picked up the novel. She hoped the tray would not be too long in coming, for suddenly she felt ravenously hungry. She began to read, and just as she was becoming involved in the story a thought popped into her mind having nothing at all to do with the entrancing Elizabeth Bennett and her family.

He has asked me to stand up with him tonight!

Five

Isabelle fanned her flushed cheeks and smiled upon her latest partner, Mr. Charquith, who had just returned her to Lady Bromley's side.

"Dare I hope you will honor me with another set, Miss Holland?"

"Gladly, sir, but I fear there are none free." Though she pretended regret, she was in truth very happy to be able to make such a claim. She thought, not for the first time this evening, upon the uncountable advantages of being Lady Bromley's protégée when attending her first ball. To enter a room filled with total strangers could have been daunting for any young girl, but the sponsorship of Lady Bromley assured her of immediate acceptance, not to speak of as many dancing partners as could be desired. Lady Bromley was a popular figure in London society and, it seemed, a friend of long standing to every gentleman in the room, who all made a point of coming to greet her and each of whom, upon introduction to Isabelle, requested that Isabelle stand up with them, until every dance was spoken for before the first strains of the orchestra filled the room. All, that is, but the second set after supper, which she had decided to hold for Lord Sutterton as he had requested, though he had not as yet appeared.

She had just completed the first set and the evening stretched enchantingly before her. Surely, she thought, Aunt Nathaniel was right about the importance of one's first ball, for the Haworthys' ballroom looked to her like a fairy land with its thousands of twinkling candles drawing sparks of fire from the jewels of the women, who were all visions of loveliness to Isabelle's unjaundiced eyes in their gowns the colors of all the gorgeous flowers in a fantasy garden. The only small cloud of disappointment Isabelle experienced was that dear Aunt Nathaniel was not here to enjoy it with her.

Her next partner, Lord Talboys, presented himself, Mr. Charquith bowed and regretfully gave up his place, and Isabelle was led out for the next set. Lady Bromley smiled upon them benignly and congratulated herself upon her discernment, for she was very pleased with Isabelle. She thought her beautiful, of course, or she would never have taken her up to begin with, despite Mrs. Holland's claims upon her benevolence, but also she found Isabelle mature beyond her seventeen years, with a proud, though not overweening bearing, and exceptional taste, if her ball gown was anything to go by. It was of palest blossom-peach gauze, with the square-cut neckline just covering her shoulders, the sleeves short and puffed, the bodice cut extremely high, the skirt flowing in a straight column from just beneath the bosom to a vandyked flounce, heavily embroidered with silver and gold thread in leaves and thistles. She wore only a double strand of pearls, which Lady Bromley recognized as Mrs. Holland's, and silver and gold ribbands threaded through her curls which had been pulled back smoothly from her face to form a cascade down the back of her head. Her large gray eyes sparkling with pleasure and the flush of color in her cheeks were as great an adornment as any jewels in the room. The singularity of her appearance rested on these as well as the French smartness of her gown.

Lady Bromley had every reason to feel complacent in her choice and only hoped Adrian would condescend to appear. For though he had said he would, had even requested Isabelle to stand up with him, Lady Bromley was not entirely sanguine about the matter. If he was enjoying his dinner companions or was in deep play at one of his clubs, he might well forget the ball altogether. Of course,

it was far too early in the evening to expect him, in any
case, so she could put it out of her mind for a time. Ah,
here was Caroline Bray with her detestable mother hovering far enough back not to spoil the effect of her daughter's practiced entrance.

Lady Caroline seemed to be suspended in the doorway
like a glittering ornament, her gown of yellow satin cov-
ered with golden bugle beads that caught the candlelight
and flashed sparks into the eyes of the beholders. When
she had captured a gratifying audience, she turned to
summon up her mother and proceed into the ballroom. She
was immediately besieged by young men.

Well, thought Lady Bromley wryly, Drury Lane hadn't
an actress to surpass Lady Caroline. Still, she was the
Catch of the Season, and Adrian could hardly do better
than take her with all speed before she and her fabulous
dowry were snapped up.

When they were at last taken down to supper by Lord
Jeremy Coke, Lady Bromley was ravenously hungry and
fell upon her lobster patties and champagne eagerly. Isabelle was much too excited to think of food and only
sipped at some lemonade. She was somewhat puzzled by
the nonappearance of the marquess. Not that she would
feel the entire ball spoiled for her if he did not come at all,
but it was certainly an acquaintance she had looked forward to renewing, apart from which he had asked her to
dance with him and it would be most impolite, even
somewhat humiliating for her in view of the fact that the
request had been made in front of several people, if he
simply failed to appear. She thought suddenly of Brimsley
Fairbrother. He would never have forgotten such an obli-
gation. She wondered that he was not here tonight, for
surely the Fairbrothers were distinguished enough mem-
bers of the *ton* to have merited an invitation.

Lord Jeremy Coke broke into these reflections and made
himself pleasant enough to cause her to forget all about
Lord Sutterton, and presently she returned to the ballroom
refreshed by the respite, to be gathered up by her next
partner and whirled away down the room.

Lord Sutterton strolled into the room in time to watch her progress and as he gazed after her appreciatively, his hand was rapped rather smartly with the ivory sticks of a fan and he turned in sharp annoyance to find the Countess of Boll beside him.

"I have a bone to pick with you, sir," she said with a coy smile.

"Oh, yes?" he replied with a lifted eyebrow. "And what can I have done to have earned your displeasure, madam?"

"It is my darling girl whose displeasure you have earned. She has been quite mopish this entire day after her mortification last evening."

"My sympathies, naturally," he said unencouragingly.

Lady Boll went on undaunted. "It was dreadfully thoughtless of you, though I am sure you did not mean to so humiliate her." She paused expectantly, but when he refused to be drawn, she was forced to persist. "Dear Caroline felt it a great deal that you so forgot her consequence as to request that—er—young woman to stand up with you tonight before making your request first to her. After all, Caroline is the daughter of an earl and—"

"Say no more, madam. I understand you perfectly," said the marquess brusquely. "Though I confess, I can hardly credit that any action of mine could disturb the perfect tranquility of Lady Caroline's self-esteem." With a cold bow he passed on, leaving Lady Boll staring after him, still trying over his remark in her mind to see if there was a compliment in it or an affront.

"Well, Adrian, your feathers look ruffled," said Lady Bromley as he bent over her hand. "What has happened?"

"Nothing of importance, dearest. How very beautiful you are tonight. Is Bromley here?"

"No fear. I cannot remember the last time I persuaded him to accompany me to a ball."

"Then I shall lead you out and flirt with you outrageously."

She laughed delightedly and felt an unexpected blush rise up her throat. Sometimes she was scandalized by the thoughts that rose unbidden into her mind about Adrian. If only he had been Bromley's nephew, instead of her own sister's son, her thoughts would not have been quite so reprehensible.

"There are plenty of beautiful young women here to-night for you to practice your arts upon, you scamp," she scolded to cover her confusion.

Indeed, there were many female eyes, young and old, studying him covertly and openly, for despite his rake-hell reputation he was still considered a matrimonial prize. The real facts of his financial position were not yet common knowledge, and as for his propensities for gambling and mistresses, they were too prevalent among the young gentlemen of London for it to be thought in any way unusual. He conducted himself with courtesy when he condescended to make an appearance in society, and had never yet created any scandal involving a young, unmarried girl. He had, in fact, a strong leaning toward older women, and the only one of these for whom he felt the least affection was Lady Bromley. Only lack of opportunity had so far prevented him from attempting to seduce her, aunt though she might be. She was a beautiful woman, who was also attracted to him, as he knew well, and he wanted her.

"You know I have an aversion to green fruit," he said, smiling significantly into her eyes and enjoying her heightened color as she took his meaning.

"Adrian, you must not—" she gasped, and then stopped, realizing the impropriety of allowing him to see that she understood his insinuation. "You are unfortunately not in a position to be choosy, dear nephew," she said with great resolution. "Naturally, I should be overjoyed to have you come to me with a choice of your own, but since I know you too well to think that likely, and that you will procrastinate until ruin is inevitable, I have found two for you myself. They are both young, true, but both very handsome, and fruit, as you well know, has a way of ripening whether we will or no. If you will take my advice, you will settle for Caroline Bray and have done with it. She is related to nearly everyone of influence in the country and her fortune will save you."

"I think I would prefer ruin. She looks too much like her mother, and that damned old harridan had the utter gall just now to reprimand me for slighting her darling lamb in public by requesting Miss Holland to stand up with me tonight before asking Caroline. Can you believe such a thing?"

Lady Bromley laughed. "Oh dear, Caroline is a bit too puffed up in her own consequence, I admit, but still—"

"I'll tell you what it is. If they can catch me, those women mean to run me between them, and you know I have never taken kindly to the bridle and bit. No, no fear I shall leg-shackle myself to such a girl as that with her damned managing mother hovering at her elbow to take up the cudgels in every battle."

"But my dear, if you persist in finding fault with every—" she began to protest.

"I will take the little Holland. Seems a biddable sort, and I can train her from the beginning in the way I intend her to go on."

Lady Bromley was too relieved to have gained her point thus far to debate the issue further.

On the floor Isabelle had chanced to look in their direction, and upon espying Lord Sutterton seated beside his aunt, felt her nerves begin to quiver. She had made up her mind he was not going to come tonight and was more sorry than glad to see him. She had decided the discomfort she felt in his presence was not worth the excitement of actually dancing with a man considered dangerous. She had met so many distinguished and entirely pleasant gentlemen this evening, and had had so many charming compliments paid her, she was perfectly content that nothing further was needed to make this the happiest evening she had ever spent in her life.

The sight of the marquess, however, caused her contentment to vanish, to be replaced by a sort of dread. She wished this dance could go on and on to postpone their meeting, but inevitably the last chords sounded, the last

steps were trod, and she must suffer herself to be led off
the floor and back to Lady Bromley. Never one to be
craven where courage was demanded, she threw up her
chin and commanded herself to stop behaving like a goosish
schoolgirl. After all, the man would not bite her!

She managed to smile and thank her partner, and turn to
curtsy to Lord Sutterton, who had risen at her approach
and now bowed her into the chair beside his aunt.

"What an entirely enchanting gown, Miss Holland. You
must have all the other young ladies gnashing their teeth
with envy," he said lightly.

"I thank you, sir, though I should be sorry to think I
had caused such an unhappy sensation to spoil anyone's
evening. However, I doubt it can be so, for it seems to me
the room is filled with singularly happy young ladies
tonight."

"I trust you include yourself among them?"

"Oh, indeed yes!" she exclaimed enthusiastically.

"Will you allow me some small share in your happiness?"

"Why, I—I . . ." she faltered, not entirely sure of his
meaning.

"Is it possible you have forgotten you are promised to
me for a set tonight?"

"Oh, of course not, my lord, I assure you," she said,
too ingenuous to even attempt a pretence otherwise as a
more seasoned girl might have done.

"Then I claim this one."

"But—but—I am promised for this one to Mr. Acton-
Page," she said, much flustered. "I put your name down
for a later set."

"Oh, Mr. Acton-Page may have that one," he said with
a hint of impatience. "Surely it cannot matter?" He held
out his arm so imperiously that she rose at once and was
led out, not even noticing the approaching Mr. Acton-
Page, who stared after them in outraged astonishment.

Sensing her nervousness from the slight trembling of her
hand, he refrained from speech until she seemed comfortable with the steps of the dance before he said, "Since you

claim so much pleasure from the ball, I must presume you are the belle of the evening, Miss Holland.''

"I think you are teasing me, sir.''

"Certainly not, child.''

"You are not so ancient nor I so infantile that you should call me a child, Lord Sutterton.''

"I beg your pardon, Miss Holland. I am so unused to conversing with young women that I feel rather elderly.''

Here he spoke the truth, for his avoidance of unmarried women was of long standing. When he had first ventured into society in London as a youth of nineteen, eager to test his abilities, he had begun a flirtation with a girl he had met at a ball. Her family were gentlefolk, but barely clinging to the outer fringes of the *ton*. Her mother, who was very ambitious for her pretty daughter, had instructed the girl not to be too nice in accepting the young lord's advances, thinking thereby to entrap a green boy before he knew what had happened to him. When she found him kissing her daughter in the drawing room, she had immediately thrown herself upon his neck and welcomed him as a son-in-law. His father had rescued him from this entanglement, at the cost of several thousand pounds to assuage the young woman's broken heart, and the marquess had learned his lesson too well to ever allow himself to become a victim again.

Isabelle Holland was his first attempt since then to ingratiate himself with so young a girl, and he found her unexpectedly different than he had supposed she would be. There was a straightforward dignity about her, surprising in one so young and, according to his aunt, so inexperienced. There were no bashfully dropped eyes, no coyness, no blushing confusion, though the color was strong in her cheeks. In fact, now he studied her more carefully, there was something strange in her manner that he could not quite define. Something a little too square about her shoulders, too outthrust about her chin, as though she were bracing herself for an ordeal. Yes, that was it! She must be frightened and commanding herself not to show it. He was intrigued and rather pleased to think she was frightened of

him. Perhaps it would not be so displeasing as he anticipated in making her fall in love with him while remaining
just a little frightened of him. Yes, he would like that very
well.

He set himself out to be pleasant and in a very short
time she relaxed and enjoyed his mildly flirtatious repar-
tee. He saw, in passing, Lady Caroline, who gave him her
most blinding smile, which he returned with a polite little
smile of his own. Yes, he thought, I have made the right
choice, since one was necessary, for though she glitters,
Lady Caroline has an old look for her young years. Too
many balls and parties, too much adulation, too much
manipulation to get her own way. And she does indeed
look very much, too much, like her mother.

When the set was ended he led Isabelle back to his aunt,
took her fan from her hand, and gently fanned her flushed
face. Lady Bromley observed this with a mixture of astonishment and amusement. Who would ever have expected to
see Adrian behaving like any other ballroom gallant?

"Is it possible, Miss Holland, that I could persuade you
to honor me with another set?"

"I have no others free, Lord Sutterton," said Isabelle.

"Of course you have not. It was foolish of me to expect
that it might be so. Perhaps you will allow me to call upon
you tomorrow morning?"

"My aunt and I shall be happy to receive you, Lord
Sutterton."

"Will eleven be too early?"

"Not in the least, sir." She laughed. "We are not
lie-abeds in my aunt's house, I assure you."

"Not even after the exertion of a ball?"

"Pho, pho, sir, I hope you do not count dancing as an
exertion?"

"Clearly you do not, for you look as fresh and adorable
as though you had just left the hands of your abigail."

Her color deepened, but she would not allow herself to
be put out of countenance, and smiled up at him as she
thanked him for the compliment with all the poise at her
command.

As the music struck up again he bent to take her hand. "I see a young man approaching with so much glad anticipation on his face he can only be your next partner, so I shall bid you good night."

"Oh, do you not dance again, my lord?" said Isabelle in much surprise.

"No, I would not spoil a perfect evening," he replied, then pressed his lips against her fingers, smiled into her eyes for a moment, and released her hand. He turned to his aunt to repeat the performance, but his smile to her was accompanied by the very smallest wink of complicity. Then he turned and strolled leisurely out of the room.

Lady Caroline and her mother watched him go with equal dismay and indignation. Later, as they were driven home, each allowed her fury to be unleashed.

"I have never been so insulted," declared Lady Caroline. "Not even the courtesy of a greeting!"

"Very ill-bred, I am sure. I am surprised that his aunt allowed him to behave so."

"I suppose you spoke to him?"

"Naturally. I could not allow him to go unreprimanded for his insult to you at—"

"I told you it would not answer," interrupted her daughter rudely. "You should have let me speak to him first."

"But I told you I intended—" cried Lady Boll indignantly.

"And I told you to do no such thing, did I not? I told you it would be better if—"

"I think I must be allowed to know more about how to handle rude young men than—"

"You may think so, but I do not. And I am proven right, am I not? In the future, I must ask that you not interfere."

"You term it interference when a mother protects her daughter from rudeness. Lord Sutterton knows very well what is due to a woman of title, and if he forgets it, it is my duty to remind him what—"

"And now he knows and what has it gained me?" cried Caroline. "Not even a proper greeting."

"I should have held myself remiss in my duty had I not pointed out to him—"

"And I told you to hold your tongue in the matter," said Caroline angrily.

"I will not be spoken to in such a way, Caroline. I will speak to your father about this," replied Lady Boll in stiff outrage.

"And he will tell you the same thing, for so he is forever telling you," replied her daughter disrespectfully.

This being too true to deny, Lady Boll disdained any answer, and the rest of the drive was completed in a cold silence.

No such disunity marred the evening for Isabelle and Lady Bromley, who, as they were driven home, were each very much pleased with the evening and with each other.

"Well, my dear, you have made me very proud this evening," remarked Lady Bromley, patting Isabelle's hand.

Isabelle raised Lady Bromley's hand and kissed it impulsively. "I am so grateful for your kindness to me, dear Lady Bromley. I shall forever be in your debt."

"Pooh, nonsense, my dear, I have enjoyed it all excessively."

"But I had thought it must be very dull to attend a ball and not dance oneself."

"Well, I suppose sometimes it would be so, for I like dancing very well, but when one undertakes to chaperone a young girl, it does not do to dance oneself. I would not be discharging my duty to you and your aunt else. But I was vastly entertained nevertheless, and happy to see my nephew enjoying himself."

"Do you think he can have enjoyed himself? He came so late and danced but the one set."

"He rarely goes to balls at all and never dances except to lead me out from time to time. I think you have made something of a conquest, my dear."

Isabelle was grateful for the darkness that hid her blush, and could not have answered had she died for it. Was it possible he had come tonight only to dance with her? The idea set up a barrage of conflicting emotions in her mind.

There was pleasure, of course, for show me a young girl who is not pleased to be singled out before all others for attention, especially by so attractive a man. There was a touch of dismay at having been seen to be so singled out before all the company, which was due to her natural modesty as well as to her inexperience. There was bewilderment at why she had been so honored, for she did not indulge herself in the fancy that she was so captivating it was only natural that he should do so. And there was, still, the vestiges of the fear she had felt with him originally. The fear had lessened to a great degree now, for he had been as easy to speak to as Brimsley Fairbrother tonight.

Though it sounded so evil, she wondered just what the term *rake-hell* implied. She could hardly apply to Lady Bromley for an answer, and she doubted her aunt would be knowledgeable on such a worldly subject. Perhaps she could ask Papa. Whatever the implication, she could not believe it was so evil as it seemed, for nothing could have been more pleasing than Lord Sutterton's behavior tonight. She knew very well her agitation when he first led her out could not have escaped his notice, and he had, with great kindness, set himself to soothe her.

She decided that her own imagination had frightened her. Perhaps his aloofness had created a mystery about him that had set society speculating. Wild surmises had become fact when repeated and added to by sensation-seeking gossips, and an image made for him that was undeserved. After all, despite his reputation, he was still received by such diamonds of the first water as the Haworthys, and Lady Caroline Bray and her mother did not disdain his company.

Late though the hour had been when her head was finally laid upon her pillow, she woke at her usual hour the next morning, surprised to find the maid had not come to draw back the curtains and bring her usual cup of chocolate. She sat up and rang the bell and presently Betsy's dour face appeared around the door.

"You are awake then, miss?"

"As you see, Betsy."

"Madam made sure you'd sleep late today," said Betsy
as she crossed to draw back the curtains. "I'll send Mary
with your chocolate. Madam asked to be told when you
was up. Will I let her know now?"

"Yes, please do so, Betsy."

The maid left and almost at once Mary appeared with a
tray, followed by Mrs. Holland. "Dear child, surely you
should have more sleep than this?" she exclaimed, bustling
across the room to kiss Isabelle's brow.

"Well, it seems not, for I feel so wide awake I could
not close my eyes again if I tried."

"Then, please don't keep me in suspense a moment
longer. Did all go well? Did you have partners?"

There followed an enthusiastic description of the ball-
room, its decorations, the gowns, the jewels, the partners,
Lady Bromley's kindness, and the inexplicable behavior of
Lord Sutterton.

"Bless us! How peculiar to have been so particular in
his attentions. A marquess!" Mrs. Holland was overwhelmed
to think of her niece being so honored. She thought,
though she did not say so to Isabelle, that it was surely
Lady Bromley who had persuaded the man to be courteous
to Isabelle, and perhaps it was done to oblige her old
friend, Mrs. Holland.

"And he asked that he might call this morning."

"Very proper. One's partners should inquire for one's
health the morning after a ball," said Mrs. Holland. Then
of a sudden she started to her feet. "Good lord! The
marquess coming here! And the lord knows how many of
the others may not come. I must see whether the maids
have dusted out the drawing room properly." She hurried
away without another word.

Her excitement infected Isabelle, who set aside her cup
and rang for Betsy to help her dress. She ate a hurried
breakfast and was seated in the drawing room with Mrs.
Holland well before eleven, when the first visitor was
announced.

"Mr. Fairbrother!" cried Mrs. Holland, unable to conceal her surprise, for her mind was fixed so entirely upon Lord Sutterton.

He halted halfway across the room. "I hope I have not come at an inconvenient time."

"Oh dear no. You are always very welcome. Please have a chair. Is not Miss Fairbrother with you?" babbled Mrs. Holland confusedly.

"My mama could not spare her this morning. She was very sorry to miss you, Miss Holland, for she wanted most particularly to hear of the ball."

"I was surprised not to find you both there," said Isabelle, holding out her hand to him with a smile.

"The illness of an uncle required our attendance," he replied with a grimace. "One's relatives have no respect for one's plans."

"I hope he has recovered."

" 'Twas only indigestion, I think, but he was convinced his last hour was upon him and demanded his relatives at his bedside. The hour was so late when at last his trouble was eased and he fell asleep that we could only stumble, exhausted, into our own beds."

"There now," said Mrs. Holland, "how provoking for you, and for Miss Fairbrother, for young ladies should not be made to miss balls."

"She was certainly not happy to do so, I assure you. Mrs. Holland, I wonder if I could persuade you and Miss Holland to come for a drive with me. The day is very fine."

"Now, I take that very kind in you to include me in your invitation," said Mrs. Holland, "but we are expecting visitors, you see, and cannot be from home this morning."

At this moment Lord Sutterton appeared as though on cue, and Isabelle colored up under the astonished stare Mr. Fairbrother turned upon her.

The marquess bowed. "Mrs. Holland, good morning. Miss Holland, I hope I find you in good health?"

"Oh, yes, thank you, very," said Isabelle faintly.

"My aunt sends her compliments to you both."

"Oh, how very kind she is. But how rude you must think me. Lord Sutterton, are you acquainted with Mr. Fairbrother?"

Both gentlemen bowed and claimed to be charmed, though there was little more than a bare civility in the manner of each, for they were mutually displeased to find the other present.

The conversation became general and rather stiffly formal until Mr. Fairbrother decided he could not, as he would have liked to do, outwait the marquess, who seemed determined to do the same. Mr. Fairbrother rose and made his adieus and left the field to the marquess, feeling rather miffed that neither Isabelle nor her aunt protested his going.

Isabelle and Mrs. Holland had both felt the situation too uncomfortable to prolong and had said nothing to prevent Mr. Fairbrother's departure. Once he was out of the room, Lord Sutterton relaxed back into his chair and became entirely genial in his manner.

"Well, Miss Holland, I trust there are no ill effects this morning from so much dissipation last night?"

"Why, sir, do I look the worse for it?"

"Indeed not. Quite the reverse, if I may say so. As though you were ready to commence again at once."

"La, my lord," exclaimed Mrs. Holland, "I should hope a few hours of dancing would not discommode a young girl who has her health. It is right strange that men can spend the whole day riding to hounds or shooting partridge and yet feel a little dancing to be a great trial to their strength."

"I daresay those who complain are those who are less fortunate in their partners than was I, for you hear no complaints from me," replied Lord Sutterton, smiling at Isabelle.

"Why, you have no right to complaints, in any case, my lord, for you danced but the one set," said Isabelle.

"Gladly would I have danced them all, had I been allowed to do so with the one fair partner I so fortunately found."

Isabelle found this compliment too overwhelming to respond to. Even Mrs. Holland was silenced by so open an avowal, but seeing the silence lengthening uncomfortably while Isabelle seemed absorbed in studying the drapes and the marquess seemed content to watch her, Mrs. Holland pulled herself together.

"Er—Lord Sutterton—er—I wonder—do you hunt?" she said, throwing out as a conversational gambit the first thing that occurred to her.

"Why yes, I do. You are interested in the hunt, Mrs. Holland?"

She laughed merrily. "You are making fun of me, my lord. Oh dear—hunting—me!" She went off into a veritable paroxysm of laughter at the picture this presented to her mind.

Isabelle began to laugh despite herself, and then Lord Sutterton joined in and after this the visit went very easily. Before he took his leave, he had engaged Isabelle to drive with him on the following morning.

Isabelle and Mrs. Holland sat for some moments in silence after the outer door had closed upon him. Isabelle could think of nothing to say and Mrs. Holland, who thought of a great many things she would like to say, thought it better to say none of them.

"What a pleasant young man he seems," she ventured at last.

"Yes," was Isabelle's reply.

They were saved the further necessity to discuss the visit by the announcement of the Misses Richmond, who had come to hear about the ball. They had, of course, danced in the homes of their friends, and attended assemblies, but had never attended anything so grand as a private ball.

The next three-quarters of an hour was spent in a description, in the minutest detail, of every aspect of the evening on the part of Isabelle, and rapturous exclamations and eager questioning on the part of Victoria and Horatia.

Mrs. Holland, having already heard the story, allowed her mind to attend to her own thoughts. Lady Bromley's nephew, a marquess, seemed to be developing particular feelings toward Isabelle. Mrs. Holland could no longer suppose that Lady Bromley had pushed her nephew into mere courtesies, for it was plain as plain that he was much taken with the girl. The question was, how did Isabelle herself feel about the marquess? She had seemed no more partial to him than to Mr. Fairbrother, but then, it was early days yet.

Listening now, she noted that Isabelle made no mention of his name, not even when she was asked to put names to her different partners of the evening. This seemed to Mrs. Holland significant. If she had been indifferent, she would have included his name with the others she was naming. Only to think, a marquess! Why, my very own niece might be the Marchioness of Sutterton!

Six

Having resolved, however unwillingly, upon marriage as an inevitable necessity, the marquess set about to cast his lures with a masterly expertise. With most young women he had encountered he knew he would have had little more to do than show an interest and the fruit would have dropped into his palm eagerly. With Isabelle, however, he sensed that more skill was demanded. There was that fear to be set at rest first, and the cool manner with which she counteracted the fear to be overcome. He felt she had more backbone than he had yet met with in a girl of her years and that at least the challenge offered some titillation to the effort that would relieve the boredom with which he had originally faced the ordeal.

As a first step when he arrived the following morning to take her for a drive, he insisted upon Mrs. Holland's fetching her bonnet and accompanying them. Isabelle, who had been put extremely on edge by the prospect of an hour alone in his company but for Betsy, who would contribute nothing except her inhibiting presence, was disarmed by this gesture, as was her aunt.

Lord Sutterton directed his coachman to drive to the Park, seated himself facing them, and set himself out to be charming. He divided his attentions between them and his compliments to Isabelle were stated in a light-handed manner calculated not to alarm her with any freighted innuendos. They only hinted delicately at his admiration of her and his pleasure in being in her company and after a time she relaxed enough to wonder at it that the prospect of being with him so alarmed her while the actuality was so pleasant.

Not long after they entered the Park they encountered Mr. and Miss Fairbrother riding in company with Mr. Tuberville and Horatia Richmond. Miss Richmond, looking very smart in her riding costume, had the dazzled air of one entered into Paradise and smiled blindly upon everyone impartially, including Lord Sutterton when introduced to him. Miss Fairbrother, on the other hand, lost her composure completely and hung her head bashfully and only mumbled a response. When attention was turned from her, she stared at the marquess, eyes starting wildly, occasionally turning an alarmed look upon Isabelle. She clearly considered her friend in danger and marveled at her courage in exposing herself to it.

Mr. Fairbrother did not attempt to hide his displeasure. His usually pleasant face was stony, his manner stiff and unbending. He only nodded distantly to Lord Sutterton and the ladies and held himself aloof from the ensuing exchange of amenities. He had, until this moment, felt fairly confident of his suit for Isabelle's hand. She had favored his company, he knew he was acknowledged by her father and relatives as a prospective husband, and she was approved of by his mother. He was aware that his mother's approval hinged in part on the rumors of Isabelle's fortune, but he was not swayed by that. He was genuinely in love with her and would have proposed even had she been penniless. He had no need to marry money, but from vague insinuations that had reached his ears, he thought that such might not be Lord Sutterton's case. Not that he discounted the idea that Isabelle's person did not attract Lord Sutterton, for she was a monstrously pretty girl, but all the same Mr. Fairbrother, apart from his natural antagonism to any rival, could not be easy in his mind to see her in the man's company, notwithstanding the presence of Mrs. Holland.

After dinner that evening, Isabelle found an opportunity to question her father on the meaning of *rake-hell*.

"Why, my dear, it usually means a young gentleman

who lives rather more for—er—pleasure than others and does so with a complete disregard for the opinions of his peers or the capacity of his purse."

"You mean gambling and—and—mistresses and such things?"

"Um—yes."

Isabelle turned away thoughtfully. She found the explanation more reassuring than otherwise, for she was not so unsophisticated in the ways of the world to expect a man of Lord Sutterton's age to have remained celibate. As for the gambling, was not Papa a gambler himself? Gaming held no terrors for Isabelle, though she was not wise enough to realize that a profligate gamester who ignored the capacity of his purse was a far cry from a prudent professional like her father, who earned his living by it.

Mr. Fairbrother and his sister called the next morning, but before he could propose any expedition, Lord Sutterton was announced. Miss Fairbrother shrank fearfully against Isabelle on the sofa as though she would shelter behind her as she was used to do with her mother on social occasions. Mr. Fairbrother's face became a mask, all good humor erased.

Lord Sutterton greeted everyone courteously and made himself very pleasant, especially with Miss Fairbrother, who finally allowed herself to be coaxed into a laugh by one of his quips. Her brother observed this sourly. Had she been a bird, he thought contemptuously, she would at this point be perched upon my lord's finger eating out of his hand.

Lord Sutterton did not attempt to outlast the Fairbrothers. He rose gracefully after a half hour and declared he had only come to deliver an invitation from his aunt for Mrs. Holland and her niece to join her in her box at the opera this evening. Mrs. Holland was mightily pleased by this condescension and with a glance at Isabelle to confirm her agreement, accepted happily. The marquess then bowed to everyone and left the room.

Mr. Fairbrother glared after his retreating back and fumed

inwardly, knowing that the marquess was bound to make one of the party to the opera or his aunt would not have used him to deliver her invitation. He salved his pride by extracting a promise from Isabelle to accompany him and his sister for a drive the following morning. When his visit was further interrupted by the announcement of Lord Talboys, he quitted the field himself, thinking that he must waste no time if he was to win the girl for himself.

The marquess, of course, was in attendance that evening and had much more opportunity to speak apart with Isabelle than usual, since his aunt kept Mrs. Holland engaged in conversation. He bent toward her, his eyes warm with admiration, encouraging her to speak, listening with flattering attention to her every word. She expanded under this treatment, telling him first of operas and singers she had heard on the Continent and then something of the life she had led there.

"Rather a trying childhood for you," he said sympathetically.

"Not really." She laughed. "I did not miss what I did not know I should have had. My only regret now is that I cannot ride."

"But that is so easily remedied. I have a lovely little mare that would suit you perfectly. Will you allow me to send her around to you tomorrow?"

"No, my lord, though I appreciate so considerate a thought," she said, aware of the impropriety of accepting such a gift. "Besides," she added to soften the refusal, "I have no riding dress, nor could I ride if I had it, for I meant that I do not know how to ride. It is only one of many accomplishments I lack."

"Ah, how I should love to be your tutor," he exclaimed so fervently that she looked up startled to meet his eyes. He smiled and he seemed to be sending her the same message she had received the first night she saw him. It was a look that implied intimacy between them, and again, as then, she could not look away from it. She had no idea how long they remained so, their glance locked, but she started visibly when Lady Bromley spoke to him. He slowly withdrew his gaze and turned to respond to his aunt.

After the evening at the opera, she did not see the marquess for three days, three days during which she became increasingly more puzzled and restless, jumping each time she heard the door knocker, thinking it might be he. She received many callers, she was taken about London in parties of young people, she went for drives with Mr. Fairbrother, but she did not see Lord Sutterton, though her eyes seemed always searching for a sight of him.

Then, when she had almost convinced herself he would come no more and it really was better that he should not, Mary came tapping at her bedroom door to say Lord Sutterton was below and her aunt desired her to come down. Hurriedly, she put the finishing touches to her toilette and went down to greet him, her pulses racing and strangely breathless, a condition she ascribed to the earliness and unexpectedness of the call. He rose smiling at her entrance and kissed the hand she extended.

"My lord," she said.

"Miss Holland, how happy I am that you are here to see me. I have heard of you everywhere and had braced myself for disappointment. I trust you have been enjoying yourself."

"Indeed, yes, very much."

"My aunt hopes that you and Mrs. Holland will be free to come to a dinner party on Saturday."

"It seems you are ever Lady Bromley's messenger, sir. She should have sent around a note and not put you to so much trouble," she said coolly.

He understood at once that she was intimating he only came at his aunt's behest and that she was displeased by his three days' absence, though she had been so busy with her friends. This was part of his plan and he was glad to see that it had worked very well.

He smiled his intimate smile and said softly, "I was hesitant to push my presence upon you, being uncertain of my welcome among so many admirers. I eagerly accept my aunt's commissions as an excuse to present myself."

"For shame, my lord, for speaking so," she said, "as though after all her kindness to us we would not always happily welcome any relative of Lady Bromley's."

"I would prefer some encouragement to hope I would be welcome though I were not related to Lady Bromley."

She colored but forced herself to answer straightly, "Of course you are so welcome, sir," before turning away to seat herself beside her aunt upon the sofa and include her in the conversation. Mrs. Holland, who had, of course, heard their words while pretending to be engrossed upon her embroidery frame, had been somewhat shocked by Isabelle's words. There seemed, to her, something discourteous in calling a marquess a mere messenger boy.

Isabelle was shocked at herself. She had not meant to reveal so much of her feelings, but she had not realized until they popped out how strongly she had felt it that he had not come to see her. She was grateful that she had not been even more explicit and could only hope that he had not understood her. Was she becoming so spoiled by the amount of attention she had received from Brimsley Fairbrother and others that she pouted with displeasure if anyone flagged in their attentions to her?

When Lord Sutterton had taken his leave she excused herself to her aunt and went to her room. She needed to think quietly about her behavior. She could not, after further thought, accuse herself of being a spoiled society beauty. She had never experienced any anxiety about whether any of the other gentlemen of her acquaintance called upon her or not, though naturally it was gratifying when they did.

What then had caused her to allow Lord Sutterton to see her displeasure? And why was she so displeased? For some time her mind refused to deal with these questions and wandered off into various memories of her few encounters with him, all, in retrospect, pleasurable, and more—yes, more exciting than her experiences with gentlemen in London had been so far. The ball, the drive, the opera, each had left her rather heady with happiness and looking forward eagerly to the next one.

She pulled herself up at this point. She was forgetting her sensible plan of looking about carefully, taking her time to make a wise choice. If she allowed herself to go on in this direction, she would be in danger of losing her perspective. Their meetings, pleasurable as they had been, were all of the most superficial substance. The marquess had been making the agreeable to a friend of his aunt's, nothing more, and the more fool she if she allowed herself to impute any more importance to it than that. There must be no more reading of intimate messages into his singular way of smiling into her eyes. No doubt he did the same to every woman he met and they all read some such message into it. It was just his way. He was an unusually handsome man of wealth and title, accustomed to women losing their heads over him. He would have little interest in Isabelle Holland with her five thousand pounds and her connection to a minor country baronet. To think otherwise was to court unhappiness, therefore he could have no place in her carefully thought-out plan for her future.

After this severe taking to task, she prepared to meet him two nights later at Lady Bromley's dinner party with her armor securely in place, and further strengthened by the fact that despite the assurance he had extracted from her that he was welcome to call upon her at will, he had not taken advantage of it since.

He made his customary late appearance at the dinner party, and after greeting his aunt, made his way at once to Isabelle, followed by every female eye in the room. He greeted Mrs. Holland and bowed over Isabelle's hand.

"Good evening, Miss Holland. I see that I need not inquire if I find you in good health," he said.

"No, my lord, I am very well, thank you," she replied pleasantly, withdrawing the hand he still held.

"I trust you still look upon London with favor?"

"Oh, indeed, sir. Everyone here is kind. They never seem to tire of giving parties to entertain their friends."

"I am sure that with such a charming guest, they have every reason to entertain."

She laughed lightly and looked about her as though deeming the compliment too superficial to require a reply.

Little devil, he thought with vexation, for he saw that she was not to be won so easily as he had hoped, and while he admired her cool-headedness, it irritated him to realize he would have to exert himself. He was not the least in love with her and felt no danger of ever being so, and had hoped the business could have been accomplished without his being forced to enact such a farce. He caught his aunt's eye at that moment, and made a small moue of displeasure, but she only smiled back encouragingly. Well, well, he thought, there is nothing for it, I suppose, unless I want to pursue the Bray girl. And her mother, he added involuntarily and shuddered in distaste. No, no, he could not do it, however less trouble was involved. He turned back resignedly to his duty.

Lady Bromley had naturally assigned him to take Isabelle in to dinner and he wasted not a moment the rest of the evening, making love to her with all his considerable ability. As a result, all Isabelle's worthy resolves of two days ago melted imperceptibly away. Before the evening was over, he had persuaded her to come for a drive with him the following day to visit the famous flower gardens of the Wickley estate only a few miles from London where the public was allowed access on certain days. He wished the girl could ride, for it seemed to him there were infinitely more opportunities for getting away from inhibiting eyes that way. He felt sure that if he could only get her alone for a few minutes she would capitulate. However, he would do the best he could tomorrow and no doubt he could contrive something.

Isabelle attempted to restore her sensible attitude in the intervening hours, but found it nearly impossible to concentrate on it. The matter seemed somehow less pressing after the hours spent in his company last night.

She persuaded Aunt Nathaniel to allow Mary to replace Betsy as chaperone and when Lord Sutterton was announced, came down in a flounced white muslin walking dress, a red velvet spenser, and a chip bonnet, looking, as he did not hesitate to inform her, thoroughly enchanting.

Mary, ecstatic to be released from her duties in the house and elevated to so lofty a position as lady's maid, sat with her back to the driver, staring about her, mouth slightly agape. It was the first time she had ever ridden in an open carriage, or indeed in any carriage at all.

They set off at a spanking pace, the marquess keeping up a rather erratic conversation, from time to time seeming to go off into a deep, abstracted silence after staring intently at Isabelle for a moment. She found it very disturbing and longed to ask him outright if there was anything troubling him, but dared not.

When they reached the entrance of the gardens, they left the carriage to stroll among the neatly laid-out flower beds, admiring the fountains and the carefully arranged vistas. There were others taking advantage of the fine day for an outing and before long they came upon Swinburn Tuberville with a Richmond sister upon each arm. Isabelle, followed by Mary, had just crossed the path to inspect a bush of pink roses abloom in unusual profusion, and was perceived by the other party to be alone with her maid.

"Why, Miss Holland! Well met," cried Mr. Tuberville, his endearing smile transforming his homely face. "Oh, would that I had another arm to offer you."

"That would indeed be a disfigurement you should be unhappy to have wished for, sir," she replied, laughing, "and greedy as well, when you have two such well-filled arms already."

"And Miss Holland has no need of an arm in any case, as mine is already at her service," added the marquess, sauntering across the path to join them.

"Ah, Lord Sutterton, I failed to see you there," said Mr. Tuberville, unabashed. "I believe you know Miss Horatia Richmond, but not Miss Victoria Richmond."

Lord Sutterton bowed to each lady and then they detached themselves and came to embrace Isabelle, chirping with excitement at the encounter.

"Well, my lord, this is a pleasant and unexpected meeting," said Mr. Tuberville pleasantly. "We have explored everything and were just on our way to find some refreshments. You will join us, I hope."

"I thank you, but we have only just arrived and have our exploring still to do," replied the marquess smoothly, not about to be caught up in a party that would present all sorts of obstacles to his plans. "You will find refreshments down that path, I believe. Shall we proceed, Miss Holland?" He held out his arm. Isabelle was compelled to take it and he led her away as she called out good-byes to her friends over her shoulder.

She was somewhat provoked at what seemed to her an unseemly haste in separating themselves from the others. She would not for the world have offended any of those good people by treating them rudely. She removed her hand from his arm, fumbling in her reticule for a handkerchief as a pretext for doing so, and afterward walked a little apart from him in silence.

"I have displeased you," he said presently. "You would have preferred to make a party with your friends."

"I would have preferred not offending them," she replied stiffly.

"Forgive me. I meant no offense, but perhaps my eagerness to be alone with you provoked me into rudeness. I will take you back to them and apologize," he said humbly.

She laughed, relenting at once at his words. "No. I will take the word for the deed. Oh, do look at that charming little bridge!"

A small humped-back bridge spanned a tiny stream chuckling over mossy stones and they walked upon it to gaze into the water. The marquess saw that Mary was staring down as though hypnotized and quietly guided Isabelle off the bridge and into a grove of trees on the bank of the stream. "Just through here I believe is an arbor where you may sit and contemplate the water more comfortably," he said, with a covert glance back to note that Mary was still rapt and had not noticed their leaving.

As he hoped, when Mary at last noticed that she was

alone she hurried off the bridge and along the path that led past the grove of trees. She would spend a long time in search of them, he thought, which, of course, was exactly what she did do.

In the meantime, he found the bench beside the stream and seated Isabelle upon it and himself beside her.

"Why, how pretty it is here," exclaimed Isabelle happily. He only sighed and gazed abstractly before him. After a long silence, Isabelle glanced about uneasily. "I wonder what is keeping Mary?"

The bridge being hidden from their view by the trees, he felt safe in replying, "Still upon the bridge. She will come presently." This was said gloomily and followed by another silence, broken at last by so heavy a sigh from him that she was compelled to turn to him.

Rather hesitantly she said, "My lord, forgive me if I seem to pry, but you seem—unhappy. Are you troubled by something?"

"Only by my stupidity," he replied morosely.

"Oh?" she said encouragingly.

"Yes, for you see, having achieved that which I have striven for for so long, I find myself too tongue-tied to take advantage of it."

She laughed disbelievingly. "You? Tongue-tied?" He did not reply and after a moment she said more seriously, "What could you have striven for that has caused such a condition?"

"Only to be alone with you for a few moments."

"I cannot think why that should cause such a state."

"Ah, because you are such a stern judge!" he cried. "And I have already offended you without meaning to."

"Why, Lord Sutterton, I do not understand you in the least. I surely cannot be called stern, nor can you justly accuse yourself of offending me."

He turned to her impulsively. "You are too good. I do not deserve your forgiveness."

"I am unaware of anything that needs it, but if your peace of mind depends upon it, you may rest assured you have it," she said as gaily as possible, attempting to lighten the atmosphere.

"You are adorable!" he cried, seizing her hand and kissing it.

"My lord!" she protested, attempting to pull her hand from his grasp.

"No, I will not give it up so easily," he said, holding it more firmly, smiling now. "I hold it as a token of the forgiveness you granted me for any offense I may have given. I know I was rude to your friends before and that when I have called and found you so surrounded by them I have behaved childishly, but it was only jealousy of the favor they have found with you. Indeed, I know too well I am not worthy to be counted among them."

"Oh, do not say so, my lord! Of course I count you among my friends," she assured him earnestly.

He stared into her eyes and, not taking his own away, raised the hand he still held and brushed his lips against it. Then quite slowly he leaned closer and kissed her lips lingeringly. She had had no time even to realize this when he jumped to his feet, his eyes wide as though aghast at his conduct, and gasped, "My God! Please forgive me! What have I done?"

She stood up, so confused she could not think, struggling to regain her composure. She fussed with the ribbands of her bonnet and brushed aimlessly at her gown. At last she stuttered, "P-p-perhaps we should go in search of Mary."

"Dear Miss Holland, I swear I did not mean to take advantage of your goodness," he said, running a distracted hand through his hair and backing away a few steps.

She turned and started back through the trees and he followed her. They regained the path before he spoke again. "I have spoiled everything now and you are angry with me."

"I—let us forget the matter, sir."

"Ah, as though I ever could! No doubt you will find it easy enough to do so."

She was saved having to reply to this by the appearance

before them of Mr. Tuberville and the Misses Richmond, who all seemed in the gayest of spirits, and when they saw Isabelle and the marquess called out cheerful greetings as they passed by, but Isabelle was much discomfitted by the meeting, since Mary was so clearly not in sight. What must they be thinking to see her wandering about without her maid?

Then, before the other party was more than a few yards away, Mary came hurrying up, crying out, "Lor, Miss, what a fright you have give me. I've searched for you this half hour! Where did you get yourself to?"

Isabelle knew the others could not have helped over-hearing this and was further embarrassed. "We stayed looking at the water, Mary. I could not think where you had gone," she said as calmly as possible. "Should we not find the carriage, Lord Sutterton?"

The trip back was difficult, but she managed to keep up a conversation, mostly connected with her expectations concerning Miss Horatia and Mr. Tuberville, to which the marquess responded with only a token show of interest. When they reached the Holland front door, Mary hopped out and hurried up the front steps while he assisted Isabelle, taking the opportunity to press her hand and look beseechingly into her eyes. She smiled and thanked him prettily for the expedition, assuring him that she had enjoyed it.

He climbed back into the carriage when the door had closed behind her and as he was driven away, allowed a smile of satisfaction to express itself. He was more than pleased with the morning and knew Isabelle was his for the asking now. Had this not been so, she would have let him see very clearly that his kiss had angered her. She had not been in the least angry and would by now be shut in her room reliving the experience and wondering how soon she could expect a proposal.

And he was right, for she had hurried at once to her room, glad not to encounter anyone, and sitting at her dressing table tried to recall their entire conversation there by the water and found in it now much that had escaped her at the time. His assertion that he was jealous of her friends, for instance, and the bit about his childish behavior. That surely explained why he had not called those three days. And to admit jealousy was surely as close as he could have come to making a declaration of love, for one could not be jealous unless one cared. Had he not given in to that impulsive kiss he would no doubt have gone on to tell her of his love.

She closed her eyes and remembered the kiss and felt almost giddy for a moment as she experienced again that soft pressure upon her lips. It had been too brief for her to register any sensation at the time, but now in her mind she could extend the fleeting moment of it and she found it indescribably delicious. No one had ever kissed her upon the lips before, except perhaps her mama, but she had no memory of that. She touched her mouth wonderingly. Lovers kissed that way, she knew from novels. Were they lovers now? Yes, she thought, with a great surge of feeling, yes, we are lovers. He has let me see his heart and I must love him.

Lord Sutterton was wrong, however, in one thing. She was not wondering how soon she could expect his proposal, for she had not learned that this is what girls now expected a kiss to lead to as a matter of course.

He came every morning, early, for four days and on the fourth found her alone in the drawing room. He had, naturally, inquired for Mrs. Holland at the door and the butler had shown him into the drawing room before going away to summon his mistress. Isabelle rose as the marquess hurried across to take her hand. "Miss Holland—Isabelle—dearest Isabelle, I must speak! You know my feelings?" He took her other hand now and held them both against his chest. She was too overcome to speak, but gazed steadily up into his face and nodded. "And dare I hope—is it possible—can you feel the same?"

"Yes," she whispered, blushing but with her head up proudly.

"Ah!" he cried triumphantly, and swept her into his arms to kiss her much less gently than he had done in the arbor by the stream. She responded with all the ardency of her young nature and there was plenty of time for her to experience all the various sensations she had missed the first time.

They sprang apart at the sound of Mrs. Holland's voice approaching the door as she ordered her manservant to have wine sent to the drawing room.

He called several days after that, but there was no further chance for them to be alone and expressions of their love had to be satisfied with soft looks and a brief pressure of hands upon meeting and parting, but Isabelle was not unhappy. Her heart was high with happiness and she treasured the secret of her love, unwilling to share it with anyone.

Then one morning a posy arrived in an ivory holder with his card and a message on the back of it to say he was called out of town for a few days on business and that he hoped she would not forget him. A week passed with no further word, but Isabelle refused to allow herself to grow despondent, for he had told her he loved her and she must trust that this separation was as unwelcome to him as to her.

A note arrived from Lady Bromley asking them to call, which made Isabelle very happy. Perhaps Lady Bromley would speak of her nephew. The marquess had, of course, gone at once to tell his aunt of his success, and though she scolded him for not proposing on the spot, he had reassured her he would waste no time in the matter and she had assumed he was doing so. Her invitation had been to help the cause by showing Isabelle every consideration.

Out of her presence and influence, however, the marquess had decided he deserved a rest from the arduous hours he had put in so far in his wooing. He had sent Isabelle the note about business and gone off to a less tedious and more rewarding wooing of his neglected mistress of the moment whom he had established in a set of rooms far away from the part of London inhabited by his aunt and her friends.

Mrs. Holland was vastly gratified by Lady Bromley's reception of Isabelle, for she was becoming more certain

every day that Lord Sutterton's attentions were too pronounced to be ignored, and surely, he and his aunt being
so close, he would have confided his feelings to her. This
demonstration of Lady Bromley's regard could only be her
way of showing her approval of the match. Isabelle herself
felt something of this and the color in her cheeks became
more pronounced as she acknowledged Lady Bromley's
warm greeting.

After a time Lady Bromley began to tease her gently
about the matter. "Do tell me, my dear, how my nephew
does, for I think you must see a great deal more of him
than I."

"Oh, no, my lady—I mean—not this past week while
he is called away on business," said Isabelle, much flustered.

Lady Bromley looked blank. Called away on business?
Why she had seen him not two days ago herself—not to
speak to, but only through a shop window as he had
passed down the road in his carriage. She hurried now into
a long explanation of an estate of his in Scotland that gave
him some problems from time to time, but she was very
angry with him. He would certainly learn from her before
this day was over what she thought of his irresponsible
behavior.

When her guests were gone she went at once to pen a
few lines to him requesting that he call upon her immediately and had her footman take it around to his house at
once. Lord Sutterton, however, had not slept at home for
this past week and was not to do so for another week, so
the note lay awaiting his return on a tray in the hallway
along with other letters, including a number of irate demands for payment of long overdue accounts.

Seven

So another week passed and Isabelle neither saw nor heard from her lover, but she was not sad, being uplifted by love. She marveled at herself, she who had scoffed at the idea of love, and turned her new experience this way and that to examine it and to secretly thrill at it.

She spoke of it to no one, not even her papa or Aunt Nathaniel. There was nothing, after all, to tell them as he had not yet proposed, and she was too shy simply to announce that she loved and was loved. She saw all her friends as usual, went to parties and even balls, where her new-found happiness shown forth from her eyes and drew even more gentlemen into her orbit. Mr. Fairbrother, dancing with her at a ball, was so encouraged by the sweetness of her smile as to think the time had come to make his declaration if he could only be alone with her for long enough. He would have been much chagrined had he known that Lord Talboys had found those few moments and made use of them, but had been firmly, but gently, refused.

One late afternoon she returned from a breakfast given by Lady Hetherington which, as usual, had not begun before midday and was still in progress when Isabelle, becoming weary, had left. She heard voices from the drawing room and went in to find her aunt entertaining a gentleman. The man rose and turned to her as her aunt called out a greeting, and Isabelle stopped dead on the threshold. Here was someone she knew, but so utterly out of context was he in her aunt's drawing room that she could not think who he might be.

"Laws, child, how startled you look," laughed Mrs. Holland. "Come and make your curtsy. 'Tis Captain Perronet come to visit you and your papa, though he had not come back from Nathaniel's club yet. He will be that surprised to see you, captain, and ever so glad too, for he has spoken of you often."

This flow of chatter allowed Isabelle to take a deep breath and attempt to still her hammering heart and recover from the shock of recognition. Her entire detestable experience with this man, forgotten from the moment she had set foot on her aunt's doorstep for the first time, now flashed through her mind and set her trembling with remembered anger and humiliation. What was he doing here?

He stood there waiting, tall and dark-browed as ever, but then a slow smile transformed the stern features and he stepped forward, bowed, and said, "Miss Holland, it is indeed a pleasure to see you again."

She sketched a curtsy, but could not bring herself to speak. Mrs. Holland frowned slightly at this, but only said, "Come, love, sit here beside me and have a glass of wine. You must be tired to death from your party. I have never really approved of this new fashion for breakfast parties—too early in the day for partying, to my way of thinking. Captain, would you be so kind as to refill your own glass and bring one to Isabelle? Then I won't have to ring for a servant and we can all be cozy together."

During this speech, Isabelle walked on trembling legs to the sofa and sank down upon it. A moment later she accepted a glass of wine from the captain's hand and gulped at it eagerly, hoping it would steady her nerves and give her enough courage to hold her head up and not allow this man to see that his appearance had in any way disconcerted her. Presently the wine did its work well enough for her to address him directly.

"I had thought you halfway around the world by this time, Captain Perronet."

"And wished me there, too, I make no doubt," he said with a laugh, "but I am grateful you thought of me at all, Miss Holland."

She bit back a denial of this, knowing it would only sound childish, and said, "Where do you sail next, sir?" in a coldly reproving voice.

"Ah, so eager to see the back of me, eh? Not that I blame you. I am a great oaf with women. My sister tells me so all the time. But to answer your question, I do not sail again. I've sold my ship and become a landlubber again."

"But what shall you do now, sir?" cried Mrs. Holland.

"Why, set up for a country gentleman, madam. I've bought a fine great property in Sussex near my sister's place and am having it done up a treat. The family that built it owned it some four hundred years, but they all died out some twenty years ago now, and it has stood empty since. A place can go down a lot when it's neglected that long."

There followed a lively discussion between him and Mrs. Holland about roofs and drains and chimneys, leaving Isabelle free to sort out her thoughts which had been thrown into a sad state of disorder by the sudden and undreamed-of reappearance into her life of this man who had been so rude to her that she had hoped never to see him again. Why, why was he here? She studied him covertly as he spoke with her aunt, his eyes bright with enthusiasm and a smile coming and going on his face. She had never seen him so animated and had to admit he was not so unattractive as she remembered him. Then, slowly, as she watched him, she made another discovery. He was not at all the old man she had thought him to be. Away from his ship and the duties it had demanded of him, his hard features were relaxed and she realized he could be no older than the marquess, perhaps even younger.

He looked at her suddenly and caught her eye and smiled. She flushed and looked away quickly, then was annoyed with herself for having been caught staring at him and for allowing him to see her discomposure. Why did her every encounter with this man lead to embarrassment for her? Why should she even allow him to embarrass her? He was nothing to her, not even a friend, merely an acquaintance.

Her papa came in with her Uncle Nathaniel to interrupt her thoughts. "Captain Perronet," cried Mr. Holland gladly, striding across the room to shake his hand heartily. Isabelle noted with astonishment that her father's face was lit with genuine pleasure, as was that of the captain. She had not realized they had so truly liked one another. Naturally, there ensued a recapitulation of all the information already given to Mrs. Holland. Finally the captain was urged to stay and take his mutton with the family and after proper demurs he agreed, and Isabelle at last was able to escape upstairs to remove her bonnet and change for dinner. For a time she toyed with the idea of having a headache and asking for a tray in her room, but discarded it as cowardly. She had done nothing to be ashamed of. It was Captain Perronet who should be ashamed for his insulting thoughts regarding her and for his hasty judgment of her for which he had never apologized. And then to just appear brazenly on the doorstep expecting her to welcome him as though nothing had happened!

So, armed with her secret love and her pride, she swept down to dinner in her old gown of blue silk, worn only when the family was dining at home without guests, her face set in a pleasantly detached expression. Captain Perronet, who had insisted upon going back to his lodgings to change, had returned and was being entertained by Isabelle's papa and Mr. and Mrs. Holland. It was clear to Isabelle at once that her relatives made him just as welcome as her papa did, which was a great puzzle to her, though she could not but admit he was more affable than she had ever seen him before. He rose as she entered and turned to her expectantly.

"Good evening, Captain Perronet," she said loftily.

"Miss Holland. A charming gown and my favorite color. I feel honored, indeed."

She at once felt ashamed of her pettiness in choosing the

gown deliberately. She dipped a curtsy and mumbled, "I thank you, sir."

"I don't know why I have such a partiality for a blue gown, but it has always been so."

"I am not accustomed to hearing pretty speeches from you, sir," she said, feeling somehow the need to defend herself again.

"Oh, aye, I know my tongue is often grating to ladies' ears, but I've been much with sister lately and she has been busy honing off the rough edges."

She raised an eyebrow and said only, "Oh?"

"I expect you're thinking she has taken on an impossible task," he said with a laugh at himself, "but then, you don't know my sister. Very determined little body she is, and up to all the niceties of behavior, having attended Mrs. Hobbes' Academy for Young Gentlewomen and made the most of her time there."

"Good heavens!" cried Mrs. Holland excitedly. "Lady Bromley attended that school. I remember well when she was sent away and how much I envied her. I wonder if your sister knew her there?"

"She knew of her, more like. You see, Lady Bromley, the Honorable Miss Edgecombe as was, was an older girl and left during my sister's first year there, so they never became friends."

The captain's stock rose in Mrs. Holland's estimation. His family clearly was of some substance to have sent their daughter to Mrs. Hobbes' school. "Such a coincidence," she said. "What is your sister's name, sir? I must mention it to Lady Bromley when we meet next time."

"She was Miss Elizabeth Perronet then, ma'am, but now she is Mrs. Ramsleigh Claypool of West Sussex. Eastbourne, to be exact, though it's a small place and you may not know it. Near Cowdray Castle, it is."

"Ah, yes. I have not been there, but I have a friend in Midhurst and that is quite near, I believe. Is your own property near there?"

"Quite near, in Chithurst."

There followed a lively flow of conversation as the older

Hollands asked dozens of questions and remembered various families in the captain's neighborhood, leaving Isabelle free to reflect upon her own ungraciousness. She told herself that there was no need any longer for her to snub the man. What had happened was in the past and she had no need to defend her reputation now. She was accepted into society, she was courted by men of the *ton*, and she was loved by a distinguished man of title. She could surely forgive a man who had not been afforded the beneficial refinements of good society. He seemed harmless enough now, and if he had appeared fearsome on his own ship, perhaps it was necessary when a large vessel and many people's lives were his sole responsibility.

She began to feel almost beatific with her own nobility of character and throughout the rest of the evening, though she seldom spoke, a tender, small smile turned up the corners of her mouth and did not vanish even when he asked to be allowed to call again the next day.

William Perronet, walking the dark streets of London back to his lodgings, whistled softly, thoroughly pleased with the outcome of his visit. All had turned out even better than he had hoped when he set out for London. The lass had been cold at first, as was only natural his sister had warned him, but she had thawed out soon enough and as far as he could make out the wind was set fair and calm seas showed ahead. He had only to keep a steady hand on the helm and he would bring her safely into port. For Captain Perronet had come to court and win Isabelle Holland for his wife.

Since the day she had left his ship she had filled his thoughts almost exclusively. The sweet oval of her face and the cool gray eyes haunted his dreams. His ship held no more charm for him. He began to dream of acres to ride with a house to go home to each evening and Isabelle Holland waiting there to welcome him. True, the sea had been his life for the past ten years, but before that he had been a country lad for seventeen, and he loved the countryside of Sussex. He could well afford to do as he liked, for he had very profitably invested the money from his trading ventures and the sale of the ship would bring even more.

Once decided on his course, he had put matters in train at once with all the dispatch and decisiveness with which he had commanded his ship. His last cargo was sold and the ship changed hands in less than a week and then he proceeded to the business of buying an estate. He had had his eye on Tall Oaks, the derelict manor house of the Garland family, even as a boy, daydreaming about being master there and of all that he would do to make it prosperous again. The solicitors were only too eager to accept his offer and he soon had an army of workmen swarming over the place to effect its restoration. He then set off for London to find and woo Isabelle Holland. He was not the man to entertain doubts and had remained serenely confident despite Liz's reiterated warnings that he might find difficulties in his path. He saw none that could not be overcome with perseverance. She had been a little uppity to begin with, but soon changed into more pleasant behavior that would no doubt improve even more in days to come.

So, on the following morning he arrived full of confidence and expectations. He found only Mrs. Holland waiting to receive him, but she greeted him warmly and they conversed as easily as would friends of long standing. However, his senses were stretched for sight or sound of Isabelle, and he was much discomfitted when she did at last appear to find her bonneted and dressed to go out. She greeted him in a friendly enough way, but did not mention her plans and he could not find a way to ask her. Presently a Mr. Fairbrother was announced and she rose at once. The captain's saturnine brows drew together and he replied gruffly to the introduction.

"I regret that an engagement prevents me from staying, Captain Perronet," she said sweetly, giving him her hand briefly, "but I leave you in such good hands I shall not worry for your entertainment."

Mr. Fairbrother bowed to all and led her out of the

room. William stared gloomily after them. "She goes out alone with that gentleman?" he asked abruptly.

"Oh, no, captain, that would be most improper. His sister always accompanies them, but sometimes she waits in the carriage when he comes in to call for Isabelle."

"He is a—a—beau of hers."

"He calls very frequently," replied Mrs. Holland cautiously.

"He is the only one?"

"Oh, dear me no, there are several young men who are very attentive to Isabelle," said Mrs. Holland proudly. "She is invited everywhere and has made many friends."

The scowl deepened for a moment, but Mrs. Holland chattered on happily about balls and dinner parties and the marquess, and excursions and ridottos and breakfast parties and the marquess, until poor William was only too happy to make his escape when Mr. Holland and his brother came and invited him to accompany them to their club.

He was not, however, the man to give up easily, despite any number of lords and marquesses, and he came the next day and the next and then the next again until he found one day that she had no engagement. Having by then hired a carriage and pair, he immediately invited Mrs. Holland and Isabelle to go out for a drive with him. Mrs. Holland looked so gratified by the invitation that Isabelle had not heart to refuse. She was accustomed now to his presence, which seemed to afford so much pleasure to her father and her relatives, and was no longer bothered by it. He treated her with every courtesy on their brief encounters and she no longer felt at daggers drawn with him each time he spoke to her.

Apart from this, she had other, more pressing, problems to think upon. She still had not heard from Adrian, and while she felt it was her duty to remain cheerful while he was occupied by his business and to trust that he must be as eager to return to her side as she was to see him, still she was beginning to sigh restively at his continued absence. If only he would write a few words to her.

Then, too, yesterday Mr. Fairbrother had taken advantage of a few moments' private conversation to declare himself to her and ask for permission to speak to her father. Much flustered by the abruptness of the declaration, she had said only that she could not give him such permission. Then Miss Fairbrother, who had only walked ahead with a friend, had rejoined them and nothing more could be said on the subject. Isabelle was annoyed with herself for her handling of the situation. After all, she had known, even expected, it to come before Adrian had entered the scene, and she had forgotten all her sensible intentions for her future. Mr. Fairbrother's proposal had therefore come as something of a shock to her. She was also annoyed with him for choosing such a time to tell her of his love, with his sister only a few yards away and likely to return on the instant, as indeed she had. Had he asked to speak to her privately, then approached the matter less abruptly, she would have had time to prepare her refusal and settled the matter once for all. As it was, she could not doubt he would speak to her again and she must decide how to tell him that it was not possible to contemplate a marriage where she did not love, not now that she knew what love was! Lord Talboys' proposal she had been able to dismiss lightly, for she did not take him seriously, and he had taken her refusal in the same way, being, she thought, rather more relieved than otherwise.

~ These problems left her little time to think of Captain Perronet. He was her father's friend, he was around a great deal, and soon, no doubt, he would take himself off back to the country. Only common civility was demanded of her in the meantime and that she gave, as now when she agreed to accompany her aunt for a drive with him.

"I hope you have not been driven about so much by your friends that you find this boring, Miss Holland," said William.

"Oh, not in the least, sir. I enjoy it of all things and would drive out every day if I could."

"Then you shall," he said promptly.

She pretended not to have heard this. "Do you plan to be in London much longer, captain?"

"You sound eager to see me gone, Miss Holland, and alas, I have only just arrived a few days ago. But I shall stay as long as it takes."

"I beg your pardon?"

"I said, I shall stay as long as it takes."

"As long as what takes, sir?"

"Accomplishing my purpose."

"How intriguing. What can your purpose be, I wonder?"

"Ah, as to that, I will be sure to tell you of it before anyone else," he said with a grin that disarmed her as much as his remark puzzled her.

"How provoking of you," she said. "Now I shan't have any rest until I know the answer."

Which, of course, was his intention, for he knew about women's curiosity from years spent teasing his sister, and he wanted himself to be in her thoughts as much as possible. "Have you seen the Tower of London, Mrs. Holland?" he asked, turning to the older woman.

"Mercy on us, sir, I should be frightened to death to go to such a place where so much blood was spilled!"

"Oh, that was all washed away long ago, ma'am. I assure you it is quite ordinary now. Have you seen it, Miss Holland?"

"No, but I should like to, I think. So much history in those walls—the two little princes and poor Anne Boleyn."

"Then I will call for you tomorrow and we will all go," he said in so positive a way that neither woman could deny him. Actually, thought Isabelle, it might answer very well to be busy entertaining her papa's guest. It would leave less opportunity for Mr. Fairbrother to renew his suit, and perhaps he would think better of it given time to cool his ardor.

For the rest of the week she was seen everywhere with Captain Perronet. He was determined to see all the sights of London and they visited Mr. Bullock's Liverpool Museum and the Egyptian Hall and Mr. Barker's Panorama in Leicester Square. He dined several times with the Hollands and engaged a box at the opera for all of them, and though Uncle Nathaniel slept through most of the performance, the rest of the party enjoyed it very much. Afterward the captain took them to a supper he had arranged.

During the meal, when the others were all speaking together, he leaned nearer to her and said quietly, "You know, Miss Holland, we sailors see so much of the uglier side of life, we fall into the way of assuming evil where none exists."

"I—suppose you do, captain," she said, feeling the color hot in her cheeks as she understood his allusion.

"It is just as evil in us to think in such a way. You have been so kind to me, I can only assume you have found it in your heart to forgive what I should have apologized for before you left my ship."

She looked at him straightly as he deserved for this handsome apology. "Yes, Captain Perronet, I have."

"You are a wonderful girl, Miss Holland. Are we friends then?"

"Indeed we are, Captain Perronet," she said warmly, much touched by the humbleness of his question. "So now you will tell me your purpose in coming to London, will you not? I have puzzled and puzzled over it, and I think I have it. You have come for furnishings for your new home! Am I right?"

He grinned happily. "No. At least—no, not if you mean sofas and tables and things of that sort."

"Ah, but I am close?"

"Yes, and one day soon, if you have not guessed it, I will tell you."

Each time she saw him she had another guess: he had come to hire servants, he had come to find a landscape gardener, and then he would tease her and change the subject. As they drove from place to place he would tell them stories of foreign lands and customs and amusing seafaring tales, causing a great deal of disbelieving laughter.

One day when Isabelle and her aunt were giggling like two schoolgirls, clinging helplessly to one another, they were hailed from a passing carriage and found Lady Bromley observing them curiously.

The captain immediately called to the coachman to pull

up and introductions were made. Lady Bromley saw a tall, boney-faced man with heavy, dark brows and sharp brown eyes. But attractive, nonetheless, she thought, especially when he smiled, for his teeth were very white against his sun-browned complexion and two long creases in his cheeks framed his mouth in a way that enhanced his looks. He seemed very much at his ease with the Holland women and they with him.

"Dear Lady Bromley, what a fortunate meeting. I have meant to write and tell you of the captain's visit, but he has kept us so busy I haven't had a moment. The thing is, his sister was at school with you! Is not that a coincidence?"

Lady Bromley thought it was hardly possible, but she acknowledged that it was indeed a coincidence. The matter was explained to her, the sister named, and though she had no memory of the woman, she graciously pretended that she did indeed remember a very pretty young girl named Perronet in the first form. "You must bring the captain to dine with me, Mrs. Holland," she said as she was driven away. Then she had herself driven at once to her nephew's townhouse and sent the coachman up to inquire if Lord Sutterton was at home.

The flustered butler came out to the carriage to explain that his master had been away two weeks now and he had no knowledge of when he planned to return.

"Where is he?" she demanded.

"He did not tell me his destination, my lady," said the man, carefully avoiding her eyes.

"Did he not?" said Lady Bromley, raising a disbelieving eyebrow. "But perhaps you may guess it. If so, you will send a message to him at once that he is to call upon me tomorrow without fail. Drive on."

Adrian sauntered in late in the afternoon the following day and Lady Bromley, who had expected him in the morning and who had waited for him all day, was in a cold fury by then.

"I hope I have not dragged you away from anything important, Sutterton," she said glacially.

"Dearest Aunt, as though anything could be more important. I rushed around the moment I awoke and was given your message.''

"It is now half past four in the afternoon. Did you only now rise from your bed?''

"But of course, darling,'' he replied lazily.

"Or at least you only just rose from some bed,'' she said with heavy sarcasm.

"Ah, darling, you are jealous,'' he murmured, kneeling at her feet to take her hand and plant kisses all over it.

She tugged it away sharply. "Please do not be ridiculous. This is a serious matter. You tell Miss Holland you love her—''

"Oh no, dearest, I never actually said that,'' he protested.

"You allowed her to assume it then, and immediately disappeared. She thinks you are in Scotland on business, but I knew better for I saw you myself last week. What if she had seen you?''

"Really, you worry too much. The girl is besotted enough to wait any length of time,'' he said carelessly.

"That may be so, but you have not any length of time at your disposal. You know that you must announce your betrothal at once and marry as quickly as possible. Ruin stares you in the face and you go off to—to pleasure yourself with your little opera dancer.''

He looked pained. "Not an opera dancer, dear Aunt. Surely you cannot accuse me of such poor taste?''

"Whatever. The point is, you must stop all this at once. I saw Isabelle yesterday with a most attractive man and they were on the very best of terms, I can tell you. I do not know if it is not already too late.''

"Pooh, nonsense. I tell you, the girl is mine whenever I choose to claim her, but if it will please you I will go to her tomorrow.'' He repossessed himself of her hand and, turning it, kissed her palm lingeringly. An electric thrill shot up her arm and her eyes closed to savor the pleasure of it.

"Well, well, what is this, Sutterton,'' cried Lord Bromley as he entered the room, "making love to your aunt?'' He gave a great booming laugh at his own joke.

Adrian stayed just as he was, only turning to answer, "Happily, sir, would she permit it."

Lady Bromley pulled her hand from his grasp and said rather breathlessly, "I am trying to persuade him that he must propose to Miss Holland at once, Bromley."

"Oh? I thought you'd settled on the Bray girl. Give you a glass of wine, Sutterton?"

Adrian rose gracefully to accept it and the moment was over. What a complacent old fool his uncle was, to be sure. He must arrange to visit his aunt someday when his uncle was out of town.

Still, he took his aunt's advice and the next morning presented himself at the Hollands', only to find that Isabelle was out. Drat the girl, he thought, irritated that he had made the effort to rise early only to find that he must do it a second time. He left his card and the message that he would call again tomorrow morning.

Isabelle, meanwhile, was strolling along a footpath in the Park on Captain Perronet's arm. They had all alighted to walk for a time beneath the trees, the sun being very warm, but after a time Mrs. Holland had espied a bench and declared she would rest for a spell. The captain and Isabelle wandered slowly away.

"Miss Holland, I think the moment has come when I must tell you why I have come to London," he said presently.

"Oh, wonderful! Tell me at once."

"I came for you," he said simply.

"For—for me?"

"Yes. I was not able to put you out of my mind for even one moment since I saw you leave my ship. I had never thought—well—you see, dear girl, I love you and. . ."

She turned, raising her hands as though to ward off the words, her face stricken. "Oh—do not—I beg you, Captain, do not . . ."

"But I must. There is this great void where my heart was before you stole it from me," he said with a little laugh, "and it must be filled. I love you too much to do without you any longer. I must have you for my own, darling girl, and then the void will be filled again.''

"You must not say this—please do not—I . . .''

"I know I am a rough fellow and you are used to these smooth London dandies, but my heart is solid as an oak and it will always beat only for you. I have a home to take you to that only waits for you to furnish it as you like, and you shall never want for anything you might desire, I promise you. I will set you up as a fine lady with a satin gown and a carriage,'' he added mischievously.

She laughed in spite of herself as she remembered Señor Hernandez, but then she sobered and held out her hand to him. "Dear Captain Perronet, I am honored that you should care for me, but it is not possible. I—you see—my heart is not free.''

"Not free,'' he repeated, uncomprehending.

"I have already given it to—to another.''

"You are betrothed?''

"No, not as yet, but he has declared his love and I have told him of mine.''

"And he did not ask for your hand at once? Why—why—what sort of fellow is this? He is only having a flirtation with you!''

"I do not think so, but in any case, I am not—I love him,'' she said stoutly.

"Perhaps it is only an infatuation and you will get over it. He cannot be worth your love if he did not propose to you at once. A man cannot be sincere if he tells you he loves you and then does not ask for your hand at once.''

"I am sorry, captain, but I cannot discuss it with you any further. Now, shall we return to my aunt? She must be wondering what has become of us.'' She turned and began to walk away.

"I will not give up this easily, Miss Holland,'' he said, his black brows drawn together ferociously.

"Please do not pursue the matter, Captain Perronet. Cannot we just forget anything has been said and remain friends?''

"Friends, aye. Friends two people must be, to my thinking, before they love one another."

"And yet we were not friends when I left your ship and you say you began to love me then," she could not resist saying, though she knew it was wrong to reply in any way.

"That is why I have not spoken before. I wanted to let the friendship grow to be sure it was not just some obsession. The first heat of love cools after a time, but friends remain friends, and then the love becomes something solid that lasts forever."

"That is beautifully said, captain, and I am sorry to be the cause of any distress to you. I have appreciated your friendship and always shall, but my heart is no longer my own. I have given it to someone and told him of it. Would you have me change my mind? Surely you cannot think me so shallow as that, nor want me if I were?"

"I only think you have made a mistake about your feelings. Where is this man? I have not seen you with anyone who could have your heart or I should have known it at once. Why is he not by your side now if he loves you? No, no, Miss Holland, I cannot believe in his love. I do not intend to give you up so easily. I will never give up until I read of your betrothal in the papers, and so I tell you, Miss Holland!"

Eight

The drive home was mostly silent, with Mrs. Holland attempting to keep up appearances with a running commentary on all they saw, which grew more desperate as the moments passed and she received very little in the way of encouragement. The captain scowled into the distance, while Isabelle stared absorbedly at the passing scene, making only token murmurs of acknowledgment to Mrs. Holland's statements. That poor lady cast covert glances from one to the other, wondering what could have happened to put them so out of sorts with one another.

Isabelle was distressed to have caused the captain this unhappiness and wished it had not happened. How could she have ever guessed he would have conceived such feelings for her. Now, she knew, they could never again return to the unfettered friendship that had grown between them this past week.

How rapid the changes in my life have been, she thought with some wonder. Not three months ago I was sitting in a gloomy rooming house in France, never dreaming that life could ever be different. Not much over a month ago I had met and detested this man who now professes to love me. How strange that here I sit now, sad because of his sadness and mourning the loss of our friendship. And barely a month ago I had not even heard of the Marquess of Sutterton, she remembered, her spirits lifting somewhat at the thought.

William was very courteous when he bid the ladies

good-bye, though somewhat stiff in his manner. Isabelle pressed his hand warmly and looked up at him beseechingly, but he did not respond. However, when Mrs. Holland asked if they would see him tomorrow, he said firmly, "You may be sure of that, madam." Isabelle turned away sadly, sensing more disagreeable scenes between them in the future.

All this was forgotten when she found the marquess's card on the hall table. He is back! Oh, how could I have gone out today and not been here to receive him, she mourned. She was not consoled when the butler informed her that his lordship would call again in the morning. That was such eons away. Why should he not return later today? She went to her room with dragging steps, unable to understand how anything could keep him away. Why had he not stayed to await her return? He must surely have known she would be back by midday. For a time, her heart was filled with resentment against him, that his eager anticipation to be with her again after such a long separation did not equal her own, and even whispered aloud, "He cannot love me as I love him," and swallowed down this bitter pill, welcoming the scalding hurt of it, even prolonging the pain, until a few tears came to ease her heart.

Then, slowly, reason returned and she allowed herself to find justifications for his behavior. He had many things to attend to, he would want to see his aunt, it might be necessary to consult with his man of business regarding the problems he had encountered in Scotland. Bah! she thought in self-disgust, I am so weak and childish, wanting my own way in everything. He has many things in his life besides me, and I have only him to think of. This is the way of it for poor women. But if we truly love we must truly trust. I will never doubt him again. I will never allow myself to express the least recrimination tomorrow, but only apologize for being away. After all, it is my own fault, not his, poor dear man.

Thus does the loving heart, unable to bear the least tarnish on the beloved, turn the resentment upon itself, absorbing the guilt gladly. She was able, after this, to indulge herself in imagining their coming reunion, though it was difficult for her to get past the moment when he would hold out his arms and she would fly into his embrace, a scene she envisioned over and over.

Before she retired for the night, she went to her aunt's dressing room. She must convince her aunt that she must be allowed to receive him alone in the morning. To do this it was necessary that she reveal her secret for the first time, which revelation put her Aunt Nathaniel into such a flutter she could barely speak for some moments, an unusual state truly indicative of her excitement. When she had recovered she was still by no means convinced of the propriety of such a meeting, but at last gave way in the interests of her niece's receiving a proposal. Of course, she said, it was strange in him not to have proposed at the time he made his declaration, but since he had not, she could see that privacy was now necessary. There followed a lengthy debate on where this meeting should take place. Despite the fact that Mrs. Holland felt it was not fitting for so grand a personage as the Marquess of Sutterton, it was at last agreed between them that Isabelle would receive him in the small back drawing room alone, while Mrs. Holland welcomed all other visitors, including, inevitably, Captain Perronet, in the main drawing room. Not to do so might arouse suspicions, especially when it was equated with the fact that Isabelle was absent. They could only pray their guests would not all arrive on their doorstep at the same moment. At last Isabelle bid her aunt an affectionate good night and went off to her bed, satisfied that all had been done that could be done, and closed her eyes to see yet once again herself flying into her lover's arms.

The event itself proved somewhat different. When she was informed that the marquess had arrived and been shown into the back drawing room, she sped down the stairs, flung open the door, and paused expectantly, her gray eyes brilliant with anticipation and the color high in her cheeks.

Adrian turned from the fireplace and said coolly, ''Oh, there you are at last, eh?''

She had not realized she had been holding her breath until this flattening and anticlimatic greeting came almost as a blow to expel it. She was so taken aback she could only stutter, ''A-a-t l-l-ast?''

''You were from home when I called yesterday,'' he explained, not bothering to hide his annoyance.

''But—but—I could not have known you—''

''It was most inconvenient,'' he said reprovingly.

At that her chin came up and her wits returned. ''Sir, I am indeed sorry that you were inconvenienced. Had you condescended to send a word to announce your arrival, I might, perhaps, have contrived to cancel my previous engagement so as to receive you.''

He saw he had gone too far and changed his tone at once. ''I was sadly disappointed,'' he said, giving her a rueful little smile.

She melted at this. ''Oh, and so was I also!'' she cried, closing the door and advancing slowly toward him. ''Welcome back, my lord,'' she said shyly. ''I—I have missed you.'' She held out her hands hesitantly and he took them and drew her nearer.

''Ah, now that is the welcome I had hoped for.''

''And the one you would have had at once, had you given me the chance to say it before accusing me so unfairly,'' she said chidingly.

''Now, who is this handsome man you have been seen driving with about London?''

''Handsome man? Oh, that is a friend of my papa's, Captain Perronet, who brought us here from France.'' She laughed. He is jealous, she thought indulgently.

''I do not trust sailors, as a rule, but I suppose I must accept a friend of your father's. Is Mr. Holland at home this morning?''

''I—believe so,'' she said breathlessly, her heart beginning to pound at what she knew was coming. Now, now, she thought, he will ask me to be his wife!

''Then I had better speak to him since I am here.''

"Speak to him, Adrian?" she breathed, daringly using his name for the first time.

"Now, don't go all missish, there's a good girl," he said, patting her cheek. "Go and fetch your papa and let us settle the matter once and for all."

"Yes—yes, of course, but—but . . ." She raised her mouth nearer his, seeking, if not the outright words she hoped for, at least a token of love. He pulled her closer and kissed her, and she, afire at the first touch of his lips, felt her senses begin to swim with passion. Then he was setting her away firmly. "Go along now, silly girl. Time a'plenty for all that when our business is finished."

She felt her heart sag with disappointment as she turned obediently away, but then she thought: trust! I must remember to trust him. He is shy now, but when we are married I will teach him to trust me with his deeper emotions, to show them to me without fear of appearing unmanly. Oh yes, when we are married, I will teach him. Her heart lifted with this thought, and she went with a lighter step to seek out her father in his dressing room. As soon as he saw her face, he dismissed his brother's valet who had been assisting him in putting the finishing touches to his morning toilette.

"Well, well, my dear, you look like a spring day with a rainbow in it. What has happened?"

"Oh, Papa," she cried, throwing herself into his arms. "I am so very happy. It is—Lord Sutterton! He—he would like to speak to you!"

There was an unexpectedly long silence after this announcement, while Mr. Holland's brows drew together. He lifted her chin to study her face intently. She began to grow anxious and some of her color faded. "Papa? What is it?"

"Is this truly what you want, dear child?"

"Why—yes—of course it is!"

"It is surely precipitate, is not it? You can hardly know him."

"Oh, Papa, of course I know him. I love him and he

loves me. He has asked to speak to you. Will you not go down to him now?''

"Yes," he said heavily, "yes, I will go down, child." He kissed her brow and held her close for a moment, and then left the room. She stared after him in bewilderment and alarm. What was wrong? Should he not be happy for her? Was it possible he found Adrian unacceptable? What if his disapproval was apparent to Adrian? Perhaps Adrian would not persist with his suit if her papa disapproved it. But surely Papa would not. . . .

Of course Mr. Holland did not, though he had not cared for the little he had heard of Lord Sutterton when he made inquiries of his brother and of his new acquaintances at his brother's club. They all of them repeated rumors they themselves had heard at only second or third hand, and Mr. Holland did not like to judge a man on hearsay. Since he trusted his daughter's judgment, he felt that he must approve her choice. He was entirely courteous and gave his consent without any demur, though his smile was less wholehearted than should have been the case. Such a nuance was, however, lost on Adrian, who knew Mr. Holland not at all and had very little interest in Mr. Holland's opinion of his character. He had experienced no doubts at all regarding Mr. Holland's consent, it being a foregone conclusion, in his own mind, that such a man would leap eagerly at an offer of marriage for his daughter from the Marquess of Sutterton.

The matter was arranged in very short order, it being agreed between them that the marquess would send the announcement to the papers and that a meeting would shortly be arranged between Mr. Holland, the marquis, and his solicitors to go into the matter of marriage settlements. The two men shook hands and a servant was then sent to summon Isabelle and her aunt and uncle. Isabelle came flying in and, clinging to the arm of her betrothed, received the good wishes of her relatives with a radiant smile.

Claiming that his aunt awaited him for his tidings, Adrian managed to extricate himself in a very short time and made his adieus, promising to call upon Isabelle the next day. The two Mr. Hollands soon left the house and Isabelle excused herself from the tearful embraces of her aunt and ran to her room to be alone. For some reason she felt strangely flat, as all the bubbles of excitement burst in the quiet she had sought to savor them.

It is natural, she told herself, as she paced about her room, after being so much in alt, to feel let down afterward. If only he had not gone away so quickly—if we could have been left alone for a time to sit down together quietly and talk. There is so much I want to tell him—so much I want to learn.

Of course, she assured herself hastily, it was natural that he should want to share the good news with his own relatives as soon as possible, just as I did myself. He loves his aunt as a mother and knew she would be waiting to hear. There were not, seemingly, all that many people he held dear, for he never spoke of any other relative or friend. She remembered her own feelings when there was only her father, and supposed he must sometimes be very lonely. She would, she vowed, make it all up to him, and her relatives would be his, and he would come to love them dearly.

Suddenly there flashed into her mind the memory of his face as Aunt Nathaniel had thrown her arms about him, tearfully wishing him happy and calling him her dear nephew Sutterton. Was it revulsion he expressed? No, it could not have been. It must be that he was shy about caresses in public. Perhaps in his own family it was not usual to express affection with caresses. She remembered then how cold he had been when first she entered the room, longing to rush into his arms. It must have been only shyness. And jealousy, she remembered with a sudden flash of happiness. Dearest Adrian. He has heard from his aunt, of course, about her having been with Captain Perronet and had not liked it. Oh, how she would change him when they were married. Her love would change him, make him more open and giving, for he would learn that he could trust her. He would not need those other things,

either, gaming and—and—mistresses, when they were together forever.

At breakfast Aunt Nathaniel told Isabelle that Captain
Perronet had indeed called the day before while she was
with the marquess, but had left very shortly after being
informed that Isabelle was feeling indisposed and could
not come downstairs. He had also told Mrs. Holland that
he would not be able to call today, and Isabelle was not
unhappy to hear this. She hoped no one at all would call
and that she could be alone with Adrian at last. She was in
the drawing room by ten o'clock, knowing it was far too
early to expect him. She had a long, restless morning
alone and at half past twelve received a note from him to
say he could not come that day after all, but would try to
come on the day after.

He did come, but the meeting was very short. He had a
most pressing engagement, he said, and could hardly even
be persuaded to sit down. He paced impatiently about the
room picking up ornaments and setting them down without
looking at them.

"But Adrian, I have hardly seen you at all since your
return," she protested. "Surely you—"

"Now, please do not go all weepy and clinging. I
cannot bear that in a woman!"

"Why, I am not in the least weepy," she said indignantly, "and as for clinging, I have had little enough
chance for that!"

"Now, now, do not fly up into the boughs over every
word a fellow says. I have a great deal on my mind just at
present and I look to you to be reasonable."

"Oh, my dear, forgive me," she cried repentantly.
"Will you not sit down and tell me about it? Perhaps I can
help you in some way."

"No, no, these are not matters for women's ears. You
would not understand. Now, I really must not stay or I
shall be fearfully late for my appointment with my man of
business."

"Surely he must await your pleasure," she protested, but timidly.

"Isabelle, there are many things to be seen to before a marriage, and the sooner I can see to them the sooner it will come about," he said severely.

She replied contritely, "Of course, my dear, you are right. I will not plague you any longer."

"There's a good girl," he said, and strode across to where she sat, bending as though to take her hand, but she rose quickly and put her arms about his neck, her mouth raised for his kiss. He kissed her, but only briefly, and she was not experienced enough to know how to make it something more. Her passion could be evoked, but she could not initiate it.

He smiled, patted her cheek, and left the room quickly. She sank back upon the sofa and thought resentfully, I wish he would not pat me in that way. I know it is his sign that I have pleased him, but it makes me feel like a—a—pet, an importunate puppy, perhaps.

She quelled such a disloyal thought by promising herself that when there was more time and they could speak together intimately, either as lovers or as man and wife, she would tell him her feelings about being patted on the cheek. In the meantime, she realized, he had said nothing about when she would see him again, but he surely would not expect her simply to sit at home waiting for his calls. She went quickly to seek her aunt to suggest they call upon the Richmonds. She found her aunt in the drawing room with Captain Perronet. He rose at once as she entered and bent gravely over her hand. There was no smile in answer to hers and she turned away from his close scrutiny.

"Aunt, I thought we might call upon the Richmonds. I have not seen them for days."

"Oh, a lovely idea. Will you accompany us, captain? I am sure you will like them very well. They are very old friends and when Isabelle first came to London, could not do enough to entertain her. Ring for the carriage to be brought around, Isabelle dear."

William said that as his carriage was at the door and as

he had no plans, he would happily accompany them and see them safely returned. Isabelle thought fleetingly of Adrian's objections to her driving about London with this man, but then remembered he had agreed that he would trust a friend of her father's.

As she went upstairs for her bonnet it came to her very disagreeably that she had denied her friendship with the captain to Adrian. Not in so many words, but by allowing him to infer that the captain was her father's friend, not her own, surely as deceitful in her as an outright lie. Why had she done it? It did not take her long to admit to herself that if she had claimed the captain as a special friend of her own, she had known instinctively that Adrian would have objected to her seeing him again, and she did not want to give up the captain's friendship.

So, not only was she deceitful, but disloyal to her friends and selfish as well, for surely it would be better for Captain Perronet if she did give up their friendship, and if she cared for his needs more than her own, she would do so. She was made profoundly unhappy by these unflattering discoveries about her character, but could not bring herself to the point of severing their friendship. She compromised by promising herself that at the first opportunity she would correct the impression she had given Adrian by explaining to him the true state of things concerning Captain Perronet.

They were shown into the Richmonds' drawing room to find them entertaining Swinburn Tuberville. The Misses Richmond descended upon Isabelle with such glad cries of welcome at seeing her again that it was some time before introductions could be made and the party disposed about the room in relative calm. Mr. Tuberville began eagerly questioning the captain about ships and foreign lands and seafaring life in general, which he professed to always have had a secret yearning for. Mrs. Richmond and Mrs. Holland settled down comfortably to catch up on gossip, while Victoria and Horatia drew Isabelle into a far corner of the room to besiege her with questions regarding the Marquess of Sutterton, knowing nothing of the sinister reputation ascribed to him by Miss Fairbrother, but being only mightily impressed with his illustrious title and excessive good looks.

Isabelle could not prevent her telltale blushes, thus causing the Misses Richmond to eye her with even greater interest.

"Why, Miss Holland—I do believe—is it possible we may wish you happy?" cried Victoria in an excited whisper.

Isabelle could not bring herself to tell an outright lie, but neither could she speak when no official announcement had been made, and the color stained her cheeks an even deeper hue.

Miss Horatia clasped her hands together ecstatically. "Oh! You have hit upon it, Victoria. It is true! Oh, dear, dear Miss Holland, how very wonderful!"

"Please—please—I beg you to say nothing to anyone as yet. At least until the announcement appears in the papers," pleaded Isabelle, much agitated to have given herself away to them so easily, but yet not too displeased to have her happiness known.

"Oh, we will not, dear Miss Holland," Miss Victoria assured her. "We understand very well how you feel. Indeed, we have news of our own that—"

"Victoria!" cried Horatia, now blushing in her own turn.

Isabelle knew at once what this news must be and turned to embrace Horatia impulsively. "Mr. Tuberville, of course, I hoped it would be so."

"But we cannot announce it until he has spoken with his parents, who are at present touring on the Continent," explained Horatia. "Is it something of the kind in your case also?"

"No, only that the marquess is to send the notice to the papers and I suppose has not had the time to do so as yet. He has a great many business affairs to attend to," Isabelle replied with a sigh.

"Ah me," said Victoria, with mock sadness, "only too soon I shall be the only one unmarried."

"Oh sister, please do not say such things," reproved her sister sadly.

"It is but a tease, Horatia, to be sure. For I shall soon have two dear married friends to invite me to their parties and introduce me to charming young men," laughed Victoria. "Tell me, Miss Holland, is Captain Perronet married?"

"No—ah—no, he is not," said Isabelle, hoping she would not betray herself with another blush. She did, but fortunately both Victoria and Horatia had turned to study the captain with great interest and so did not see it.

"He is a good looking man," murmured Horatia, "do you not agree, sister?"

"Indeed. So—so manly, such a commanding presence," said Victoria enthusiastically.

Several days passed with no further visits from the marquess, but Lady Bromley honored them with a call. She found Mrs. Holland and Isabelle entertaining Captain Perronet, Miss Victoria, and Mrs. Richmond. Mrs. Richmond soon rose to leave, taking a most reluctant Victoria with her, but Captain Perronet held his ground.

Lady Bromley was too much a lady to allow her displeasure to become evident and asked him very civilly how he did.

"Very well, my lady."

"And will your stay in London be of a long duration?"

"I hope not too long. I do not care for London."

"You must convey my regards to your sister when you return to Sussex," she said graciously and turned her attention to her hostess.

Clearly meant as my dismissal, thought William with grim amusement. How well she does it. Centuries of practice in dealing with the lower orders there. He found her an attractive woman, but did not like her. Too much facade, he thought, to be entirely trusted. He did not approve of her as a friend for Isabelle and thought even more strongly that it would be a very good thing to take her right away to the country, away from all these artificial, high-in-the-instep people. For despite what she had told him, he did not really believe that his suit would fail. How could it, when his love was so strong and sure. This silly notion of having already given her heart to another was the foolish product of a young girl's dream of romance. She had been the object of an idle flirtation on the part of some glib drawing-room dandy. She was much too honest and true herself to think anyone could play such games, but then those very qualities would eventually show her the truth. He must just be patient, and near at hand, and someday she would be his.

Mrs. Holland was becoming much agitated. She was only too well aware that Lady Bromley had called as a representative of Sutterton's family to extend their approval of the match, and was also aware of Lady Bromley's increasing displeasure at the captain's presence. Mrs. Holland wished she had the ability, which no doubt Lady Bromley possessed, to dismiss unwanted visitors without insulting them unforgivably. She would not insult dear Captain Perronet for all the world, but she did wish rather exasperatedly that he would take himself off now before Lady Bromley became impatient and went away without expressing her feelings about the betrothal. Of course, the dear captain did not know of the betrothal, so could not know of the purpose of Lady Bromley's visit, so no blame attached to him. Oh, why had not Sutterton sent the announcement to the papers so these social contretemps need not arise?

However, she need not have worried. Lady Bromley had no intention of leaving without having her say, and settled herself down into a long, detailed account of the various illnesses besetting an aged relative, and of all the various remedies attempted for their cure. William became so restive at all this dreary information that before long he rose to take his leave. When he was gone, Lady Bromley rose at once to embrace Isabelle and assure her of how happily she welcomed the match.

"You will need to learn to be very firm with Adrian, Isabelle, as I have learned to be since my dear sister's death. He is sometimes willful and thoughtless, I fear, but a darling boy for all that, and I've no doubt that marriage and a family will settle him down."

Isabelle flushed. She did not like hearing Lady Bromley

call her nephew a thoughtless and willful boy. He was seven and twenty at least and it seemed to her undignified to have him named so.

"Captain Perronet seems to have become quite the old family friend," Lady Bromley continued. "Has he been told of your betrothal, Isabelle?"

"No. I have not liked to speak of it before it is formally announced."

"Ah, that is something I meant to take up with you. Why has not the announcement been sent to the papers?"

"Why, Adrian has been to busy to attend to it, I suppose."

"Too busy?"

"Yes, there are a great many things to be attended to before a man in Adrian's position can marry. I do feel badly to cause him so much extra worry and work, and I do try not to be too impatient at seeing so little of him, especially just at this time, for I know all will be different once we are married."

This speech caused Lady Bromley to once again hurry home to pen a note to her nephew demanding his immediate attendance upon her under pain of her extreme displeasure should he fail to come at once. He came within the hour and Lady Bromley wasted no time in telling him of the madness of his behavior, which would, did he not mend his ways at once, cause all to come to naught.

"And let me add, the handsome sailor is still very much in evidence, and if I am any judge, much besotted with the girl. He is not a rival I would welcome, were I in your precarious position."

The marquess went that afternoon to instruct his man of business to insert the announcement of his betrothal to Miss Isabelle Holland into the papers. It appeared two days later and for many days was the *on-dit* of the *ton*, causing many young girls to sigh with envy and many mothers to gnash their teeth in frustration at having such an eligible man snatched from under their very noses by an unknown chit of a girl of no rank, whose connections were negligible and whose beauty was nothing out of the way.

Speculation regarding the size of her portion increased the amount by several thousand pounds, that being the only asset she possessed as far as most could see that could account for her snaring the elusive Marquess of Sutterton.

On the day of the announcement, Adrian appeared in the late afternoon on the Holland doorstep, so late that it was clear he expected to be invited to stay for dinner. The invitation was delightedly extended by Mrs. Holland and graciously accepted. Isabelle was made excessively happy by this unexpected visit and by the radiance exuded by the marquess in an amiable temper.

This temper had been coaxed into being by Lady Bromley, who had insisted that now the announcement had appeared he could not simply assume his duty done and go about his own business. He must be seen frequently in Isabelle's company, and most especially on this particular day, since she would be expecting him as would her family.

Thus it was that the marquess charmingly complimented Mrs. Holland on her cook and well-trained servants, and Mr. Nathaniel Holland on his excellent wine cellar. Isabelle's papa was congratulated on raising so remarkable a daughter, while Isabelle herself was complimented by many long and admiring glances and smiles.

Lady Bromley would have been proud of his performance. He bade them good night and was walked to the door by Isabelle, where he kissed her with great expertise and went on his way very well pleased with himself for having made a sacrifice of his evening to do his duty. Tomorrow, he thought, a note and a posy should do well enough, then the day after that a drive in the Park to expose the alliance to the stares of the *ton*, and so forth. With management, the business need not take up too much unnecessary time.

By the time he reached his club it had occurred to him that married life would actually be much easier than all this necessity for planning meetings. As her betrothed, he thought, I am expected to dangle at her shoe strings, but as her husband I can go my way unhindered. How dense of him not to have seen this at once. Yes, best proceed with the business as expeditiously as possible.

Nine

Isabelle had just been handed Adrian's posy and was reading his note with disappointment not unmixed with resentment when Mr. Fairbrother was announced and requested an interview alone with her. His face was somber when she entered the room and he bowed gravely.

"Forgive me, Miss Holland, if this visit is unwelcome to you at this time, but I was so nonplussed by what I saw in the *Gazette* this morning I could not rest easy until I had come myself to verify the truth of the matter."

"Your visit could never be unwelcome, sir," she said evasively.

"So I had assumed until now. Indeed, I had assumed a great deal more, it seems," he said accusingly.

"I think I cannot be held to account for what you may have assumed, Mr. Fairbrother," she replied trenchantly.

"Perhaps not, perhaps not, but I think you must admit these assumptions were not discouraged."

"I admit no such thing, sir. Not being aware of your assumptions, how could I then either encourage or discourage them?"

"We are speaking at cross-purposes, I fear."

"Then be so good as to explain your position quite baldly, Mr. Fairbrother, and I will do my poor best to understand it."

"I read this morning that you are betrothed to the Marquess of Sutterton. Can this be true?"

"It is true, sir," she said with simple dignity.

He stared at her reproachfully for a long, silent moment. She kept her chin well up and looked back at him steadily. At last he said, "Then I have indeed assumed that which was never true. I had thought you understood my purpose, and was encouraged to believe you were not averse to it."

"Whatever your purpose may have been, I have certainly never encouraged it, Mr. Fairbrother."

"I thought you understood that I—I had become very fond of you," he said miserably.

Her heart melted at his evident unhappiness. "Mr. Fairbrother, indeed I am sorry if you thought I understood any such thing. No such words were ever spoken between us. Of course, I thought you enjoyed my company or you would not have sought it, just as I enjoyed yours and your sister's. But I think you must absolve me from ever encouraging you to think there was more than friendship between us."

He was too fair-minded to resist this honest assessment of their relationship so far. He knew he had been remiss in not declaring himself the moment he knew his own heart. He had been too careful when a more impetuous lover might have attached her affections at once. He bowed. "Allow me to felicitate you, Miss Holland. I wish you well with all my heart," he said, and then walked rapidly out of the room.

Isabelle had barely recovered from the agitation this confrontation had caused before Captain Perronet was shown in.

"I have come to say good-bye, Miss Holland," he announced sternly.

"Oh—I am sorry—I—let me ring for my aunt to come down," stuttered Isabelle.

"That will not be necessary. It is with you I would speak. I said I would not give up until I saw your betrothal announced in the papers. Well, I saw it this morning, but I have changed my mind. I still do not give up. I think you have made a mistake and that you will come to your senses before it is too late. I will be waiting for that moment. My love for you is as strong as it ever was, and my confidence in our future is unchanged. I will be waiting.''

With that he marched out of the room with no farewell, his harsh voice still echoing from the walls. Isabelle felt limp, as though battered by a strong gale. On trembling legs she made her way up to her room and locked her door behind her. She then threw herself across the bed and burst into such a paroxysm of tears as she had never experienced in her life.

Mr. Fairbrother meanwhile had unburdened his unhappy heart to his sister who, while sorry for his failure, refused to allow him to censure Isabelle for it.

''But she must have known my feelings,'' he cried. ''I was with her nearly every day!''

''Oh, no doubt she was not unaware of your partiality, but if you never said anything, what could she do? In these matters the man must lead the way. Why did you not speak?''

''I was waiting for some indication of her own feelings.''

''Then you are more foolish that I gave you credit for,'' she retorted with sisterly scorn. ''A woman cannot show her own feelings until the man has declared himself. What did you expect from her, sighs and blushes and fluttering lashes? You would have been repelled by such behavior and she would have been labeled a flirt and too forward in her conduct by everyone else. Oh, you men make me very cross.''

Despite the lowness of his mood, his mouth twitched at this from a pert miss of fifteen who had had, as yet, no experience with men at all. ''You are very severe, Mouse.''

''Well, you deserve to have your hair combed with a foot stool for being so chicken-hearted. Oh, I see it all. You wanted to be sure you would not be refused if you offered, for you never could bear to look foolish, Brim, as well you know. But one sometimes must just throw one's hat over the windmill. You are too careful of your dignity.''

A much chastened Mr. Fairbrother went away to find what comfort he could from his friends at his club, thinking dismally that in future he would be careful not to fall in love ever again.

William also needed comforting, despite his brave words to Isabelle and the bellicosity of his attitude and, as usual, he sought it from his sister, Elizabeth Claypool.

Mrs. Claypool was very like her brother in appearance, being taller than average for a female, though extremely lithesome and graceful in her movements, and her dark eyes glowed softly from beneath a modified version of his heavy brows. Her character and manner, however, were very different from her brother's. Never having had to make her way in the world or to command a ship as had he, her inborn serenity of temperament had developed unimpeded. Four actively mischievous sons had discovered that her quiet displeasure was far more effective than any punishment dispensed by their more volatile and impatient father. Being some ten years William's senior, she had always had somewhat the same effect on him.

Squire Claypool had inherited his position and the estate that had been his family's for several hundred years. In marrying him, Mrs. Claypool had certainly "married up," but in fortune and antiquity their families were equal, and in education she was his superior. Claypool Grange was a large, comfortable mansion set about with ancient shade trees and well-tended gardens and, except when they were having lessons with their tutor, rang with cries and halloos of boys at play. They greeted their uncle boisterously, but sensing his mood to be somewhat dour, they soon left off trying to climb upon him and went galloping off. Mrs. Claypool knew at once that all was not well with her brother but wisely forebore to notice it.

"Will seems hipped about something," remarked Mr. Claypool that night in the privacy of their bedroom.

"Yes, so he does," replied his wife as she sat before her glass deftly plaiting her thick mane of dark hair into its nightly braid.

"Did you ask him why?"

"No," she said composedly, "he will only deny it and

become impatient. He is not to be pushed into confidences. He will tell me himself when he is ready.''

And so it was. He sought her out some days later where she sat reading in the shade of a giant cedar tree and threw himself prone in the grass at her feet. She smiled briefly in welcome, but when he did not speak returned to her book and for a time all was silent but for the sound of bees in the flower beds and a light breeze soughing through the cedar branches.

Presently he said, "I'm very troubled in my mind, Liz.''

"Having watched you stump about the place for three days now like a bear with a sore paw, I assumed something was bothering you.''

"You remember my mentioning Miss Holland and her father that I was going to visit in London?''

"Yes, of course I remember,'' she said truthfully, for how could she have forgotten the first girl her brother had ever mentioned voluntarily in her presence. "I hope you found them well?''

"Oh, yes, well in health . . .''

"But . . . ?''

"She is betrothed,'' he said harshly.

"Good heavens, that was very quick off the mark, was it not?'' replied Mrs. Claypool, knowing the whole story in that moment. It was surely as she had thought when he first spoke to her of a Miss Holland: her brother, at long last, had lost his heart—and now had lost the girl as well. Oh dear!

"Too quick by half. She has been taken in by some Regent's Park saunterer,'' he growled.

"Why, have you met the man?''

"No, but I have met his aunt and did not care for her.''

She had to laugh. "Lord, Will, how ridiculous you are. as though you can judge a person by his relatives. Remember Great Uncle Jeptha who was deported for stealing sheep? Would you want to be judged by—?''

"Yes, yes, you need not spell it out for me. But I know it is so, just the same. He is not the man for her.''

"And who is?" she asked quietly.

"I am. Oh, Liz, my heart is sore indeed, for never have I felt so sure of anything as this. She seems made for me, as though she had been fashioned from the stuff of my dreams."

Mrs. Claypool felt a lump rising in her throat at such poetical words from her usually blunt-spoken brother. That he could speak of such deep feelings at all showed her the terrible depth of his pain. "Did—did you tell her of your love?"

"Yes, and only then learned . . ." He proceeded to tell her all Isabelle had said and what he had replied. Then of the announcement of her betrothal in the papers.

"So you did not see her again?"

"Yes, once before I came away from London. I told her I would not give up no matter how many announcements they put in the papers," he said fiercely.

"And then changed your mind?"

"Changed my mind? Of course I have not changed my mind!"

"Then why are you here? Surely you cannot think to have any influence upon her at this distance."

"Oh—I—I wanted to talk to you about it—ask your advice. What must I do, Liz, to make her see how wrong she is?"

Poor Mrs. Claypool was put in a dreadful quandary by this appeal, for what, indeed, was there to advise him to do? There was so much that was unreasonable in his conviction that the girl was wrong in her choice and the assumption that the man could not be worthy because the aunt had made a bad impression on him. Yet his unhappiness was so great she could not say these things to him. In his present state, reasonableness could make little headway with him. Clearly, he must finally make up his mind to get over the girl, but that would take much longer if he stayed moping in the country. Perhaps in London he would meet another girl to put Miss Holland finally out of his mind.

At last she said, "If you truly mean that you will not give up, I think you must stay near at hand."

"Go back to London, you mean. Yes, I know that I must, though I detest the place, and I dislike the idea of hanging about like some—some lovesick cowherd with straw in my hair."

"Little chance you could be taken for that, Will." She laughed. "I think, though, it could not hurt to be—well—seen about, just as a friend of the family, you know. If you are indeed right about her choice, it may well be that she will have need of a friend. There is much that you need to be doing in London in any case. You will need to consult with Tilbury's if you are to have a carriage by the time your house is ready, not to speak of furnishings."

"I've no heart for all that—I had thought she would—" He turned away abruptly.

Her heart ached for him. He had clearly meant that Miss Holland as his intended bride should have her say in the way the house would be furnished. "Well, well, there is time in plenty for all that, the builders will not be finished for months, I suppose. But you will need horses, you know—at least a matched pair for your carriage. Perhaps Mr. Holland could help you with that. And you will need staff, of course, a housekeeper and a cook."

Somehow these practical plans for his future soothed him, or perhaps it was only her words about his being in London in case Isabelle should need a friend that fit in so well with his hopes. In any case, he decided he must hasten back to London. Why, even now she might need him!

Though Isabelle had no real need of him at that moment, she did miss his company. In view of his last words to her, harsh as they had been, she had fully expected to at least encounter him from time to time in her aunt's drawing room. She had been vastly surprised and not a little cast down to learn he had left London entirely. Had his words then been only the bombast of a disappointed suitor, or the result of not getting his own way as he must be accustomed to after all his years commanding a ship? Not that it mattered a whit, she assured herself hastily, for she certainly did not want or expect him to continue with his suit.

Her days alternated between notes and posies from Adrian and morning visits or drives in the Park with him. Between their meetings she had much to keep her occupied, not least of which were almost daily fittings for her wedding clothes, the gift of her uncle.

He had very kindly begged her to give him and his wife this great pleasure immediately after he had learned of her betrothal. "Mrs. Holland and I have no daughter to do this for, and it would give her the greatest happiness to do it for you, so I beg that you will allow her to."

She could not refuse a gift offered so delicately without appearing graceless. After several visits to the silk warehouses, the dressmaker's work had begun and was still going forward at a great rate. Apart from this there was a constant flow of congratulatory visitors, and invitations accepted before her betrothal was announced that she saw no reason not to fulfill, including two balls. To her deep humiliation, Adrian did not appear at either of them. The first one she had mentioned to him and assumed he would attend since she would be there. She touched upon the subject ever so lightly the next time they met, now allowing the least reproach to tinge her remark. He only replied that he had simply forgotten the matter entirely.

"These things are so much more important to women who like to show off their gowns to one another," he said carelessly.

"There is also the love of dancing that I believe is not exclusive to women," she said. "Shall you go to the Pomroys' ball on Friday?"

"Good heavens, no. I detest the Pomroys as much as I detest balls. You must go if you like it, certainly."

She felt a surge of annoyance at this assumption that she only awaited his permission, but she only said, "Oh yes, I shall certainly go." On the night she regretted her words, for she knew from the ball the previous week that a great many eyebrows had been raised at her appearance without her fiancé. She felt she could not back down, however,

and gritting her teeth she sailed into the Pomroys' ballroom with a smile, but her mind could not hold back the
resentment she felt against her beloved for this neglect. He
could have made the sacrifice, she thought, surely not so
very large a one to just put in an appearance for my sake.
He need not even have danced with me, only stood beside
me for a brief time to give me countenance.

Such mutinous thoughts had surfaced before this. There
seemed to her, in their occasional times together, a lack of
that loverlike attention she had expected. His attitude was
distinctly off-hand, his caresses brief and somewhat busi-
nesslike. She remembered longingly that day when he had
kissed her so passionately and she had fallen so instantly in
love with him. She had thought such moments would only
grow after she accepted his offer. Was it possible such
ways were considered in bad taste? Did he despise her as
common for being so greedy for caresses?

There was no one she could consult in such a matter, for
she could not bear to seem to be complaining of his
conduct, any more than she could have borne to hear him
criticized, for that would have seemed to cast doubt on her
judgment.

There was to be a very grand dinner party at Lady
Bromley's in a few days to introduce her to Adrian's
relatives, and both dread and eagerness were equal in her
anticipation of the event. Her own family would be around
her, and of course, Adrian would be by her side this time,
for Lady Bromley had demanded that he be present despite
all his protestations against the party. Besides this support,
a new gown of white silver lamé on gauze had been made
for the occasion, which became her very well, so she had
every reason to believe that the evening would go well
enough and she would not make too bad an impression on
the relatives.

She entered the room on her father's arm, and her hand
trembled so he put his free hand over it and smiled reassur-
ingly at her. Mr. and Mrs. Nathaniel Holland followed
behind them. Lady Bromley came up at once and all
conversation stopped as every eye in the room turned to

the door. It seemed to Isabelle that the room was jammed with people, and for a moment the walls seemed to spin as she felt the pressure of so much concentrated interest. She clutched desperately at her papa's arm.

"Remember Madame Gascoigne," he murmured. Isabelle instantly felt better, for Madame Gascoigne had been a massive French woman with the heavy forearms and large red hands of a butcher. Isabelle, at fourteen, had refused to pay the sum demanded for meals, claiming them unfit to be eaten. Surrounded by her portly husband and four beefy sons, Madame Gascoigne had adamantly demanded her money. Isabelle had been just as adamant in her refusal, finally threatening to call the police. The Gascoignes had retreated in a body at the very word and no more had been said about a charge for meals.

Isabelle still trembled, but she greeted Lady Bromley with a composed smile and allowed herself to be led about the room for introductions. They were, with one exception, people well past middle age, who all treated her with every courtesy. The exception was an extremely pretty auburn-haired girl of some four and twenty, whose flour-white complexion colored furiously whenever she was addressed, exposing a sensitivity and shyness painful to behold. She was the daughter of a cousin of Adrian's, and despite her blushes when introduced to his bride-to-be, managed to raise her eyes long enough to reveal an unveiled hostility that shocked Isabelle immeasurably.

The reason for it was revealed only when Adrian appeared, late as usual. Isabelle happened to be looking at the girl when Adrian paused in the doorway to greet his aunt and uncle, and saw the girl lean toward him involuntarily, almost yearningly, and her eyes rarely left him the rest of the evening, though Adrian ignored her.

Indeed, he did not greet any of the guests besides Isabelle and her family, only looking about and nodding coolly before remarking in a voice he did not bother to lower, "Still the same rum-looking lot as ever, I see. How boring of you to let us all in for such an evening, my dear aunt."

"Behave yourself," whispered Lady Bromley furiously before calling out to the company, "Come, my dears, we will go in to dinner now."

Adrian took Isabelle in and sat beside her, but seemed more engrossed with the food set before him, and especially with the wine, than with his partner.

"You are out of sorts tonight, Adrian," she said sympathetically.

"Yes, I am. I dislike these people very much and see no point in your being forced to suffer an evening being introduced to them. It is highly unlikely you will ever see any of them again. Certainly not in my house!"

"They seem pleasant enough," she ventured cautiously.

"Oh, yes, when they think there might be pickings, but when one goes to them for help they can become very unpleasant indeed."

Isabelle pondered this enigmatic statement, but did not dare inquire further into its meaning when so many eyes and ears were strained in their direction. She turned to Lord Bromley on her left and began a conversation safe to be heard by all and left her beloved to brood over his wine.

After dinner when the gentlemen had rejoined the ladies in the drawing room, the shy cousin had paused a moment before Adrian where he stood with Isabelle as though to speak to him.

"Well, well," he said, "it is Cousin Mary, is it not, or is it Marion?"

Blushing, her eyes on her shoe tops, she murmured, "Mary, Cousin Adrian. I—I—am happy you . . ." She stopped and dragged her eyes up to his face with an effort to gaze at him adoringly. Isabelle's heart went out to her as she realized the girl was in love with her cousin.

"Heavens, Cousin Mary, I see you still suffer the same lamentable want of conduct. Whatever do they teach girls these days," he added, turning to Isabelle with a laugh. The poor girl went a deeper scarlet and tears filled her eyes as she turned blindly, stumbling against a table as she hurried away. Isabelle watched in horrified pity, her blood seeming to freeze in her veins at such unnecessary cruelty. She stared at him for a moment and then turned away to her Aunt Nathaniel without speaking to him.

She was grateful for the fact that the party broke up very shortly after that. At the door a venerable old gentleman in the primrose satin coat and knee breeches now extremely out of date came up to wish Adrian happy. Adrian was civil enough to him, but as the old man tottered off, before he could possibly be out of range of Adrian's voice, Adrian said to Lady Bromley, "Silly old court card. Too miserly to buy a decent set of new clothes."

Isabelle was silent in the carriage going home, while her relatives expiated upon the guests and the menu. Her farewell to Adrian had been extremely cold and brief. She could not look into his eyes and pulled her hand from his hastily before he could bend to kiss it. He had looked puzzled. She tried to keep her mind blank now as she was jounced over the cobblestones, but a frail cold wisp of cloud seemed to wreathe in and out of her mind, pushing insistently for attention. She held it off as long as possible, but at last it found its way out and said its piece.

I do not like him.

Lady Bromley, meanwhile, was taking her nephew severely to task for allowing himself to exhibit himself before Isabelle in such a light. "I am used to your arrogance and bad manners, as are all your relatives, but she was put in a great disgust with you."

"You exaggerate as always," he replied, lounging back in a chair, hands in his pockets, long legs stretched out before him.

"No, I do not. I saw it very clearly. And all because most of them have refused to lend you any more money, you must insult them."

"Well, I told you I did not want to come to this party."

"Nor I to give it, knowing you as I do. But it was expected of me and since I put myself out for your benefit, the least I expected was courtesy from you. Now you must repair the damage as best you can, if that is possible. You must be quick about it, too."

"Oh, I have already made up my mind on that. I have decided the sooner the better for me. I shall go at once and demand that we set an early date for the wedding and set an appointment with her papa to meet with my solicitors for the marriage settlements."

"Thank God for that," breathed Lady Bromley fervently.

Ten

Having been inspired by the idea that his convenience would be better served as a married man than as a betrothed one, Adrian wasted, for him, little time setting things in train. Of course, he could not go to Isabelle on the next two days, for he was engaged to go to the races at Epsom with a party of his fellow carousers and their bits o' muslin, and rooms had been already engaged for two nights at an inn famous for its cellar. It was, therefore, three days later before he saw Isabelle again. He attributed her withdrawn mood as she greeted him to a fit of the sulks because of his negligence and set about cajoling her into better spirits. He took her hands and brushed his lips back and forth over her fingers before kissing each one separately. When her eyes remained resolutely lowered, he tilted her chin up with one finger, forcing her to look at him.

"Now, what is this? Are you cross with me?"

"No, my lord," she said, lowering her gaze after the briefest of glances.

"No, my lord," he mocked, "and you dare say that when you address me so? Am I to address you as Miss Holland now? Come, come, Isabelle, you must not be cross with me because I was called away for a day."

"Two days," she murmured.

"Two days. I agree it was two days and stand corrected. I should not have gone if I could have avoided it, as you must surely know. Say you forgive me."

"There is nothing to forgive. I am sure you are free to come and go as you please," she replied, but without warmth.

"I see what it is. It is a lap dog you wanted, I think. But I must tell you, Isabelle, I am not of the sort who will sit by your side by the hour to hand you your embroidery frame or help you wind your yarn. I am no such namby-pamby drawing-room dawdler as that, nor do I believe that is what you love me for. Is it? Is it, my dear?" he insisted when she did not answer at once.

"No, of course not," she muttered, trying to draw away from him. But he would not release her and pulled her closer into his embrace and kissed her. She willed herself to respond, but could not, though she put her arms about his neck and did not resist him further.

She knew she appeared to be pouting and wished she could conduct herself better. The dreadful admission she had made to herself on the night of Lady Bromley's dinner party to honor their betrothal had weighed down her spirits so dreadfully that it was difficult to cast it entirely aside in his presence and pretend that all was as it had been. She had, in the two days of his absence, wrestled mightily with herself over the revelation and had finally decided that she must not judge him on his behavior of that evening. She knew he did not care for his relatives other than Lady Bromley, and had not wanted his aunt to give the party. He had not behaved well therefore, and had exhibited his displeasure as might a naughty child. It was most reprehensible, but surely not beyond her understanding and forgiveness.

Thus had she talked to herself these past two days and tried to subdue this serpent of discord that had crept into her nest against her will, a serpent that must be annihilated for her peace of mind. She thought she had succeeded until she was actually in his presence, but now found she was not guileful enough to pretend to be happy when her heart was so heavy, and she could not bring herself to meet his eyes directly lest any trace of her disloyal thought should still be discernible there.

Adrian, however, felt the arms go about his neck and was satisfied that he had won her over. He drew away from her slightly to smile quizzically at her.

"There, I believe it is my dear girl again. Now we can proceed to other matters. A date must be set, you know."

"A date? Oh!"

"Yes—oh! You have not set the date of our marriage yet. And I must tell you, I will not like to be put off so that you may buy more bonnets and kickshaws for your trousseau. I want it to be as soon as may be," he said sternly, as a man whose patience has already been sorely tried by delays.

"I am sure you may name any day you choose."

"Then I say this day fortnight," he said promptly, "and please tell your father that I will send him a note later today setting a time to meet with my solicitors."

A fortnight! Isabelle was filled with dismay at his words, but having given him leave to name what day he would, she was reluctant to sound childish by immediately protesting when he did so. After all, this was the man she loved and had agreed to give herself to, and if he had behaved badly and earned her disapproval, no doubt there were faults of her own that he might point out to her if he chose, and she would not expect him to stop loving her because of them.

Later in the day her papa came to her holding a note from the marquess. "My dear, here is Lord Sutterton requesting me to meet him at his solicitors' on Thursday. He says you have set a date."

"Yes, Papa," she said calmly, naming the day.

"It is rather sudden, is it not?"

"He would have it so, Papa."

He studied her face, sure all was not well with her in some way. "Is there something bothering you, my dear girl?"

She felt a lump forming in her throat at the kindly concern in his voice and for some reason felt inclined to throw herself onto his bosom and weep, something she had not done with him since she was a small child. However, she fought back the tears and forced herself to smile and answer brightly, too proud to allow him to think her less than blissful in the knowledge that her lover was so eager to claim her for his bride.

Mr. Holland found Lord Sutterton's solicitors, Grooby, Mudge and Tornish, in Lincoln's Inn, in a gloomy set of rooms reached by a narrow, dark stairway. No doubt the meager amount of light admitted by the one grimy window accounted for Mr. Mudge's perpetual squinting frown, or perhaps it was the louring, crammed shelves all around the room, which seemed to be threatening to tip out their red-tape-tied bundles onto the inhabitants at any moment. Mr. Holland found both the frown and the shelves equally unpleasant, but he refused to allow himself to be intimidated. He smiled calmly and acknowledged Adrian's introduction to the solicitor before taking the chair offered him.

"Now, Mr.—er—Holland, in order to—er—get our business—er—concluded as quickly as—er—possible," began Mr. Mudge in a voice as dry and dusty as his office, and then continued in a lengthy peroration, made even more lengthy by his nervous interjections every few words. Mr. Holland felt his nerves began to twitch with irritation and stole a glance at his future son-in-law to see if he were similarly affected. Adrian, however, seemed inured to Mr. Mudge's style, or perhaps resigned to it, for he only stared glassily at the dim yellow square of the window and tapped his fingers on the arm of his chair.

When Mr. Mudge said, ". . . so, it will be—er—best to begin with Miss Holland's—er—settlement," Mr. Holland broke in at once, hoping to speed things along somewhat.

"I agree. I would like it left entirely in her own name, with, of course, the income from it to be received by her husband during her lifetime. The money would of course be left as she willed it upon her death."

Adrian sprang from his chair. "What? You surely cannot be serious?"

"My lord," interrupted Mr. Mudge, "please calm yourself. I think this is best left to—er—myself. Mr. Holland, Lord Sutterton naturally feels that as her husband it will be his duty to have the charge of all finances in his own household.''

"I have no objection to that at all, nor, I am sure, would my daughter feel it necessary to take that duty from him, but I would be remiss in my duty to my daughter if I agreed to sign my daughter's entire fortune into her husband's hands. What if there should be an—ah—estrangement, or what if he should die suddenly before there was an heir? Her money as well as his would then pass into the hands of the next in line to the title, and my daughter would be left unprovided for.''

"I think Lord Sutterton can be trusted to provide for his own wife, sir,'' said Mr. Mudge reprovingly.

"I would not dream of not trusting Lord Sutterton to behave honorably, but I am speaking of unforeseen future circumstances which must be taken into consideration now. Surely that is not unreasonable?''

"This is b-b-beyond anything insulting to me, sir,'' stuttered Adrian rising again abruptly and banging his fist on Mr. Mudge's desk, sending up a cloud of dust.

"My lord, my lord,'' soothed Mr. Mudge, "please let us not become—er—heated. These matters can be—er—worked out if we all remain—er—calm. Now, Mr. Holland''—he turned briskly toward the visitor and all trace of his nervous manner of speaking disappeared— "I quite see your point, indeed it is well taken. Naturally, the marquess cannot care for the implication that he is not capable of caring for his own, but I am sure he would be agreeable to setting aside a portion of the dowry to remain in his wife's name, just in case any such dire circumstance as you mentioned before should arise. In fact, it is usual to do so. What sum would make you feel comfortable?''

Mr. Holland smiled ruefully. "It is not such a large dowry that I could feel comfortable at dividing it at all.''

"Perhaps we could come at it more easily if we could just put down the exact sum of the total,'' replied Mr. Mudge smoothly, picking up his pen and dipping it into the inkwell expectantly.

"Five thousand pounds," said Mr. Holland at once, in an effort to be as expeditious and cooperative as possible.

"Ah yes, five thousand pounds. Then let us—let us—" He faltered to a stop and looked blankly at Mr. Holland for a moment. Then his face brightened, "Oh, I see, you mean you would agree that five thousand be set aside in her own name out of the sum total?"

"Mr. Mudge, that *is* the sum total," said Mr. Holland.

There was a stunned silence while this information was assimilated, then Mr. Mudge's pen fell from his nerveless fingers and rolled to the floor. just as Adrian exploded from his chair, shouting, "What is that? What do you say, sir?"

"I said that my daughter's dowry is five thousand pounds, Lord Sutterton," said Mr. Holland calmly.

"That cannot be possible! I was told—my aunt said—"

"I am sorry if you are disappointed in the amount, my lord, but I fear it is so despite what you may have been told." Quite suddenly, Mr. Holland found himself feeling more cheerful than he had for weeks.

Again a silence held the roon, while Mr. Mudge stared at Lord Sutterton and Lord Sutterton stared at Mr. Holland, who met his gaze openly. After a moment Adrian swung away to stare out the window. Presently he said tautly, "There is something not quite straight in all this, sir."

"In all what, Lord Sutterton? I can see that you expected a great deal more, but a dowry is hardly a thing we Hollands feel quite nice to discuss openly, and certainly no one has asked any of us outright for the—ah—sum total. Since you did not ask when you came to me for my daughter's hand, I assumed it was a love match and money was of no importance to you."

"I think a family as prestigious as my lord's is entitled to expect him to bring something into the family with his marriage, Mr. Holland," said Mr. Mudge loftily.

"You mean there is a price to pay for the great honor conferred upon her," said Mr. Holland tartly.

"The family is an ancient and powerful one, sir, which would confer honor on any who joined it."

"The Hollands, you will find, are an even more ancient family, Mr. Mudge, and as for honor, we look up to no one. Our escutcheon is unblemished."

Mr. Mudge was silenced for the moment and no one spoke until Adrian turned back to face them. "This need not be an insoluble problem. Isabelle has relatives who I am sure would be happy to—"

Mr. Holland rose abruptly to his feet. "There can be no question of any such thing, sir. I find such a suggestion reprehensible."

"I am sure your sister-in-law would not find it reprehensible to be connected to the Marquess of Sutterton," Adrian fired back.

Mr. Holland drew himself up. "My sister-in-law, my lord Sutterton, while she might happily give any amount of money to her niece to secure her happiness, would find your suggesting such a thing as intolerable as do I. She may be a tradesman's daughter, but she was taught never to sell her soul for a mess of pottage, as evidently some of those who look down upon her are willing to do."

"I find your words offensive, sir, and I resent your coming over all moral after the trick your family has played upon me."

"Sir, you pursued my daughter, professed to love her, and asked me for her hand in marriage. I see now that you were motivated by some baseless gossip that my daughter is a great heiress. I think, if the truth were told, it is you who has been playing tricks. I will bid you good day." He bowed to each man and walked out of the room.

"Give me a pen and paper," Adrian ground out savagely between his clinched teeth. "At once, you fool!"

Mr. Holland strolled along home, feeling almost lightheaded with relief. He had not realized how heavy a weight had descended upon his mind after giving his daughter into the keeping of a man he could not like, no matter how hard he had tried for Isabelle's sake. He began to whistle softly to himself, but suddenly he remembered that it was now his duty to seek out his daughter and tell her of the events just passed. He sobered down at once, for however relieved he felt at having his own opinion of the marquess justified, Isabelle would be bound to feel very differently about it. She had chosen the man, after all, and was in love with him. What if, despite the despicable conduct displayed this morning, the marquess truly loved Isabelle and persisted in wanting to marry her despite the smallness of her dowry? Perhaps it had only been shock that had brought out his display of temper, and once reconciled to the facts he would realize that his love for her came before everything. Then how would it look to Isabelle if her father had come running with this tale to her lover's disparagement? Perhaps the best thing would be not to return home at once, but to stay out of the way long enough for the marquess to recover his temper and act accordingly.

Mr. Holland dithered, not sure of what would be best. He knew she would be waiting anxiously for his return, but what was he to say? If he reported truthfully and the marquess remained faithful in his suit, he, Mr. Holland, would be guilty of sowing the seeds of doubt and possibly discord into their married life. No, no, he could not do it. Better to wait and see which way the marquess acted, than to cause Isabelle even one moment of unnecessary unhappiness.

It was, therefore, a totally unprepared Isabelle who received, one hour later, the note from her betrothed, written in the solicitor's office and dispatched by messenger at once.

Dear Miss Holland,
    I think it must be as clear to you, as it has slowly become to me, that we are not suited. In both our interests, therefore, I think it is best to recognize the fact and agree to part.
                        Your obedient servant, madam,
                                            Sutterton

The stark brevity of the words and the unexpectedness of the message so froze Isabelle's mind that she read the note three times with incomprehension. She sat down and stared before her for a few moments before slowly raising the paper once more before her eyes. She read it slowly and as the meaning sank into her mind, she felt an ugly jerk of nerves through her whole body.

Mrs. Holland came rushing in at that moment, stopped, and looked about in bewilderment. "Where is your papa? I made sure I heard the knocker and I'm that nervous to hear how the meeting—why—Isabelle—dearest child—you're as white as a pillow sham—what has happened?"

Isabelle stared at her for a moment and then with a queer little smile said, "I have been jilted, Aunt," and fell back upon the sofa in the first swoon of her life.

When Mr. Holland entered the house some time later it was to find it strangely silent, yet electric with tension. The butler who admitted him looked discreetly bursting with significant news and a housemaid hurrying up the stairs turned wide eyes over her shoulder for an instant before disappearing.

With Mr. Holland's first flickers of apprehension, his sister-in-law came rushing down the stairs. "Oh, Peregrine, what on earth have you done?" she cried reproachfully.

"Done? What do you mean, what have I done?" he said somewhat indignantly.

"You have never really approved of the match, I knew that all along, and now I suppose you have let him know it."

"I did no such thing."

"Then what happened? Were there words between you and the marquess?"

"Suppose you tell me what is afoot here," he said sternly, to call her to order.

"She had a note from him—Oh, Peregrine, he has jilted her!" Ah, thought Mr. Holland, I should have guessed that after what I saw today. "Oh, the poor child," continued Mrs. Holland, the ready tears slipping down her fat cheeks. "The disgrace! Was it something you said to him, Peregrine?"

"Yes," said Mr. Holland a little grimly, "I suppose you could say that. Where is Isabelle?"

"I have put her to bed. She fainted!"

"I will go up to her. Alone, if you please, my dear," he added when Mrs. Holland began to follow him.

He found Isabelle propped up against her pillows, sipping a glass of warm milk. Certainly she was paler than usual and her expression was far from happy, but he was relieved to find her less devastated than he had feared from his encounter with Mrs. Holland.

"Well, my dear, here is sad news," he said, bending to kiss her forehead. "Has it made you ill?"

"It was only the shock, Papa, that caused me to faint. You know I have never been given to fainting. Then Aunt fussed so I thought it better to give in and be put to bed to give her something to do to relieve her feelings. But what of you?"

"I? What could be wrong with me?"

"I—we—feared—I do not know what exactly." She laughed shakily. "Hard words, even blows, I suppose. I know you did not really care for Adrian."

"It was not my place to object to your choice, Isabelle. I admit I never could seem to get next to the man, but, well, that is all by the way. I know you want to know what transpired at our meeting, and to tell you at its simplest, the marquess evidently expected a very large dowry in exchange for bestowing the title of marchioness upon his bride."

"But—but then why did he choose me?"

"I can only tell you what I believe to be true from something he said, and that is that he was led to believe that you had such a dowry."

"But how can that be? The matter was never mentioned between us. In fact, I never mentioned it to anyone at all, except for Aunt Nathaniel when we first arrived and she asked me."

"My dear, we shall probably never know for sure where such an idea came from, but knowing his aim was to marry for money, we must count it as a blessing that you

are well out of it. Will you tell yourself that and not allow
your spirits to be laid too low by this blow? I know first
love seems like last love, but believe me, it is not neces-
sarily true. You are still very young and all of life is still
before you.''

"Yes, Papa," she said, turning her head away so he
would not see the tears forming, but reaching out her hand
to him. He pressed it between his own for a few moments,
then went quietly away.

At Mrs. Holland's insistence a doctor had been called to
examine Isabelle, and the busy housemaid who showed
him upstairs was, unfortunately, the person who had come
upon the marquess's note, dropped and forgotten after
Isabelle had fainted. The maid could not read it herself,
but had shown it to the butler who had read it out to her.
She now whispered the news importantly into the doctor's
ear as they climbed the stairs, and when he had pronounced that a few days in bed to settle her nerves was all
that his patient required, he went away bursting to impart
his news to his next patient. As this happened to be a
woman patient of great social ambition, she hurried off to
visit the Dowager Duchess of Halford where she had
entree, and titillated a group of the dowager's friends with
the delicious *on-dit*. By breakfast time the next morning,
half the *ton* knew that Miss Holland had been jilted by
Lord Sutterton and had ordered their carriages early in
order to spread the news to the other half.

None of this was known to the Hollands at once. All
had remained in the house to support Isabelle if she had
need of it. She had refused to remain in bed, despite all
her aunt's pleadings, for she had found lying quietly alone
only produced a dreary repetition of "Why? Why? Why?"
or bouts of murderous rage where she had fantastical
visions of confronting him and either annihilating him with
scorn and disdainful words or in some more violent manner with fists, nails, teeth, knife, or pistol in a perfect fury
at his betrayal of her trust. All this, the first day, filled her
conscious moments and was too unpleasant to face for a
second one. Unable to bear such thoughts, and unable to

delve more deeply into her real feelings for the time, she rose from her bed and attempted to go about her life as though nothing had happened. She decided that when questioned about her betrothal she would make small remarks to imply some doubts in the matter, and hope that eventually it would be accepted that the match had been called off and the subject could be dropped.

Unfortunately, this admirable program was doomed to failure, since the matter was already spread over the town. She found that wherever she went she faced avid speculative looks, prodding, innocent-sounding questions, or buzzing conversations that stopped abruptly when she entered the room. After a week of this, her air of composure began to erode. She became listless and pale and given to bouts of tears. She began refusing invitations and could rarely be coaxed even to go for a drive to take some air. If visitors were announced, she disappeared upstairs into her room. She felt she had become an object of pity and was ashamed.

One morning as she and her aunt sat at breakfast, Captain Perronet was announced. Isabelle started, her eyes wide with apprehension. "No—no—I cannot—you must receive him alone in the drawing room, Aunt!"

"Oh, my dear, our old friend—surely you—"

"No. Please go in to him at once, Aunt. Tell him—tell him I am out—or ill—no—not that or he will be sure to come again. Just tell him I am out."

Mrs. Holland attempted to remonstrate with her, but Isabelle was adamant. She could not face Captain Perronet. At last, Mrs. Holland gave up and went away alone to the drawing room and Isabelle fled to her room.

"My dear Captain Perronet, this is delightful indeed," cried Mrs. Holland, advancing across the drawing room, her hand outstretched.

"Very kind of you to receive me," replied William with great relief, for he had not been certain of gaining admittance at all after his last visit to the house. It seemed, however, that Isabelle had kept silent about that or otherwise Mrs. Holland would not have been so openly warm in her greeting. He should have known Isabelle was not the sort of girl to speak of a private interview and set her relatives against him.

"I think it is kind of me after you went away without telling me or bidding us good-bye," laughed Mrs. Holland, patting his arm kindly to take the sting out of her words. "I hope there was no serious trouble at home that caused you to leave so abruptly."

"No, no, all is well there—just something I had to—er—attend to."

"Well, we have missed you. Sit down, sir. Will you take a glass of wine?"

When they had chatted comfortably for some few moments, he cleared his throat nervously and said, "And how is—is Miss Holland?"

Mrs. Holland was a bit flustered but finally said, "How long have you been in town, captain?"

"But an hour, madam. I came straight from my lodgings as soon as I washed off the dirt of my travel."

"Ah, me, then of course you will not have heard of what has befallen us. My poor, dear niece!"

William turned pale and started to his feet in alarm. "What has happened? Please tell me at once!"

With many sighs and a few tears, Mrs. Holland told him Isabelle's sad story. As she spoke the color slowly returned to William's face and he sank back into his chair. Ah, the villain, he thought savagely, the villain! How I shall punish that dastardly coward for hurting my Isabelle! At the same time, beneath his ferocious need to avenge this wrong, he experienced a great sighing relief and gladness.

He came every day and at last, on the fourth visit, Isabelle came down to receive him when he arrived while her aunt was out. She walked slowly toward him, her head high, her gray eyes cool and withdrawn as when he had first known her. She did not give him her hand, only bowing her head in greeting. "Good morning, captain. I am sorry my aunt is away from home and not here to receive you. Will you have a seat?"

"Isabelle, my dear friend, you must not be stiffish with

me, even if I deserve it after my behavior at our last meeting," he said, and reaching out, he possessed himself of her hand, which he bent to kiss lightly and then held in both his own.

Her hand felt warm and comforted by his clasp, but she nevertheless withdrew it and turned away to a chair. The raw wound upon her feelings could not yet bear the weight of comforting. She felt that to accept it would cause her to break down completely and she was too proud to allow that, even before her family. She saw no one else now, not even the Richmond sisters, who had called several times and written solicitous notes inquiring after her health, for Mrs. Holland had excused Isabella by telling them she was laid up with an infected throat. Isabella did not know whether they knew the truth or not, but assumed they must, that everyone in London knew and delighted in the fact that the penniless nobody had been jilted by the marquess. Actually, she was correct in that so far as the *ton* was concerned, but only because it was such a delicious scandal to relieve the tedium of their days. In another week or so something new would arise and they would pounce upon it eagerly and forget all about Miss Holland and the marquess. Isabelle was too new in the ways of the *ton* to realize this and thought herself disgraced forever. When she thought of the marquess's curt note rejecting her, it seemed her very soul curled in shame.

She could not bear the thought of people looking upon her with pitying eyes either and so had till now refused to see anyone but her family. She still did not understand what had prompted her to come down to receive the captain today after successfully avoiding him until now, but somehow she had not cared to have him think her a coward.

She turned now to indicate that he should sit down opposite her, and said, "My aunt tells me you have been in Sussex, sir. Does the work go well on your new house?"

"Splendidly, thank you, though I spent very little time there actually. I visited my sister."

"I hope she is keeping well?"

"Very well."

"And the children?"

"They too," he said so shortly that she fell silent and stared at her hands "Isabelle," he burst out at last, "this is ridiculous!"

She looked at him then, steadily, and it seemed to him there was something imploring in her gaze which caused him to subside. "Perhaps you will like a glass of wine, captain?"

"Yes. That would be pleasant," he said meekly, and she rose to ring for the servant.

"Do you make a long visit this time?" she inquired in her queer, new formal way that sat so oddly upon her, he thought. He began to sense, however, how fragile was her control and knew he must go very slowly if he was to regain a place in her life. He was as determined upon this as he had ever been, but as impatient with social foolishness as well, and found it a very trying situation.

"I must order a carriage made and buy some cattle, and my sister tells me I must begin to look for furnishings. I am hopeful that you will advise me on that."

"I fear I know little of such things, never having had a house of my own to furnish, but I am sure my aunt will be very happy to assist you."

"Well, even you must know more than I," he said with a grin.

For a brief instant a smile trembled on her lips in response and then the door opened to admit the footman with a tray, and the moment was lost. While the wine was being served, Mrs. Holland returned and came in to them and the conversation became general.

Altogether, however, William was not displeased with this first meeting. She had consented to see him at last, at any rate, which he could sense had taken some courage, and if patience was required on his part, then he would be patient.

In the meantime, there was something he must do to satisfy his own sense of honor. That swine had dared to treat Isabelle in a despicable way and must be punished for it or he felt he would never be able to rest easy. The only problem was that he didn't know where to find the marquess or what he looked like.

For some days he haunted the streets where the better clubs were located, hoping he would somehow meet up with the marquess, perhaps by hearing him addressed by name, but he had no luck at all. At last he inquired, casually, of Mrs. Holland where Lady Bromley resided.

Mrs. Holland stared at him in astonishment for a moment. He muttered something about his sister having inquired in a letter. Mrs. Holland gave him the address with no further comment.

The next few days he hung about in the neighborhood, but when people began staring at him suspiciously he realized it was hopeless and began to despair. However, one afternoon he accompanied the two Mr. Hollands to Mr. Nathaniel Holland's club, and as they strolled down the street they passed a group of gentlemen talking together. Both Mr. Hollands pointedly looked away and passed by. After they had gone some steps, Isabelle's father murmured with loathing, "That was Sutterton."

William whipped about. "Which one is he?"

"The blond one to the left."

"Excuse me for a moment, gentlemen," said William, and went marching back the way they had come and straight up to the group.

"Lord Sutterton," he said loudly.

The marquess turned in surprise and surveyed him. "Yes?"

"I would like a word apart with you."

There was a look in his eye that Adrian did not care for at all. "I am busy with my friends, as you can see," he said insolently.

"Would you prefer me to say what I have to say before them?"

Feeling there was safety in numbers, Adrian said in a voice of extreme boredom, "If I cannot persuade you to go away."

"My name is William Perronet."

"I cannot say that news conveys anything to me," replied Adrian languidly. Then he saw approaching them the two Mr. Hollands, and suddenly realized who was speaking to him.

"We have a mutual acquaintance whom you have treated despicably," said William with cold rage. He drew off his gloves, slapped them together, and deliberately struck Adrian across the face stingingly. "You are a contemptible, fortune-hunting cur. Here is my card. If you wish satisfaction, your seconds will find me at Long's Hotel." He held out the card and when Adrian did not take it, flicked it at his feet and turned and walked away.

Adrian's friends watched him intently. Adrian attempted a laugh. "The man must be drunk," he said.

"But surely you must act, Sutterton. The man struck you!"

"I never duel with men with whom I would not sit down to dine," said Adrian with an attempt at lightness.

His friends shuffled uneasily, exchanging covert glances. They did not know who William Perronet might be, but all of them recognized Mr. Nathaniel Holland. Any man Mr. Holland chose to give his friendship to must be a gentleman. They found it difficult to believe the marquess was afraid to meet the man, but unable to account for his attitude in any other way. At last, unable to meet his eye, they made their excuses and melted away, leaving him alone.

Before the day was over the story was all over the *ton* and in the weeks that followed, Adrian found himself shunned by men who had heretofore been glad to call him friend. Nothing William could have done could have been more devastating to the marquess than to publicly exhibit him as a coward.

As they walked away, William found his arm taken on either side by the Holland brothers. They did not speak of the matter then, nor, indeed, ever, but William understood their feelings entirely.

Eleven

William had need of all the patience at his command in the days that followed, for his encounters with Isabelle were rare and vastly unsatisfactory, since she continued to hold herself at a distance from him as though she existed behind a shield of glass. He called most days and Mrs. Holland was only too happy to welcome him and give him assistance in the matter of furnishings for his new home, and both Mr. Hollands gladly accompanied him to Tattersall's to inspect horses and to the carriage-makers. Isabelle, however, took no part in any of these expeditions.

William was quite often persuaded to stay for dinner and naturally Isabelle took her place at the table, but while always courteous and expressing herself as glad to see him, she was less than forthcoming conversationally. She never initiated any subject and rarely contributed to any unless addressed directly. This was a daunting situation for a man of William's temperament. He was a plain-spoken man, unused to conversational subleties, and was always fearful of inadvertently saying something that would cause her pain. Also, it was difficult for him to be in the presence of her unhappiness without wanting to fold her in his arms and comfort her as he would a child. He realized now that had he not already declared his love for her, he could have been of much more comfort to her, perhaps even have persuaded her to confide in him about her feelings. Surely she must now have discovered she had been mistaken in her feelings for that dog; that it had not been true love but only a young girl's infatuation with the glamour of a titled and much-sought-after man. Surely she could not really have loved him?

This was the question also exercising Isabelle's thoughts during the long hours she now had at her disposal and spent, for the most part, alone in her room. She had relived every moment she had spent in Adrian's company, remembered each word exchanged between them. There had not been, after all, so many that she had any difficulty in recalling everything.

Her first shattering discovery was that rehearse those words as she might, nowhere in them had he ever actually said that he loved her, or even words approximating it that could have been construed to have the same meaning. How then had she been so deceived as to think he had? She who had always prided herself on her clear thinking and hardheadedness? She who had disdained the idea of falling in love as girlish nonsense that clouded one's judgment? And clearly she had had the right of it there, for had her judgment not been befogged by love, she would have realized sooner all the things about him that she did not like: his insensitivity, his selfishness, his outright cruelty, all things she had insisted upon disguising to herself until she could do so no longer and had been forced to admit to herself that she did not like him. Was it possible that she had still loved him even though she did not like him? Since she had not immediately asked him to release her from their betrothal, she supposed that this must be so and writhed with humiliation at the thought of it. Looking back, she saw now that every meeting with him after their betrothal had held something hurtful and slighting to herself in it, apart even from his reluctance to make love to her.

This last, of course, was the acknowledgment that above all others caused her the deepest pain, for it meant, to her, that she was not lovable, that her only appeal to him had been the fictitious dowry, an admission so lowering to her self-esteem as to nearly destroy it. She imagined everyone thought of her as a green, ignorant girl with no

pretensions to beauty or wealth or rank, throwing herself at
the first titled and supposedly wealthy man to come her
way in her eagerness to achieve the married state. This
thought was so demoralizing she could not bear to meet
any of her former friends for fear she would see the
contempt in their eyes.

She longed to be able to forget the entire affair, if only
for a few moments, but she could not. She simply went
around and around with the same thoughts, which caused
her to feel slightly headachy most of the time and so
thin-skinned she must hold even her family at a distance so
that no kind word or caress could cause her to break down
completely. She still had enough pride to refuse to allow
anyone to see her do that, most of all William Perronet,
though she found after that first meeting she did not mind
meeting him again in the company of her family.

So William had to be content with merely her presence,
a smile of greeting or good night, and an occasional few
words of casual conversation. He wrote to his sister, more
for the relief of expressing his feelings than because he had
anything to report. She responded advising patience and yet
more patience, for it was far too early to expect a girl of any
sensitivity to have recovered from such a blow and be
open to another proposal.

In his frustration, William was glad to be taken up with
great enthusiasm by the Richmond sisters after meeting
them in the street one day. He accepted their invitation to
walk home with them and see their mother again, who,
they assured him, had conceived a very high regard for
him at their previous meeting and would be delighted to
renew the acquaintance.

William welcomed any distraction and accepted at once
by extending an arm to each young lady. Mrs. Richmond,
indeed, seemed excessively happy to see him and soon he
was comfortably seated, a glass of wine in one hand and a
biscuit in the other, discoursing upon his new horses and
carriage and manor house in Sussex.

All the ladies hung upon his words, but it was left to
Miss Victoria to respond to him, Miss Richmond having

retired rather into the background and Mrs. Richmond contenting herself with smiles and nods of approval to everything he said. When he took his leave, Mrs. Richmond asked him to dine with them the following evening and he accepted gladly, for he could not dine with the Hollands every night, and the nights when he was left to his own devices were long and lonely for him. He had taken to walking the dark and silent streets of London well into the early morning hours in an effort to exhaust himself, for of late sleep had become more and more elusive to him.

The only other guest at the Richmonds' the following evening was Swinburn Tuberville, and having already met and liked one another, he and William were glad to renew their acquaintance. William saw at once that Miss Richmond and Mr. Tuberville had reached an understanding, though there had been no official announcement as yet. They were very comfortable together in company and though behaving with every propriety, William noted that when they thought themselves unobserved, their eyes sought each other at once and they exchanged very tender and loving looks. He envied them excessively.

Dr. Richmond hurried in just before dinner was announced and shook hands in a rather distracted way with William. He was a nervous, harried-looking little man, clearly still much in awe of his stately, well-born wife. Mrs. Richmond was at her most affable this evening with two young gentlemen, one already affianced to her eldest, to grace her table and no other, possibly more attractive, young women to distract their attentions from her daughters. This Captain Perronet now would, she thought, do very nicely for dear Victoria. Oh! the glory, the relief from strain it would be to have them both married. She had been quite in despair that they never would find husbands, dear good girls though they were, until chance had thrown dearest Tuberville in their way. The captain, of course, was not so well-born as Tuberville, but must surely be possessed of a grand fortune, having bought a large estate and being in the process of such extensive renovations, apart from the furnishings, the horses, and the carriage being made to his own specifications. He must surely be intending to look about for a wife now, and he was such a fine, upstanding figure of a man, far handsomer than dear Tuberville. Looks, however, were not everything, she thought, casting a fond and doting eye upon her future son-in-law, and breathing a silent prayer of gratitude to Isabelle Holland, who had been the instrument of so much rejoicing in Mrs. Richmond's heart.

Her gratitude was not nearly so fervent as that of her daughters, however. Victoria was truly proud and glad of her sister's good fortune, and both girls congratulated themselves for their perspicacity in seeing at once that nothing but good could come of their friendship with dear Isabelle. And now, again due to her, here was this wonderful sea captain come into their lives.

The dinner was lengthy, featuring some seven courses of excellently cooked food which both young men partook of heartily, and William was able to forget his pressing problem under the lighthearted badinage of young Tuberville and the attention lavished upon him by the women. When the gentlemen rejoined the ladies after dinner, Tuberville and Miss Richmond retired at once to the far end of the room while Dr. Richmond took what was clearly his accustomed chair opposite that of his wife before the fireplace. William saw that Miss Victoria sat alone upon a sofa in the middle of the room and was looking expectantly up at him. He good-naturedly went to sit beside her, though he would have preferred a more general conversation to a tête-à-tête.

"Ah, captain, a moment to speak quite quietly at last. Tuberville is so volatile, is he not? He quite takes us out of ourselves with his fun, but much as I enjoy it, I do sometimes long to speak of more serious things."

"Why, Miss Victoria, you quite frighten me. Nothing too serious, I hope."

"Oh—well . . ." Victoria flushed and fluttered her fan. "You must not take me up so quickly, captain. I meant only—well—ideas and—and such things as opposed to jokes and *bon mots*."

"Ah, I see. Well, I fear I am so well-fed my brain has gone to sleep when it comes to ideas. You will have to start us off if we are to get anywhere along those lines."

Victoria felt her usual facile mind go blank for a moment, then she said the first thing that occurred to her. "Have you seen anything of dear Miss Holland since you came back to town?" She could have bitten her tongue in vexation the moment the words popped out, for dearly as she loved Isabelle, she knew it was very poor policy to discuss another, and prettier, girl at this moment.

William's expression sobered somewhat. "Yes. Yes, I have seen her a few times when the Hollands were so kind as to ask me to dinner."

"Oh, do tell her how much we have missed her and long to see her if you happen to go again. Now—I understand that you have a sister living in Sussex also."

William was as happy to change the subject as she was, and went into great detail about Elizabeth and his four nephews, and from there into great detail about Tall Oaks, his new manor, which delighted Victoria greatly, for she could see he loved the place and it seemed to her his confiding in her in this way brought them close together. He surely didn't tell just everyone these small details.

At last she sighed, "Oh, how beautiful you make it sound. How I should like to see it!"

"Well, well, perhaps you will one day and find it all less beautiful than I make it sound and be disappointed."

Victoria's heart beat with almost painful happiness. He must mean her to see it or he would not speak so, she thought breathlessly. Unfortunately, the tea tray was brought in at that moment and their delightful privacy was brought to an end. Victoria kept expecting him to ask if he might call again the next day, but he did not. However, just as he and Tuberville rose to take their leave, Tuberville suggested that he join them the next morning for a ride in the Park and William said he would have been happy to do so but that he had already engaged himself to go shopping with Mrs. Holland in the morning. He then suggested that he would like to come the day after if they were to ride, and the matter was arranged. William would meet them all here on the day after tomorrow at ten in the morning. Dear, dear Tuberville, sighed Victoria happily.

As usual, Isabelle did not appear when he went to call for Mrs. Holland the next morning, nor had he expected it. He had hoped, just a little, but had not truly thought she would join them. As they were driven along to Robert Dodsley's at Tully Head, where the finest furniture was to be found, William told Mrs. Holland of his meeting with the Richmonds and of the dinner party.

"I take it that Miss Richmond and young Tuberville are betrothed," he said.

"Oh, yes, it is so. They only await his parents' return from the Continent to announce it. He has written them and they have approved, for her dowry will be quite substantial. Mrs. Richmond was a Terwhitt, you know, oceans of money, and she the only child of her parents."

"Miss Victoria asked about Isabelle. She says they have not met for some time."

"No," said Mrs. Holland, "she will see no one. No one but you."

William took some comfort from this, for though she held herself apart still, at least she allowed him to see her. She trusted him. That must count for something.

Though he had purchased a handsome pair of grays for his new carriage, he had not as yet bought any other cattle, so he was obliged to hire a mount from a livery stable before joining the others the next morning. For a time they all rode together, but then Tuberville and Miss Richmond dropped back and William found himself alone with Miss Victoria. She was very gay, almost roguish, this morning, flashing her eyes at him and teasing him about his livery horse. It gradually was borne in upon William that she was flirting with him. This came as something of a shock when he realized it, for he had never been flirted with by a genteel young lady before in his life. For a time he quite enjoyed it and responded in kind, to his astonishment. But then he began to think of the implications of what he was doing. Never could he be so cruel as to encourage so nice a young woman as Miss Victoria to think he was serious when his heart was so irrevocably given elsewhere. He decided he must set the matter straight at once, but could not imagine how he was to do so.

He was glad when the others rejoined them at last and relieved when the outing was over and the young ladies delivered safely back to their home. He was again invited to dinner for the following evening and, though uncomfortable about it, could think of no graceful way of declining. In the interval he pondered on what he must do. To simply repulse all her advances, and really, he thought, it was not quite fair to call them so, but still he must think of them so, would be cruel. Not only were they very kind to him, but they were good friends of the Hollands. Nor would it answer to refuse all further invitations, for they would not understand the reason and be hurt. At last he decided he must take Victoria into his confidence—make an ally of her. Naturally, he would only tell her of what obtained to himself. He could not mention Isabelle's name or any of her problems, for to do so would be betraying Mrs. Holland's confidence. That story was Isabelle's to tell if she chose.

Consequently, when he and Victoria were again seated upon the couch in the Richmond drawing room after the usual hearty and elaborate meal, he confessed to her that his heart was very heavy and he desperately needed someone to speak to, someone of sensitivity and understanding.

"Oh, Captain Perronet," breathed Victoria fervently, "you make me very happy. I should be so honored to serve as your confidante. I do not know if I am wise enough to advise you—"

"Oh, it is not advice I seek, only someone to whom I can unburden myself from time to time. You see . . ." He paused, feeling several kinds of fool as well as miserable to be speaking of his feelings to anyone but Isabelle, and on top of everything guilty to be using this innocent girl in such a way as she gazed so trustingly into his eyes. Still, he thought, he must stop any tendency she might have to imagine herself developing a partiality for him. For a moment he saw himself as an egotistical fool for thinking such a thing possible, but then he remembered the way they seemed always to be paired and the flirting, and he knew he must act whether he wanted to or not. Besides, having gone this far, and she now waiting suspensefully for him to continue, there was nothing further to be done but to plunge in. He sighed and continued, "You see, Miss Victoria, my unhappiness stems from my own foolishness in allowing myself to give my heart to someone who is not free to accept it."

Any disappointment Victoria might have felt at this declaration, and indeed there was some for though she was not yet in love with the captain, she was very willing to be with the least encouragement from him, was instantly swamped by her pity at this dreadful confession. "Oh, oh, Captain Perronet, I am so truly sorry," she breathed, reaching out an impulsive hand to touch his arm. He patted the hand gratefully and she withdrew it shyly.

"I knew I could count upon your sympathy, dear lady," he said.

"But of course you can, just any time at all you feel the need to speak of it I will be only to happy to hear you. Can you tell me—I do hope—the—the lady is not—not married."

"Oh, dear me no. I hope I would not be so foolish as that," he said truthfully, though how he would have felt on the subject had Isabelle actually married the man, he could not imagine.

Victoria breathed a sigh of relief, for it would have been truly shocking to her if such had been the case. She longed to ask more, but knew it was not wise. If he wanted to tell her more details, he would do so. In the meantime, she must show him only sympathy and friendship, and who could know what might come of it? Perhaps he might tire of his hopeless passion and come to see that warmth and friendship and sympathy were more worthy of love.

Isabelle, meanwhile, was dining alone with her aunt, her father and uncle having an engagement elsewhere, and presently, in search of topics for conversation that would not distress the girl, Mrs. Holland reported that Captain Perronet dined tonight with the Richmonds.

"Really? How nice of them to entertain him," said Isabelle.

"Oh, they have quite taken him up. He has dined with them before and ridden with the girls in the Park in company with Mr. Tuberville. He is definitely betrothed to Horatia, you know."

"Yes, I did know," replied Isabelle rather absently, for her mind had presented her with the picture of the four of them riding and she wondered if Victoria looked as handsome on horseback as did her sister. She remembered suddenly the day she had taken him to the Richmonds' and how Victoria had admired him and said how handsome he was. Could it be possible she was setting her cap for him? No, that was an uncharitable way of phrasing it, for desperate as Victoria was to find a husband, she would never go about it in so vulgar a way as that phrase denoted. But still—oh, she thought impatiently, what does it matter? I'm sure he is able to take care of himself in the matter, and surely he is free to marry where he chooses.

She tried to forget about it, but it persisted in buzzing about in her mind like a bee trapped in a bottle, and she was not helped by her aunt, who brought up the subject again after the tea tray was brought into the drawing room.

"You know, my dear, it wouldn't surprise me in the least if Victoria were to lose her heart to the captain. It would really be a fine match for her and I'm sure she would make him an excellent wife," she said comfortably.

"Oh, no!" Isabelle exclaimed involuntarily before she could stop herself.

"Why do you say that?" asked Mrs. Holland in mild astonishment. "He surely needs a wife now he has retired from the sea and bought his fine home. And I'm sure he can support her handsomely. Of course, she will have a very nice portion herself, so they should be quite comfortably off."

"Yes, I suppose you are right. I just had not thought

them suited somehow,'' said Isabelle humbly. Of course, she thought, everyone would look at it in the same light, and though she could not forget his declaration of love to herself, it was also more than possible, even probable, that his feelings had changed by now and he sought love elsewhere. She could not blame him—indeed, as his friend she should be glad if it was so. She was more withdrawn than usual for the remainder of the evening and quite early declared she would go to her bed. As she took up her candle from the hall table she said casually, ''The next time the Richmonds call, I shall come down. I have missed them.''

Mrs. Holland's pleasure knew no bounds. At last, she thought, the darling girl is letting go of her grief and shame. Before she went to sleep herself she penned a little note to Mrs. Richmond to say she hoped she and her dear girls would give her the pleasure of a call in the next few days.

Victoria and Horatia were truly happy to see Isabelle again, and even Mrs. Richmond, in charity with the whole world now that her eldest daughter's future was secured and her youngest looked to be in the way of making a conquest, was warm in her greeting. And if there was just a tinge of pity in it—well, everyone knew something dire had happened in the matter of Isabelle's great alliance. Nothing had been said to any of Mrs. Holland's friends and none of them were close enough to the *ton* to be privy to any of their gossip, but there could be no mistaking the matter. Isabelle's sudden retirement and refusal to see her friends was evidence enough.

If that were not enough, her appearance now would certainly confirm one's saddest suspicions. She was pale and somehow pinched-looking, as though she were cold and had not had enough to eat lately, with large mauve circles beneath her eyes. She spoke very quietly and seldom, but there was little need for her to say much, both Richmond girls being in rare form and chattering along breathlessly.

Horatia, being the eldest and betrothed, was deferred to by Victoria, who only interjected little explanations when she felt her sister had not expiated greatly enough on her glorious future and the merits of wonderful Tuberville. But at last all was said that could be said on the subject and Horatia, as was their time-honored custom, turned the conversation to give her sister equal opportunity to shine.

"And you will never believe, dearest Isabelle, who has been calling upon us with, I believe, certain intentions," she said, giving Victoria a look freighted with meaning.

"Sister, hush!" cried Victoria, blushing to her eyes.

"Oh, is she not the slyest thing in nature?" laughed Horatia. "All those after-dinner tête-à-têtes with the captain. What can it all mean. I ask you?"

"Isabelle, you must pay no attention! She is such a tease," said Victoria.

"Do you mean Captain Perronet, Horatia?" asked Isabelle quietly.

"Why, of course! Tuberville says he is a fine man and Mama and Papa adore him. Oh, yes, we are all fond of the captain," she said significantly, with another mischievous look at her sister.

Victoria blushed even more furiously and began to speak of a new gown she had ordered for the assembly they were to attend in two weeks, and soon the talk turned to fashions and the gowns worn by various of their friends to parties they had attended since last they had seen Isabelle.

Isabelle noticed, however, that Victoria could not seem to help interjecting, "The captain said . . ." or "Captain Perronet does not care for . . ." into the conversations, coloring up a bit at each mention of his name.

Having seen them once, it was impossible for Isabelle to refuse to come down on subsequent visits and over the next two weeks she was regaled with a great deal more of Horatia's teasing and Victoria's blushing referrals to the captain's opinion upon everything imaginable. She saw the captain occasionally during this time at her aunt's dinner table, but he never mentioned the Richmonds unless Mrs. Holland questioned him about them directly. Isabelle would study him covertly as he responded, but could detect nothing in his manner or voice to give her a clue as to his feelings.

She never failed to go down when he came to dinner, but she only toyed with the food placed before her and between his visits she began to spend more and more of the day in bed, claiming she was somehow quite exhausted.

"Well, of course you must be when you eat nothing," declared Mrs. Holland trenchantly. "The body must have food for energy, and then you must be weakened from taking no exercise." Despite her scolding, Mrs. Holland was terribly worried, for it seemed to her that Isabelle was going into a decline. She consulted her brother-in-law, but he only declared that his daughter had a very healthy constitution and great good sense and would eventually rally. Meantime, she must be allowed to deal with her unhappiness in her own way. This might have satisfied him, but it did not lighten Mrs. Holland's mind in the least. At last she confided her worries to William.

". . . and I am just about at my wit's end, I do declare," she said to him as she finished her long list of worries regarding Isabelle.

William's heavy brows drew together broodingly as he thought for some time about what she had told him. As usual, he thought of his sister and wondered what she would advise. Then he thought he saw an answer. "Do you know, Mrs. Holland, I think she needs to go right away from here and from all of us."

"But where could she go? Do you mean to the seashore or something? I suppose I could take her, if I could persuade her to come, though I loathe such places myself."

"No, not the sea. Those places are filled with society anyway, which she doesn't need. I thought perhaps—well actually, I thought of her going to stay with my sister."

"Oh, well—I don't know, I'm sure," said Mrs. Holland doubtfully. "She doesn't know your sister and then your sister might not care for it, you know."

"Pooh! She never minds anything. Yes, I am sure it will answer very well. If you agree, I will write her at once and get her to come up to town and meet Isabelle and invite her for a visit,'' he said with growing enthusiasm for his plan.

Mrs. Holland was still doubtful. ''It is very kind of you, of course, and it would be kind of your sister, should she agree to it, but I hardly think Isabelle could be persuaded to go.''

''Nonsense, you don't know my sister. She is very persuasive when she sets her mind to something.''

Appealed to by her brother, Mrs. Claypool thought the matter over for two days before discussing it with her husband. He urged her to go. ''Do you good to get away, Liz, and old Will would never ask you if the matter wasn't important to him.''

Consequently, Mrs. Claypool set her household in order, ordered the traveling carriage for first thing the next morning, and told her maid to pack a box for her. When she arrived at William's hotel where he had reserved rooms for her, she found him awaiting her impatiently.

''Oh, Liz, this is good of you,'' he cried, enveloping her in a bearlike hug.

Her reply, muffled by the broad shoulder into which her face was pressed, was somewhat plaintive. ''Yes, darling, but if you smother me to death, it will all be for nothing.''

He laughed and released her and then laughed even more as he surveyed her, for his embrace had knocked her bonnet askew and she looked comical.

''Very unkind to make me look the fool and then laugh at me,'' she said crossly, untying her bonnet and removing it. ''Please go away and let me wash off some of my dirt from the journey and change my gown. Come back in half an hour and for heaven's sake, order some refreshments. I'm fair parched from the dust of the road.''

He grinned and left her, and with the help of her abigail Mrs. Claypool carried out her program and then dismissed the girl. When William returned, he was followed by a waiter bearing a well-stocked tray of wine, bread, and cold meats. Mrs. Claypool attacked the food with a hearty

appetite and at last sat back with a sigh. "Now," she
commanded, sipping her wine, "tell me everything."

So William recited the long, sad tale and finished, "We
had thought, Mrs. Holland and I, that the worst was over,
for she had finally said she would like to see the Richmond
girls again after so long, but then she seemed to sink even
lower and now rarely stirs from her bed."

Mrs. Claypool thought over all he had told her, especially the points relating to Miss Victoria Richmond, and
saw a great deal that she was sure William would never
suspect. She thought he was right that Isabelle should go
right away from London and agreed to attempt to persuade
the girl to come home with her for a long visit. "But only
on condition that you do it my way, William," she said
firmly.

"Well, of course I will," he said eagerly.

"You haven't heard my condition yet," she warned.

"Condition? What is it?"

"That you will stay right away until I say you may
come."

"But—but—what—" he protested.

"William," she said sternly, "the girl needs to get
away from all of you, not just London and the *ton*. She
needs time to think in an atmosphere where everything she
sees does not remind of her of all that has happened."

"She must do nothing else but think, I should imagine,
lying there alone day after day."

"She is not really thinking yet, she is just remembering
and feeling ashamed. Some distance between herself and
all these events will help her to really begin to think about
it. All of you remind her constantly of her misery. This is
the way to do it, believe me, William. You must allow me
to know best in this matter."

William gave in without further protest, though the
prospect of weeks in Sussex with Isabelle practically within
walking distance and he not allowed to see her was extremely disagreeable to him. However, if this was the way
it must be, he was willing to try anything. At his sister's
direction, he sat down and penned a note to Mrs. Holland

informing her that his sister was unexpectedly in London and he would bring her to call the following morning if this was agreeable. The messenger was instructed to wait for a reply, which came very promptly with Mrs. Holland's effusive agreeableness to making the acquaintance of Mrs. Claypool.

Having dispatched her response, Mrs. Holland hurried upstairs to inform her niece of the impending visit and of the absolute necessity for Isabelle to be downstairs on the following morning to meet Captain Perronet's sister.

Isabelle knew there was no way she could refuse to do so, and indeed she rather wanted to. She took more trouble than usual with her dressing the next day, but the result was not pleasing, she found as she studied herself in the glass. She turned away in disgust. What do I care for all that, she thought, what possible difference can it make to anything. Mrs. Claypool will just have to take me as she finds me.

Mrs. Claypool found her to be an unusually pale and unhappy looking girl, and her heart melted with pity. She instantly decided she would take her home and feed her up—and she must ride for exercise, she decided. When I get back to the hotel, I shall write to Ramsleigh to look out a mount for her.

Mrs. Claypool and Mrs. Holland had a great deal to say to one another, while Isabelle sat beside her aunt and listened. William sat apart and tried not to look at Isabelle. Presently, Mrs. Claypool turned to Isabelle.

"Are you enjoying London, Miss Holland?"

"No, I do not care for London much," said Isabelle quietly.

"Nor I. I only come up if it is unavoidable. And it is especially dull now I expect, with the Season nearly over and everyone going away. Do you have any plans for the summer?"

"No," said Isabelle simply.

"No? Why I should have thought—good heavens, Miss Holland, I wonder if I might persuade you to come to me?"

Isabelle stared at her uncomprehendingly for a long moment, she was so taken by surprise. "Oh—why—I thank you but I am afraid I could not—"

"Oh, please do not say so," cried Mrs. Claypool. "But then, of course, I cannot blame you. I fear it would be fearfully boring, for we have no assemblies or balls or gay parties. Yes, of course, for a pretty girl I suppose it would be dreadfully dull."

"Oh—please—no—I did not—I do not . . ." protested Isabelle, much embarrassed. "I mean I really have no interest in such things—I . . ."

"Then do say you will come, dear Miss Holland," cried Mrs. Claypool, leaning forward eagerly. "You would be doing me the greatest kindness in the world, for with Ramsleigh out on the estate all day and my four dear little boys running about, I do get lonely for the sound of a female voice." Mrs. Claypool told this bare-faced lie with all the smooth conviction of a seasoned diplomat.

"Well—I—I . . ." Isabelle glanced helplessly at her aunt.

"Dear Mrs. Holland," said Mrs. Claypool, "could you possibly spare her to me for a nice long visit?"

"Gracious me, Mrs. Claypool, I should be happy to do so if Isabelle would like to go. I must say, it would do her good to get some fresh air for a change. London is so stifling in the summer."

"There! It is settled, is it not? Do say yes, Miss Holland."

"Yes. Yes, I should like it very much," said Isabelle shyly.

Then Mrs. Claypool arranged to take up Isabelle two days hence at ten in the morning and they would drive to Claypool Grange together.

While Isabelle walked to the door with Mrs. Claypool, William lingered behind for a moment with Mrs. Holland.

"My, my," whispered Mrs. Holland. "I never dreamed it would be so easy as that."

"I told you my sister was very persuasive," replied William proudly.

Twelve

The journey to Claypool Grange was not an overly long or tiring one to Isabelle. They broke their journey in the late afternoon and stayed very comfortably at an inn used by generations of Claypools on their trips to and from London, where they were always treated royally, and arrived at Claypool Grange on the following morning about midday. Mrs. Claypool was the most companionable sort of person to travel with in Isabelle's present condition, which was more or less a state of being suspended in space. She stared dreamily out at the lush green English countryside, in full early summer flower, commenting from time to time upon some view or a beautiful hedge tangled with pale pink wild roses. Mrs. Claypool responded gently, never taking these occasional comments as an excuse to start up a conversation, always allowing Isabelle to lapse back into silence.

Isabelle was not really thinking, except to wonder now and then at her very presence in this carriage. She was not sure why she had agreed to visit Mrs. Claypool, leaving behind everyone dear to her to go into the country with a perfect stranger. Not that she had any fears about Mrs. Claypool. She had liked her on sight and further acquaintance only confirmed her first impression. Still, she was somewhat dazed with her present position, though perfectly content with it, as though she had been given permission, or had given it to herself, to drop her obsessive self-accusatory thoughts and allow her mind a period of peace.

She had had a good appetite for the excellent roast chicken they had been served for dinner at the inn and retired early to a deep, sweet sleep, to wake feeling better than she had done for weeks. Mrs. Claypool had taken note of Isabelle's lighter step and brighter eyes and congratulated herself on having been right to take the girl away from London. Another two or three weeks, she thought, and she will be armed to face up to the dreadful business in a more realistic way. Whether this would eventually work to her brother's advantage, Mrs. Claypool would not venture to guess at the moment. Thus far, she had seen no signs of any interest on Isabelle's part in William. During their brief first visit she had noticed that Isabelle's conduct toward William had been friendly but withdrawn, just as it had been with Mrs. Claypool herself. He had been there to take his farewell when they had set off on their journey and received the same treatment. Since then, his name had not been mentioned, but then, nor had any other name. Mrs. Claypool, however, did not despair, for there was the curious business of Isabelle's renewal of interest in the Richmond girls after learning of William's visits with them, and her subsequent seeming relapse. Perhaps the unbetrothed youngest Miss Richmond had had hopes that William might develop a partiality for her and had allowed Isabelle to see her own feelings. Perhaps Isabelle's regard for William was deeper than she knew herself and the possibility of his transferring his affections to Victoria Richmond had depressed her so much it had affected her physically. After all, they had become good friends before he had declared his love to Isabelle and proposed marriage, and any girl, unless she had an absolute disgust for the man, develops a fondness, even a proprietary interest, in a man who proposes to her. If all this were true, there was some hope for William.

He had urged his sister to allow him to escort them into Sussex, but she had been adamant in her refusal. When he then declared his intention of traveling down on the follow-

ing day, she had urged him to stay in London for as long
as possible, since the frustrations of being close to Isabelle
but not allowed to visit would be torment for him. He had
finally agreed to stay as long as he could bear it.

Though he did not confess it to his sister, one reason he
was reluctant to remain was the problem of Victoria Richmond. He knew he would continue to receive invitations
from them and continue to be forced into intimate little
conversations with her, and it seemed to him his plan of
avoiding any possibility of her developing expectations
where he was concerned had not worked in quite the way
he had anticipated. He was becoming very nervous and
guilty about the situation.

Having already engaged himself to ride with them on
the day after Isabelle's departure, an engagement he had
hoped to cancel by pleading the necessity of escorting his
sister and Miss Holland into the country, he found himself
again alone with Miss Victoria, as though the arrangement
were by now established custom accepted by all. He knew
as well that he would again be invited to dine and afterward, another established custom, he would be in private
conversation with her until the tea tray was brought in.

Today, instead of roguish eyes and flirtatious teasing, he
received many warm and sympathetic smiles to reassure
him of her readiness, nay, eagerness, to receive his confidences as an intimate friend. He found this much worse to
bear.

Inevitably, at the end of the ride he was invited to dine
the following evening. Desperately, he invented previous
engagements for the next three evenings. Then he must
come on the fourth evening, they insisted. He gave in with
good grace, but determined that he would leave London on
the morning after that dinner.

He dined with the Hollands on two of the intervening
evenings and alone on the other. When he arrived on the
fourth evening at the Richmonds', his resolve was strengthened by the reception he received. Mrs. Richmond greeted
him with a very nearly proprietary air and Dr. Richmond

shook his hand with unusual warmth and called him "dear boy," causing William the most exquisite discomfort.

At the first lull in conversation during dinner, he took the opportunity of announcing his departure the following morning for Sussex. There were immediate outcries of protestation. He improvised wildly about an urgent summons from the man in charge of renovations requesting his immediate presence.

"But surely you cannot need to leave so abruptly, dear Captain Perronet," cried Mrs. Richmond, much dismayed.

"I fear there is a problem that demands my attention at once," replied William firmly.

"Then do say you will return the moment it is settled," begged Horatia pleadingly.

Victoria remained silent, but cast him what he could only construe as a reproachful look. She remained subdued for some time, staring pensively into her plate, but before dinner was finished she had rallied and responded to Swinburn Tuberville's comical quips with her usual good nature. Afterward the girls played duets together while William and Tuberville lingered nearby and encouraged them. William felt sure this had been planned while the gentlemen were having their port to avoid the customary tête-à-tête between himself and Victoria. He applauded her good sense and breathed a sigh of relief.

Victoria was resigned but game, urging him as he shook her hand in farewell to write at any time he felt the need to unburden his heart.

"That is very kind of you, Miss Victoria," he replied, humbled by her goodness.

"Oh, not at all, I do assure you, Captain Perronet. And I—we—do hope you will not stay away too long."

He strode away happily down the street and to his bed at once, eager to be gone as early as possible the following morning.

At that moment, Isabelle was already deeply asleep. She had spent the day, as she had the ones preceding it, in long walks about the estate after an early morning session with the squire, who had set himself to teach her to ride.

He had found a gentle chestnut mare for her named Beauty, and while she trotted in a slow circle about a stable boy who held the horse on a leading rein, the squire called out instructions and encouragement. She had recovered from her initial soreness to find to her amazement that she enjoyed riding very much.

"Of course you do," exclaimed the squire when she told him. "You have a natural seat, bred in the bones for centuries in families like yours."

Isabelle had taken a great fancy to Squire Claypool. He had treated her from the moment he met her as a younger sister, chivying her to eat more, ordering her to drink a glass of port each night for her health, and treating her first rather frightened overtures to Beauty brusquely. To please him, she ate more, and though she detested port she drank it down obediently, and now looked forward eagerly to her lesson on Beauty each morning.

She wrote of these things to her aunt and her father as she had promised to do, but other than that she gave little thought to London or anyone there. It seemed to her she had reached a haven and she allowed herself to float through each day mindlessly. Mrs. Claypool encouraged this mood as much as possible by never referring to anything to do with the past. She was always around during the day if Isabelle sought company, but never initiated any conversations. At dinner she spoke of her children and her neighbors, while the squire talked of estate problems. Isabelle could enter into these subjects or not as she chose.

As for the four little boys, she was aware of their presence, but rarely encountered them. They had a nurse and a tutor and spent every moment that could be snatched away from them about their own affairs as far away from the house as possible. They ranged in age from six to eleven, and while she had been introduced to them and told their names, she had not yet really sorted them out. They were very shy and if they accidently encountered her, usually ran away at once.

Mrs. Claypool had given her an outgrown riding dress of her own which Isabelle had accepted gratefully. "But it is sadly worn, I fear. I shall have my seamstress make one up for you.''

"Oh, this is perfectly lovely,'' said Isabelle vaguely.

"Nonsense. You must have your own.''

The seamstress was duly summoned and work begun, but Isabelle, though allowing her measurements to be taken, showed no further interest in the new riding dress. She was now allowed to go for rides about the grounds accompanied by a groom, and was perfectly content in Mrs. Claypool's old dress. In fact, she had little interest in clothing at all, wearing the same gown down to dinner every evening, the old blue one that William had admired. Her entire interest was now given over to physical things, walking and riding and savoring the beauty of the rolling Sussex countryside. She could sit beneath a tree for long moments awed by the veining of a leaf. She seemed to have developed an extra sense that was captivated by birds and insects or the intricately delicate structure of a wild flower.

After a week of riding, she had persuaded the squire that since she never left the grounds there was no need for a groom to accompany her, and she set off every morning with a packet of bread and cheese in one pocket and an apple in the other and roamed at will for most of the day. It was on one of these excursions that she made, at last, acquaintance with the Claypool sons. She walked her horse out of a stand of trees and saw them sitting in a row on the bank of a stream. They all sat absolutely still and silent, arranged neatly from smallest to largest like stairsteps.

She pulled up abruptly and smiled as she watched them. They had not heard her approach, apparently too deeply concentrated. She began to pull the horse around, but then changed her mind and dismounted, looped the reins about a sapling, and walked up to sit down beside the smallest boy. Four heads snapped abruptly toward her and then as abruptly back to the fishing pole each held. They did not speak or even exchange glances among themselves, so she turned her own eyes to the stream and kept her silence. The water burbled and sparkled in the sun further out, but here where they sat, a deeper hole had been formed by the formation of the rocks, and the water slipped by more smoothly, dappled with sunlight by the overhanging trees.

It was a warm day, but here a light breeze stirred the air pleasantly and she took off her bonnet to feel it lift the damp hair about her face. She stared into the water and became almost hypnotized by it as, seemingly, were the boys. They had caught nothing so far, she noted, but that seemed to be unnecessary to their enjoyment. She lost track of time in her contentment and had no idea how long she sat there before stirrings of hunger brought her back to awareness. She reached into her pocket and fetched out the napkin-wrapped bread and cheese and held it out. Each boy took a share and they sat silently munching. Since she had only one apple she kept it in her pocket.

Presently she put her bonnet on, rose, and went back to her horse. With the aid of a handy stump, she managed to get back into the saddle and rode away. Tomorrow, she thought, I shall bring more apples.

When she joined them the next day, she was handed a fishing pole of her own, thoughtfully already baited, and again sat dreaming away at the water while time passed sweetly. Again she passed out the bread and cheese, and when it was consumed, handed out the apples. When she rose to go, they all flashed shy smiles at her.

This routine became part of Isabelle's day, a part she found herself looking forward to, the high point of her day, in fact. It was several days before the carefully kept silence was broken. She didn't know whether it was because they had come to trust her not to be an admonishing adult, or simply because it was the first occasion one of them had found it necessary to speak. It was directly after they had finished the simple picnic provided by Isabelle.

"I am thirsty, Ram," said the youngest quietly.

"Oh, very well," said Ram in a resigned sort of way, putting down his pole. The others followed suit and they all rose. After a second's hesitation Isabelle scrambled to her feet and followed as they set off single file up the stream. When they reached a place where the stream narrowed and ran shallowly over large boulders and rocks, they sat down and removed their shoes and stockings and waded into the water. Isabelle followed suit and, hitching up her skirt, stepped in. The water was numbingly cold and clear as glass, but after the first shock Isabelle found it delightful. The boys scooped the water up in their hands and drank and when Isabelle tried it she found it delicious.

The boys began to frolic about, leaping from stone to stone, but Isabelle contented herself by wading to a large flat rock and perching there, her feet dangling in the water. The boys called out to one another, their voices high-pitched and sweet, the sun warmed without burning, the water tumbled singingly over the rocks, and Isabelle experienced a moment of such exquisite happiness she was quite stunned by it.

But this is real, she thought, for it is not dependent on any other person, only myself and the day, with nothing between me and sun and water and sweet air. Oh, if only it could go on like this forever. The mind, however, is contrary, and had no sooner presented her with this perfect moment than it presented her also with its contrast—the happiness she had thought she had felt when Adrian had proposed.

She shuddered away from the memory, but it spread itself before her mind, complete in every detail, memorized from those days in London after his letter. Now, in this clear, unshadowed light she saw those days as febrile, uneasy, even unnatural, as of course they were, for there was only a pretence on one side with herself on the other flinging herself, mothlike, against his destructive flame. What if I had been an heiress, she wondered, and the marriage had gone through? Would I by now have learned his true feelings about me? Or would I still be fighting the knowledge, excusing and forgiving his indifference, still sure in my girlish ignorance that I could break down those defences and teach him to trust?

Yes, she thought despondently, no doubt I would be doing just that, since I did not understand him in the least

and still do not. How could I have thought I loved someone who was such a stranger to me? Will I ever understand?

"Miss Holland."

She jerked back to the present and found the four boys
lined up at the edge of the stream. "Oh—oh, are we
leaving? I was daydreaming," she said, making her way
as quickly as possible over the slippery stones to join
them. They all resumed stockings and shoes and marched
back. The boys took up their positions again on the bank
and picked up their fishing poles, but Isabelle thought she
would not wear out her welcome and, with a smile and a
wave, she mounted Beauty and rode back through the
trees.

She managed to regain some of her earlier mood as she
rode home, giving herself up to the elements around her,
and as she approached the house up the long avenue
between the double rows of oak trees she was nearly happy
again. She pulled up Beauty and sat for some moments
staring at the house, its stones softly mellowed by the late
afternoon sunlight to a honey color. It was so solid, so
rooted into the English soil, so—right. Yes, she thought, it
was something like this I dreamed of before I came to
England.

That evening at dinner she said, "I have become very
fond of your little boys. We—we fish together."

"Yes, so I hear," replied Mrs. Claypool, her eyes
twinkling.

"They told you of it?"

"Yes. They seem to have taken quite a fancy to you."

Isabelle blushed with pleasure. "Oh—really? They are
such nice children. I am ashamed to confess, however,
that I have forgotten their names. At least—I mean, I
know the eldest is called Ram."

"But then, what do you call them?" asked Mrs. Claypool.

"Why—why nothing. We do not speak."

"Not speak? That is confoundedly rude of them!" said
the squire.

"Oh no—not at all," protested Isabelle quickly. "We
fish, you see, and one must keep very quiet."

"Young scamps." The squire laughed with indulgent pride. "More likely they are too shy to speak to a pretty young girl. In any case, they are Ramsleigh, the fourth of that name, Oliver, William, and little David, in order of age. If they get pesky, just you tell me and I'll see they leave you in peace."

"Oh no, they are so kind to allow me to be with them and I assure you I enjoy every moment of it."

The next day when she came into the stable yard, all four boys were prancing about on their ponies and when she had mounted they rode out with her as though the matter had been previously discussed and decided upon. She was absurdly pleased as they streamed along in her wake chattering happily. The sun was just up, sending long shadows across the ground, busy red squirrels scolded as they skittered up and down the trees, and the air was still dewy fresh and cool. The boys followed wherever she led them and at her usual time to go there she went to the stream. They all dismounted, tied up their horses, and took up their customary positions on the bank. Ram fetched the poles from the hollow tree where they were cached and they all settled down to contemplate the water.

In the days that followed they rode, they fished, they waded in the stream, with sometimes an expedition to inspect a badger sett they were keeping their eyes on, or a trip to where the first blackberries were beginning to ripen. How is it possible I can be so happy when I have been so unhappy, Isabelle wondered, until at last she was forced to acknowledge what she had really known for some time, but refused to admit, that she had not been unhappy so much as humiliated. She had not wanted to know this about herself, because it seemed to her shameful to admit to such petty-mindedness. There was a certain nobility connected to suffering for love, but none at all to being made ill by the thought of what people would say about one. The sort of person she had always thought herself to be should not care what mean-spirited people said of her, as long as her friends remained true and so long as she retained her own self-respect.

There, of course, was the real core of the matter. She knew now that self-respect was what she had lost in the process of falling in love with Adrian, because she had not truly loved him. She had allowed her head to be turned like the most foolish, green girl by the romance about him that she had created in her own mind before she had ever met him. Then his good looks, his air of being slightly dangerous, and finally his pretence of passion for her had completed the job. She had at once cast herself into the role of reformer. She would change him, tame the wildness, domesticate him until he knelt at her feet, awed by her wisdom and good sense. She had not really loved him, for she had not known him. She had been attracted by his wickedness because it would give her a role to play that she fancied herself in.

The romance had begun to tarnish the moment she had said yes, for she had allowed him to treat her in the most shameful way with hardly a protest, all to protect her self-righteous vision of herself as the woman of strong character whose love would redeem a famous rake-hell. After Lady Bromley's betrothal party, she had not been able to hide from herself any longer the fact that she did not like him really, but even that revelation had not caused her to face the matter. She had found excuses for his conduct and told herself she must forgive him because she could not bring herself to admit she had made a mistake when she had always been so sure of her clear-headedness. What? Isabelle Holland to admit to such an enormous error of judgment? Isabelle Holland to admit to being so weak-minded she could fall in and out of love in a matter of weeks?

These admissions now were not thought out all at once in her mind, but gradually rose to the surface and clarified themselves in the sweet silence on the bank of the stream, or on her favorite rock with her feet dangling in the water, or as she rode back alone in the afternoon leaving the boys to their play.

One morning as they rode along David said, "When Uncle Will comes, we will go ratting in the hay barn, Miss

Holland. It is the greatest fun in the world. Would you like to come with us?''

She started a bit. ''Well—I doubt that will be any time soon. He will be enjoying himself in London still, I expect.''

They all looked at her, puzzled. Oliver said, ''But Uncle Will is not in London. He is in his own house here, not five miles away.''

She felt strangely agitated by this news, but she only said, ''Oh, I did not know. Has he just returned?''

''Oh, no. He has been here ever so long. Almost as long as you. But it is not like him to stay away from us. He always comes here at once. It is really very bad of him to stay away so long,'' said William sadly.

''Mama says he is too busy with his house, but it does seem strange to me that he can't find even a moment to go ratting,'' said David.

''I think your mama is probably right,'' said Isabelle. ''There is a great deal to be done when you are doing over an entire house.''

She did not really believe this, any more than the boys did. It was because he did not want to see her that he shunned this place. No doubt he had completed his conquest of Victoria Richmond quickly and had hurried down to make his house ready to receive his bride as soon as possible. Naturally he would be made uncomfortable by meeting me under the circumstances, Isabelle thought contemptuously, trying to overcome the hurt, for he should have come at least once in all this while to inquire of her health as an old friend. She tried to put the news of his presence out of her mind, but it persisted in rankling her and destroyed much of her new-found peace of mind.

Poor William was in a much worse state and had been fuming about the exile imposed upon him by his sister continuously since his arrival. He had written her the first day requesting permission to visit. Mrs. Claypool had ordered her carriage and had herself driven to his house at once.

''Well, William,'' she said as he handed her out of the carriage, ''you are getting along very well. The gardens look quite beautiful. They were laid out by Capability Brown, did you know that? I am glad to see you did not consider it necessary to change anything.''

"I wanted the place to be just as it was when I first saw it as a lad. But don't let us stand here nattering about gardens, for the lord's sake. How is Isabelle? Is she well enough for me to see her?'' he demanded impatiently.

Mrs. Claypool glanced at her footman, who still stood at the open carriage door and murmured, "*Pas avant les domestiques.*'' Then chidingly, "Well, are you not going to invite me inside, Will?''

"Why are you whispering to me in French, Liz?'' he said crossly.

"Will, take me into the house at once please,'' she demanded as sternly as possible, and to make sure he did so, turned away and began to mount the broad stairway to the front door. The house of ancient pink brick was of four stories at the central portion, and extended by three-story wings at either end, with tall pedimented columns across the central portion and a balustraded terrace all along the front. Once inside, William led her across the oval entrance hall, laid in black and white hexagonal marble tiles, to his library in one of the wings. There were only a few books on the shelves as yet, very little furniture, and the windows were still undraped, but it was a pleasingly proportioned room and Mrs. Claypool looked about approvingly at the improvements he had made, even sniffing appreciatively at the faint scent of fresh paint.

William rang for refreshments and when they had been served with wine and cakes and the door closed behind the butler, he turned to her impatiently. "What on earth are you being so mysterious about, Liz?''

"Not mysterious, discreet. It was not a subject to discuss before my servants. It will only set them gossiping and speculating, and Isabelle may overhear something, or one of the children.''

"Well, well, I suppose you are right, but what of Isabelle?''

"She is very well, I think, and—''

"Then why should I not—"

". . . and," she continued, as though he had not rudely interrupted her, "already looks much better. Her color has improved vastly and she is eating and sleeping well. Ramsleigh is teaching her to ride and she seems to have quite taken to it."

"Then why—" he began eagerly.

"But she is not yet ready for you," she said firmly.

"Oh, Liz, how can you know that?"

"Because I just do know it. She rarely speaks, and never of London or anything connected with events there. I think she has closed her mind to it all for the time, or at least I hope she has."

"But surely that cannot be good. She should talk about it, get it all out of her system."

"For you that might be best, or even perhaps for me, but not for her. She must be allowed to work it out in her own way and she will come to it eventually. And your hopes will certainly not be improved if you come barging around every day making protestations which she is totally unprepared to hear now."

"Barging around? I hope a formal call by me would not be termed barging around!" he said indignantly. "And I resent the implication that I would be so insensitive as to make protestations, as you call it, at this early stage."

"Oh, you would not mean to, but you would be bound to say something sooner or later in your downright, captain-on-the-bridge way."

He continued to protest, but she would not be swayed. That had been three weeks ago and nothing had changed. He wrote her notes nearly every day, and when they became blustering and demanding, she would again order her carriage and drive over to calm him down. He felt very hard done by. Of course he would not attempt to see Isabelle without Liz's permission, having given his word, but Liz was surely being unnecessarily strict, he thought.

Several days passed after she heard of William from the boys before Isabelle mentioned his name to Mrs. Claypool.

She had had no intention of doing so, but the words seemed to pop out of their own volition.

"The boys tell me that your brother has returned from London," she said.

"Yes, that is true," replied Mrs. Claypool noncommittally.

"I—they are hurt that he has not come to see them."

"Oh, well, he has spoiled them, I am afraid. But he is very busy now setting that place in order."

"Oh yes—yes, of course he must be." A long silence ensued while Mrs. Claypool placidly embroidered a rose petal and Isabelle stared at her hands. At last she raised her eyes and said, "He is well, I trust?"

"Yes, very well."

"You have seen him then?"

"Several times, when I happened to be passing the house. I like to see how the work is progressing. The gardens are finished and are so beautiful. Just as I remember them."

Isabelle said no more then, but a few days later she mentioned him to Mrs. Claypool again. "Did—did your brother say anything to you about Miss Victoria Richmond when you visited him, Mrs. Claypool?"

"Miss Richmond? Oh, that is the daughter of those friends of your aunt, is it not? No, her name has not been mentioned," said Mrs. Claypool, happy that the question had been phrased in such a way that she could answer it truthfully, for indeed the name had not passed his lips on any of her visits since his return. "Shall I inquire of her the next time I see him?"

"No! Oh—that is—I only—it is of no matter at all. Is the work progressing well on the house?"

"Very well indeed. Perhaps one day you would care to come with me and see what has been done."

"Yes—yes, I—perhaps we could all go. I am sure the boys would be glad to see their uncle."

"Well, we shall see," said Mrs. Claypool with, to Isabelle, somewhat disappointing vagueness.

Thirteen

The next morning Isabelle appeared in the stableyard in her new riding dress, which had been ready for her wear for over a week but ignored until today. It was very smart, having been copied from one recently shown in *La Belle Assemblée*, being of a very fine merino wool in bright green, embroidered down the front and on the *à la militaire* cuffs with black braid. With it she wore a small riding hat of black beaver with gold tassels and cordon. She was made extremely self-conscious by the stunned silence that greeted her appearance. The boys stared in open-mouthed amazement.

"Well, shall we go," she said, nervously pulling on her Yorktan gloves as she walked up to Beauty. The groom seemed not much less astonished than the young gentlemen and did not jump to her assistance at once as he usually did. She turned to lift an eyebrow at him and he flushed and hurried forward to fling her up into the saddle. She rode off at once, but was disconcerted not to hear the clatter of hooves over the cobbles as usual when the boys were following. She did not look back, but she had an anxious moment.

The boys exchanged looks and then moved after her. Isabelle breathed a sigh of relief. She had not thought of their reaction when she put on the costume after breakfast or even of why she chose to wear it now after having shunned it for so long. Mrs. Claypool, however, who had watched from the breakfast room window as Isabelle walked around the house to the stable in her new riding dress, had become thoughtful, and that evening, when Isabelle appeared at the dinner table in a different gown than the old blue one, Mrs. Clayppool decided that the time for action was now at hand. The next morning she had herself driven to her brother's house.

"Now, William," she said decisively when he had taken her into the library, "I think we can begin to think more positively about Isabelle. I do not think she is entirely aware herself of a change in her thinking, but I am positive of it."

"Do you mean—can she possibly . . ." faltered William painfully.

"Does she love you, do you mean? I think it is becoming possible, and that we must do everything we can to foster it."

"I will not have her—coerced!" exploded William, rising to his feet, his heavy brows drawn together into a straight forbidding line across his brow.

Mrs. Claypool's own dark brows, very like his though less heavy, also drew together. "Coerced? Can you truly believe I would be party to anything such as that?"

William backed down. "Well—I—what do you mean then?"

"I mean that I plan to allow you to meet, but," she said forcefully as he started forward eagerly, "in company, formally, as it were, with no intimate conversations."

He looked gloomy. "I fail to see what that will accomplish."

"It will accomplish much, if you do as I say. You must not look at her with love-sick eyes all the time she is in the same room with you. You must speak to her in a friendly, but reserved way. You must be evasive if she makes any inquiries about Miss Victoria Richmond—"

"Victoria Richmond? What the devil has she to say to all this?"

"Oh, William," she sighed, "what a babe you are in these matters, to be sure. Isabelle has conceived the notion that you and Miss Victoria have developed an attachment."

William turned a fiery red and strode away to the window to hide his confusion. "How on earth could she have thought . . ." he muttered in a strangled way.

"Well, you went about with the Richmond girls quite a bit."

"I was invited to dinner and to ride, but I never requested permission to call. It became rather—difficult, as a matter of fact."

"Of course it must have done, for the older daughter being betrothed you were naturally invited for the sake of Miss Victoria."

He was very much embarrassed, but would not discuss Victoria's behavior and his own discomfiture even with his sister. He only said, "I still cannot see what all that nonsense has to do with Isabelle."

"I believe Miss Victoria allowed her own feelings for you, her expectations even, to become apparent to Isabelle. It was directly after that requested visit that she seemed to become worse in her health. I think, William, that she felt more for you than she knew even then. After all, you had declared your love and proposed, rather forcefully. Then she learns, while still distressed at being jilted by that dreadful man, that you have apparently transferred your affections to Miss Victoria."

"Does she think so little of me? Picture me as one of those drawing-room dandies who make love to every woman they meet?" he thundered, truly outraged.

"No, no William, do be calm," soothed Mrs. Claypool. "Remember, she had already been rejected by one man, and in such a state a woman will imagine no man could love her."

"Then I must tell her—reassure her—"

"That is precisely what you must not do! Now listen to me, Will, I know I can never hope to make you understand, so you must just trust me. I will make up a dinner party and you will be invited. You will behave just as I have instructed you."

"Can't say I like this way of going on," he grumbled.

"I have never cared for flimflammery. I like everything plain and aboveboard."

"Yes, I know your ways very well, Will, but believe me, they will not answer in this case. She must be allowed to doubt and worry and become fretful before she will understand her feelings."

"I shall never understand the Byzantine workings of a woman's mind," declared William, throwing up his hands in surrender.

Mrs. Claypool sighed again for the obtuseness of men in such matters, at least of men like Will, who were truly innocent. No doubt, had he not already been so firmly attached to Isabelle Holland, Victoria Richmond would have swallowed him up in one gulp. Not that that made the girl in any way evil. It was only that she wanted a husband and William was an attractive prospect, easy enough to fall in love with and unwary enough to be an easy conquest. In truth, taken that Miss Richmond was a well-brought-up girl, it would have made life much easier all around if things had worked out that way. As it was, though she had grown very fond of Isabelle, Mrs. Claypool knew there was still a very chancy row to hoe before anything positive could come about for Will.

When she reached home, she sat down at once to make up a list for her dinner party. About twelve, she thought, should make enough people to prevent intimacy, but not too many to intimidate Isabelle. She wrote out her invitations for a week from that day and gave them to her footman to have them delivered. The guests were all old friends and neighbors.

At dinner that evening she mentioned the matter. "I want to reintroduce William to them as a neighbor. Of course, many have met him from time to time on his infrequent visits."

Isabelle was staring at her like a startled deer, but she did not voice any objections, Mrs. Claypool noted. It is because of William, she thought. She does not really care to meet my neighbors, but she wants to see William, I am positive of it.

"Good idea, my dear," declared the squire with pleasure, for he enjoyed parties. "It has been much too long since we have seen anyone. Be sure to invite old Symes. His sister-in-law is visiting. Jolly woman."

"Oh dear, I did not know. Of course she must be included, but now my table will be uneven. I shall need another gentleman, Ramsleigh."

"If you have asked the Pooles, their son is home for a few weeks."

"The very thing! I shall send them both notes in the morning. You will like young Mr. Poole, Isabelle. Extremely handsome and most pleasant."

Isabelle smiled briefly, but did not comment. She could not prevent herself from flinching at the thought of meeting all these people, but told herself she must get over this silliness. She could not spend the rest of her life shunning company, and besides, these were country people who in all likelihood had never heard of Isabelle Holland, much less the scandal connected to her name.

The next morning she reassumed Mrs. Claypool's outgrown riding habit, deciding it was much more appropriate for fishing and wading with the four little boys. She admitted to herself that she had only worn her new one because of the possibility of meeting William. She had not wanted him to see her shabby. Now, however, she knew that she would not meet him. He clearly had no desire to see her or he would have called upon his sister long ago. She wondered how Mrs. Claypool had persuaded him to come to dinner, since he must know he would encounter her there. Well, he shall see that I go on very well without his friendship, she thought proudly, and I shall look out the grandest gown Aunt Nathaniel packed and be very gay on the night and perhaps flirt a little with the nice, attractive Mr. Poole.

In the event, she gave Mr. Poole such a blinding smile he was struck quite dumb and could barely speak. She was aware of the effect she had had upon him and was not displeased, since William was watching. He had arrived before the other guests by about a quarter of an hour, but it had been a very difficult time, with William very stiff and, it seemed to her, so cold that conversation between them had been limited to brief greetings and some talk about the weather. Isabelle had been relieved when other guests were announced, the Pooles and their son being the first. After them had come the rest, one couple after another, until the Symeses arrived with their visiting sister, a Mrs. Deene, who Isabelle thought at first glance to be distressingly ill-favored. She was a widow of perhaps five and thirty, tall and full-figured. Her eyes were slightly popping, her chin receded, and her hair was a nondescript brown. She was very warm and friendly, however, and when she smiled, revealed teeth of shining white perfection. It was a most attractive smile and drew the eye away from her less pleasing features.

Isabelle found that the gentlemen gravitated toward Mrs. Deene, with the exception of Mr. Poole who, having recovered his aplomb, set himself to amuse Isabelle. She forced herself to join his effort and smiled and laughed and replied with as much vivacity as she could summon, though she found it an empty experience. Mr. Poole was very young, not more than nineteen or twenty, and while handsome and pleasant mannered, was too callow a youth to be interesting. She resolutely kept her eyes upon him, but she was very much aware that William had moved into Mrs. Deene's orbit and was engaged in a very animated conversation with her. Mrs. Claypool had assigned her brother to take Mrs. Deene in to dinner, so their conversation continued on the way to the table as they walked directly in front of Isabelle, who was on Mr. Poole's arm.

Their gaiety lowered Isabelle's spirits immeasurably. Why did he find it so easy to speak with this strange lady and yet act so stiff and formal with his old friend? She divided her attention between Mr. Poole and Mr. Symes on her other side, and refused to even look at the other end of the table where Mrs. Deene seemed to be entertaining everyone in earshot as well as her own dinner partners. As a consequence, Isabelle failed to notice how often William's eyes turned in her own direction, or the fact that Mrs. Claypool stared at him until she caught his eye and frowned slightly at him and shook her head. He looked mutinous for a moment, then sighed and turned his attention back to Mrs. Deene.

It wasn't until the ladies retired from the table leaving the men to their wine that Isabelle discovered for herself Mrs. Deene's fascination. She did not really speak much to her, but she watched as Mrs. Deene spoke with the other women. She leaned, very relaxed, against the arm of the sofa, her cheek propped against her hand. Her heavy body looked voluptuous in such a pose and as she spoke her eyes and teeth sparkled. When she laughed it was a rich, throaty chuckle that was irresistible. Why she is ravishing, Isabelle thought in astonishment, and could not take her eyes from the woman. The more she observed her, the more attractive she became. Isabelle was bewildered by her own reactions, and tried to discover wherein lay Mrs. Deene's allure. She is—is—sensuous and extremely feminine, she thought. Why, it just comes from her in waves. No wonder the men are drawn to her. No doubt were I a man I would be drawn also, she thought rather forlornly, remembering how animated William had become after the woman had arrived.

When the gentlemen rejoined them, she saw William look at her as he entered, but when he caught her eye he only smiled vaguely and went on across the room to Mrs. Deene's side. The evening was over for Isabelle and it took every ounce of pride she could call to her aid to enable her to get through the remainder of the evening without allowing her boredom and unhappiness to show. All she had wanted was a few moments to speak to William and perhaps to discover the true state of affairs regarding Victoria Richmond. Not that she would have been able to ask him outright, but she thought she might somehow know if he would only speak to her as a friend, instead of treating her as the merest acquaintance who bored him too much to exert himself enough even to be pleasant.

When the last guest had gone, except for William, she rose at once and started for the door, but he was there before her to open it. "Will you not say good night to me, Isabelle?"

"Oh, of course. Good night, Captain Perronet," she said in a brittle voice. He reached for her hand, but she turned away abruptly and fled across the hall and up the stair.

William turned to his sister, his face registering his consternation. "Liz, I cannot like this! Now she is angry with me. I cannot bear it."

"You were splendid, Will, just splendid," said Mrs. Claypool bracingly. "Everything is going just as it should do. You go along home now and try not to fret."

"May I not call tomorrow?"

"No, but perhaps in a few days I will bring her with me one morning and you may give her a tour of your house."

When he was gone, Mrs. Claypool went along to Isabelle's room and tapped softly. After a moment the door was flung open to reveal Isabelle, still in her evening dress, her cheeks flaming with color, her eyes shiny with hastily dried tears.

Mrs. Claypool pretended not to notice these signs of distress. "I hope you did not find the evening tiring, my dear."

"Tiring? No—no, of course not. It was very pleasant," said Isabelle gallantly.

"I am glad you found it so. Mrs. Deene is very amusing, is she not?"

"Yes, very. She is amazingly attractive."

Mrs. Claypool laughed. "Amazing is just the word. It is always a shock when one discovers that sort of charm in a person so unblessed with beauty. The poor woman has not had a happy life either, for all she is so cheerful."

"Losing her husband, you mean?"

"No. No, that was, in a way, a blessing for her. He died before he had spent every last penny she had brought to the marriage. It was not a good marriage, though I gather she was much in love at the beginning. He was wildly handsome, they say, and penniless. He married her for her money and then neglected her dreadfully while he spent it on gambling and other women. There was hardly anything left when he died, but no doubt there is enough for her to live on and I expect she will marry again very soon.''

Isabelle shuddered at a story that was so very nearly her own, and cried out, ''Oh—oh—'' before the tears she had checked so hastily at Mrs. Claypool's entrance welled up again to brim over and run down her cheeks.

''Why, my dear, I am sorry. I should not have told you so sad a story at the end of the evening when you must be tired. Here, let me help you out of your gown and into something more comfortable.''

She turned Isabelle around firmly and began to unbutton her gown. ''It is only—only—oh dear, it is so difficult to speak of it,'' Isabelle said, still crying.

''Well then, dear child, you need not do so. Though it is my opinion that it is just those difficult things it does us the most good to speak of.''

Isabelle was silent while Mrs. Claypool drew off her garments and slid her nightgown over her head and tied the ribbands at the throat. She then helped her into a negligee and led her to the chaise longue before the fire. ''Would you like some warm milk to help you sleep?'' she asked kindly.

''Oh no, nothing at all. You are very good to me, Mrs. Claypool.''

''It is very easy, my dear, as I am very fond of you.''

Isabelle reached for her and Mrs. Claypool sat down beside her and took Isabelle in her arms. Isabelle cried in earnest then, but finally sighed and relaxed against her shoulder, taking the handkerchief the older woman put into her hand and mopping at her eyes. ''It is only that it could so easily have happened to me.''

''What could, child?''

''Marrying someone who—who only wanted my money, or at least what he thought was my fortune. When he found out how small my dowry actually was, he jilted me.''

"That is very terrible, of course. You have been unhappy since then, I imagine.''

"Well, I thought I was, but now I realize that I was relieved, for by that time I had come to dislike him.''

"Then that is not so dreadful as it could have been,'' said Mrs. Claypool comfortably.

"No, the dreadful part is that I discovered my supposed unhappiness was only humiliation. That was very hard to accept about myself.''

"Well, one is never glad to learn that one's feelings are less than noble, but I think of the two I would prefer to suffer from humiliation than a broken heart, though it is a baser emotion.''

This practical view of the matter swept through Isabelle like a refreshing breeze. She sat up and smiled at Mrs. Claypool. "Goodness, how clever you are. I wish I had spoken to you of all of this weeks ago.''

"I doubt you would have accepted it then. You've worked it out for yourself and no lesson is ever so well learned as that. Someone else preaching at you would never have served for a girl with such an independent spirit as yours.''

Isabelle was made shy by this praise and could not speak. She threw her arms about Mrs. Claypool and hugged her heartily. "Thank you, dear Mrs. Claypool, for listening to all my foolishness.''

"You are very welcome, my dear, if only you will call me Liz. I am not really old enough to be your mother.''

"Liz, then—happily.''

Mrs. Claypool called upon her brother early the next morning, knowing he would be extremely fretful until he saw her. He hustled her into the library and closed the door. "I have hardly slept all night, Liz. I have decided I cannot go along with your scheme, whatever it is. I will not be a party to—to enmeshing her while she is still so heartbroken and unhappy—''

"Nonsense,'' interrupted Mrs. Claypool. "She is not in

the least heartbroken, and never has been. She was ashamed
before all her friends, she told me so herself. Of course,
one would be humiliated by such a thing, but she did not
admit those were her real feelings until after she came
down here away from all of you and had peace and quiet
to think it all through. Now, having been right about that,
you must give me best, Will, and allow me to be right
about the rest of it."

He was made much too happy by the news she had
given him to argue further and Mrs. Claypool took her
leave feeling rather smug. Unaware of that good fairy,
Mrs. Claypool, working in her behalf, Isabelle spent the
next few days as she had all those preceding, in riding out
with the boys. She tried to be cheerful while she was with
them, but after she rode away from them in the afternoons
she would begin to brood again about William's strange
behavior toward her. She felt he had betrayed their friendship and sometimes the tears would rise in her throat and
the brilliantly sun-filled afternoon would turn gray and
desolate. At other times she would become angry and hold
imaginary conversations with him in which she told him
how cowardly she thought him for turning away from her
just because another man had done so, forgetting all about
those daily calls in London.

She longed to speak to Mrs. Claypool about it, but
could not bring herself to mention his name. If only Mrs.
Claypool would bring his name up herself, but she never
did. Had she visited him since the dinner party? Had he
told her about Victoria Richmond, or—horrible thought—
about a new interest in the alluring widow?

It was nearly a week before Mrs. Claypool asked her
casually at the breakfast table if she would like to accompany her on a visit to Tall Oaks. "We could ride over, if
you like. I haven't ridden for sometime and would enjoy
it," she added, coming around the table to pat Isabelle on
the back.

Isabelle had gasped with surprise at Mrs. Claypool's
first words, inhaling a crumb of toast. She finally managed
to choke out her agreement to the plan and left the table to

go upstairs and change into her riding dress. The new one, of course. She dressed as quickly as possible, for she had heard Mrs. Claypool giving orders for their mounts to be brought around to the front of the house and she wanted to go to the stables to tell the boys she would not be joining them this morning.

They were all mounted and prancing about on their ponies. They accepted her excuses philosophically, except for little David, who said wistfully that perhaps Mama would allow them to come along.

"She won't," said Ram. "We are not allowed to go until the builders are finished. She says there is too much trouble for us to get into with all that lumber lying about and the wet paint."

"Then do remind Uncle Will about the ratting and that he promised," said David.

Isabelle said she would be sure to do so and took her leave of them. She found Mrs. Claypool just coming down the steps, looking very smart in her riding dress and a tall crowned hat with a white plume curling down to caress her cheek.

"Why, how quick you have been," she called out to Isabelle.

"I wanted to tell the boys I would not be joining them today."

"That was nice of you. I fear I had forgotten they would be expecting you. Were they disappointed?"

Isabelle laughed. "Not so very, I think."

At first the ride was so pleasant Isabelle forgot the end of it, but as they came closer her heart began to lurch uncomfortably in anticipation. She dreaded the coming encounter in a way, for his aloof manner at the dinner party and his avoidance of her company presaged a dismal outcome. Yet she felt compelled to speak to him, to learn once for all if he were indeed betrothed. Not that it mattered to her, she told herself firmly, but she felt she must know. She had a right to know. Yes, that was just the thing in a nutshell. He owed her at least that confidence as her professed friend. She raised her chin resolutely and determined to somehow force him to speak to her as a friend.

They turned into the gates of Tall Oaks and cantered down the long avenue. On either side there was the deer park, though none were visible. After several turnings the grounds took on a more cultivated look, though in a way that preserved an air of naturalness. A final turn brought the house in view and Isabelle pulled up her horse without any consciousness of doing so. Here is truly an English country home, she thought, sighing in appreciation.

"I know what you mean," said Mrs. Claypool hearing the sigh. "It is like a dream of peace, is it not? When Will and I were children, we would ride here often just to look at it. I think he determined to have the place even then. It had only stood empty a few years at that time and did not look so run down as it did when Will bought it. But he has restored it beautifully. You will see."

Just then William came out of the front door and when he saw them approaching he raised his hand in greeting and started down the broad white stairs that fanned out gracefully to the gravel drive. Mrs. Claypool called out cheerfully and waved her riding crop. Isabelle only smiled tentatively.

A groom came running and while William helped his sister to dismount, the groom came to help Isabelle, then led the horses away to the stables.

"Well, Isabelle, at last you have come to see my new home."

"I would have come any time, captain, had I been invited," she said.

"I—I . . ." William faltered, then caught his sister's eye and pulled himself together. "I have not liked to invite anyone while the place was in such a shambles, but I thought as an old friend you would forgive the unfinished state we are in."

Isabelle was warmed by this speech and smiled up at him. "Of course I will—"

The sound of rapidly approaching carriage wheels interrupted her and they all turned. The carriage drew up with a flourish and from the window smiled Mrs. Deene and beyond her her sister Mrs. Symes.

"You said we might come any time, Captain Perronet, so we took advantage of the fine weather to accept your invitation," Mrs. Deene called out gaily.

William flashed a glance at Isabelle, his previous words ringing in his ears, and saw her smile fade away and her gray eyes turn cold, and knew she was remembering them also. Why, why, he thought in despair, was I so foolish as to invite this woman? Surely I only said something vague about when it was finished I would welcome them. He forced himself to go forward and hand the ladies out of their carriage with as good a grace as possible.

"Dear Mrs. Claypool—and Miss Holland! What an added pleasure it is to find you here. I did so much enjoy your dinner party, Mrs. Claypool. Such lovely people in this neighborhood, I am sure I could stay here forever. I was just telling Catherine how fortunate she is in her neighbors," said Mrs. Deene, flashing her riveting smile impartially upon the company.

Mrs. Claypool bowed gracefully, not at all displeased with these unlooked-for guests. "Do take us inside, William," she said. "I am sure we are all eager to see what improvements have been made."

He led them into the house and from room to room, while they all exclaimed enthusiastically over everything. All except Isabelle. She, he noticed, said nothing at all. When they had inspected all the apartments on the first two floors, he led them into the drawing room where refreshments had been laid out.

"How lovely for you, Captain Perronet, to have your sister so nearby to advise you," said Mrs. Deene, accepting a glass of wine.

"Yes, it is very helpful," he agreed.

"I think single gentlemen need a woman's advice when furnishing a house," she continued.

"Well, I have had that. Miss Holland's aunt in London was so very good as to help me," he answered, glancing at Isabelle with a smile. She met his look without any

expression and he remembered those dreadful dinners on
board ship when she had seemed to be looking right
through him as though he did not exist. Well damnation,
he thought, becoming angry, how could I have known this
dratted woman would take me up so quickly on such an
indefinite invitation?

"This is so very much a family house, one expects at
any moment to hear the chatter of children. I am sure that
after all your years of adventuring, you mean to set up
your nursery at last," Mrs. Deene said teasingly.

William was flustered, but managed to say, "I think
when a man reaches my age, Mrs. Deene, his thoughts are
bound to turn to making a home and family."

"Your age, indeed! You make yourself sound to be
tottering upon the brink of senility, sir." She laughed
infectiously and everyone joined her. All except Isabelle,
who stared fixedly into her lap. She was not finding Mrs.
Deene nearly so amusing and charming as she had at their
previous meeting. The woman was clearly in search of a
husband, had set her sights on William at their first meeting, and had come here today to inspect what she hoped
might be her future home. At any moment now she would
start dropping hints about draperies or some such thing.

"I see you have decided on blue for your drawing room,
captain," said Mrs. Deene, "and very wise, too. The
room seems to demand it. However, I think you will find
some gold and rose accents will be needed."

Isabelle could hardly believe her ears, even though she
had prophesied just such a speech. She clinched her teeth
against a rising tide of rage. What is it to me, she thought
angrily. As well this woman, though she is much too old
for him, as Victoria, or any other women for that matter. I
am sure he is free to choose whom he likes for all of me.

Presently Mrs. Claypool suggested that his guests might
like to see something of the gardens and they all trooped
out again into the sunshine. Isabelle, the long skirt of her
riding dress looped over her arm, stalked along behind the
group, her head high, her shoulders rigid with anger. As
soon as she decently could, she suggested to Mrs. Claypool

that as they still had the long ride ahead of them perhaps they should start back soon.

"Of course, my dear, you are right," said Mrs. Claypool agreeably, turning to lead the way to the house. "We will just say good-bye now, everyone, and you must carry on. There is so much more I am sure you will like to see."

"But of course we will come to see you off, dear Mrs. Claypool," declared Mrs. Deene.

William went to order their horses brought around while the ladies waited in front of the house. Soon Isabelle and Mrs. Claypool were being waved farewell as they trotted off down the drive. Such effrontery, fumed Isabelle silently. See us off, indeed! Just as though she were already the lady of the manor. I wish I had spent the morning with the boys.

Suddenly she remembered her promise to David, and wheeling Beauty about she trotted back. Mrs. Deene had put her hand on William's arm and they had turned back to the gardens.

"Captain Perronet," Isabelle called out. They all halted and turned surprised faces at the coldness of her voice. "Your nephew asked me to remind you about the ratting." She then wheeled and trotted off up the drive without another word.

Fourteen

William was in a dreadful state. The inaction forced upon him by his sister as a condition for her help irritated his sensibilities almost beyond bearing. He had always been a man used to making instant decisions and acting upon them. When he had made up his mind to retire from the sea, he had moved immediately to divest himself of his ship. Having decided many years ago that one day Tall Oaks would be his, he had decided the time had come and pushed through the purchase of it with all expedition possible. And having realized his love for Isabelle Holland, he had wasted very little time in declaring it.

The setback he had received in that project had been severe, but he had never swerved in his determination to persevere. When her betrothal had been severed, he had felt justified in holding to his course. Surely now she would be his. He had been sensitive enough not to press his suit immediately, but had been sure his continuous presence and sympathetic friendship would eventually win the day for him. However, her apathy had come to frighten him finally and he had turned to his sister for help, thinking that with Isabelle in Sussex and so near at hand, his dream must surely quickly reach fruition.

Now, however, he felt things had only gone from bad to worse and he chafed under the restraints imposed upon him, as well as the regimen demanded by his sister. There was something sly about it all that disagreed with his usual method of dealing with problems. He knew Liz was the most honest woman of his acquaintance, and certainly not in the least sly, but he simply could not grasp what all this hide and seek was supposed to accomplish.

Look at the disaster yesterday had ended up in, the day he had looked forward to so eagerly, the first time she was to see his new home, the home he hoped would one day become her own. He had been so sure that at last he would have an opportunity to take her apart and speak to her on their old footing, let her see how very deeply he wanted and needed her. Instead, those women had appeared almost at the same instant as he had told her he had invited no one else but her because she was an old friend, and had seen the dawning warmth of her response. The first words out of Mrs. Deene's mouth had seemed to prove him false and his plan for the day lay in ruins around his feet at that moment. And all the while Liz had gone about looking like the cat who had licked up all the cream. What on earth did she mean by it? Why should she be so pleased to see Mrs. Deene, when she must have known very well what his hopes for the day had been?

He stomped about the house, glaring balefully at everyone he encountered, causing the painters to apply their brushes with nervous zeal and his housekeeper to scurry away to take refuge in the linen cupboard.

Feeling the need for immediate and positive action, he decided he would go to the Grange now, at once, and take matters into his own hands. He went to the stables for his mount and rode off with firm resolution, but by the time he reached the gates his resolve was weakened by the thought of his sister's disapproval and of breaking his word. He rode off furiously in the opposite direction in an attempt to appease his frustration. It helped to some extent, and when he returned to his house he dashed off a note to Liz to inform her that it was his intention to call within the next three days, whether she would have him or no. He sent a groom with the note to the Grange with orders to wait for a reply.

Mrs. Claypool saw no reason to deny his request, since it had never been her plan to keep them apart forever, but only long enough to give Isabelle some breathing space to think without any pressure. Mrs. Claypool had known very well that having William about the place all day would be too constant a reminder of recent events to allow Isabelle to distance herself from it all. Apart from this, knowing William as she did, she had been quite sure he would not have had the patience to hold his own feelings in check for long, and to have forced his profession of love upon Isabelle before she was ready to hear it might have caused her to feel that he had betrayed her trust in him as a friend.

That Isabelle had learned he had been in the area nearly as long as she herself had been and had not called, had been a fortuitous accident that had forwarded Mrs. Claypool's plan. She had seen that Isabelle had been hurt by his apparent disinterest in her welfare and that she had leaped to the conclusion that he had formed an attachment to Victoria Richmond.

Mrs. Claypool had known at once that though she might not admit it, Isabelle was jealous, as Mrs. Claypool had suspected when she heard of Isabelle's reaction to Victoria's visit in London. To be jealous, one must care to an extent beyond pure friendship, in Mrs. Claypool's opinion, and she had set about to foster the feeling in Isabelle. Mrs. Deene's unexpected appearance yesterday at Tall Oaks had been another happy circumstance to promote those feelings. Isabelle had not been any slower than Mrs. Claypool herself to realize that the woman would not be averse to marrying an attractive man of means and living in the neighborhood near her sister, even though the man might be some ten years her junior.

In the ordinary way, Mrs. Claypool was not a schemer or a matchmaker, but this was for her brother's happiness. She also felt it would be for Isabelle's happiness, and she was very fond of both of them. She therefore wrote her brother to call in three days' time, but if he would please allow her to continue to advise him, she would suggest that he remain circumspect in his conduct with Isabelle until he received some evidence that she would welcome a declaration from him. Mrs. Claypool thought that in three days matters might reach an appropriate boil.

There could be no doubt that this accurately described Isabelle's state of mind by the time William appeared. Though she rode out with the boys in those intervening days, and fished and sat on her rock in the stream, there was no peace to be found there for her any longer. The serenity she had recaptured by acknowledging her true feelings and her faults in regard to Adrian and her betrothal, was gone, to be replaced by an undefined restlessness. If she was riding she wanted to be sitting by the stream. Once there she became fidgety with her thoughts and longed to be on Beauty at full gallop with the wind whipping into her face making thought impossible.

She tried desperately to set her mind in order, attempting to set out some plans for her future. Very soon now I must return to Papa, she would decide, for after all I cannot impose upon Liz's hospitality forever. Besides, they would all be so much more comfortable if I were gone. The boys would not like me so well if they knew their uncle stayed away because I am here, and Liz and the squire must resent it somewhat that they are deprived of the company of a dear brother.

He must have a great disgust of me, she would think, but this thought always sent her thoughts glancing off in all directions at once. There was no coherency or order, only brief, randomly presented pictures: Mrs. Deene, her hand possessively upon William's arm, both turning surprised faces as she delivered David's message—William and Victoria riding together—William telling her he would never give up until he had seen her betrothal announced in the papers—riding in the carriage with him and Aunt Nathaniel one day in London, laughing and lighthearted— Victoria Richmond ensconced in the drawing room at Tall Oaks being respectfully addressed as "Madam" by the housekeeper—or even more dreadful, Mrs. Deene in that role!

Oh, to the devil with him, she would finally tell herself to interrupt such thoughts. Let him choose one of them and

get on with it, and let me go away and get on with my own
life. I do not care. I do not care. I do not care! She became
moody, alternating a fit of the dismals that dropped a pall
over the dinner table with a determined hectic gaiety that
deceived no one, not even the usually unnoticing squire.

"What the devil's ailing that girl?" he complained to
his wife one evening in the privacy of their bedroom.

"Oh, just youth, my love. She will come about soon, I
believe. You must not let it disturb you."

"No, I won't if you say it is all right. I know very little
about the ways of young girls, with only those four young
scamps you have presented me with." He came up behind
her where she sat before her dressing table and smiled at
her in the glass. "I should like a daughter, I think, just
like you. You are looking particularly adorable tonight,
Lizzie." He pushed her negligee from one rounded, white
shoulder and caressed it before bending to kiss it. No more
was said or thought about Isabelle Holland that night.

Mrs. Claypool did not tell Isabelle that her brother
would be calling. She feared Isabelle might deliberately
stay away from the house if she knew he was to be there to
punish him for what she deemed a falsehood. He came at
midday and was forced to kick his heels impatiently for
two hours before Isabelle came wandering into the drawing
room in search of Liz, still in Liz's old riding dress, her
hair, teased out by the wind of a full gallop, curling in
little untidy wisps about her face.

She stopped abruptly as she came face to face with him.
She stared at him as though he were an apparition, as
indeed he seemed to her. He had been so much in her
thoughts she imagined for a moment she had summoned
up a particularly solid image of him.

"Isabelle!" he said, coming toward her with outstretched
hands to take her own before she could prevent it.

No apparition, she realized then as he clasped her hands
warmly within his own. She snatched them away and
looked about with a hunted sort of expression. "I—Liz—
where is she?"

"Oh, some matter of housekeeping," he said impatiently, "but Isabelle, I—"

"Uncle Will!"

William whipped around, startled, just in time to catch David as he launched himself into his uncle's arms.

"David, for the lord's sake, where have you come from?" cried William in a strangled voice, for David had his head in a bear hug. "Let go, you young devil!"

"Uncle Will," shouted Ram as he came running in followed by his brothers. "We saw your horse in the stable . . ."

"Have you come for the ratting?" cried Oliver.

They all crowded about him, laughing and asking questions, and in the ensuing hubbub Isabelle made her escape. She hurried back out to the stable, had Beauty resaddled, and rode away with all possible speed.

She was in such a turmoil she had little awareness of where she went. She was, of course, shocked by his unexpected appearance, but uppermost was anger at—she really knew not what exactly. She could only keep thinking, how dare he! At last she slowed Beauty to a walk as they entered a copse of trees and regained some of her composure. What on earth is the matter with me, she wondered. Why did I behave in that idiotish way? Am I to be routed by that—sailor? It was only that he surprised me so, with my hair all straggling every which way and the old riding dress and everything. I should not have been so cowardly otherwise. It was really very bad of him, and then to pretend to be so happy to see me. Why should he be happy to see me when he is without doubt betrothed to Victoria by this time, apart from carrying on a flirtation with Mrs. Deene.

I shan't go down to dinner, she decided. He is bound to be asked to stay and I will not go through such an evening. I will slip into the house by the servants' entrance and ask for a tray to be sent up.

Mrs. Claypool, meanwhile, had returned from her errand to the housekeeper's room to find her brother the center of the clamorous and undivided attentions of all four of his nephews. He threw her a harassed and imploring look, but she only smiled and did not interfere. After all, her boys had missed their uncle's company through no fault of their own and deserved some time with him. Eventually they coaxed him out to the barn to look over the situation regarding their ratting expedition. He sent her a reproachful glance as he was led away and it was not much less than an hour later before he could escape and find her again to tell her of his earlier encounter with Isabelle.

"She simply disappeared in an instant and I have not set eyes on her since. Where can she have got to?"

"I cannot say, my dear, but she is bound to return for dinner. You will stay?"

"Well, of course."

By this time, Isabelle had returned as planned and was safely in her room, but though she had decided to send word she would not be down to dinner, she had not done so as yet. Instead, she had ordered up a bath and after than had asked Mrs. Claypool's abigail to help her arrange her hair. Though she had made no such conscious decision, she would go down to dinner. As she dressed, she awoke to the fact that she was acting contrary to her own resolution. But I must go down, she argued with herself in justification, it would be cowardly not to do so. Am I to be routed from the dinner table as well? I will not give him the satisfaction! With head high, she sailed down the stairs.

William stood before the fire with the squire. Mrs. Claypool sat nearby on a sofa. They all looked up with smiles as Isabelle entered, and William nearly gasped aloud in admiration, but contented himself with stepping forward and making a little bow. She nodded coldly and moved around him to seat herself beside Mrs. Claypool.

"Well, well, Isabelle," said the squire appreciatively, "you are as fine as fivepence tonight."

Isabelle flushed, furious at having attention called to the fact that she had taken more trouble than usual with her dressing tonight. She wished she had worn the old blue, but had feared William would remember it and think she had worn it to please him. Instead, she had put on a gown of white silk with short puffed sleeves in the new French mode. The low round neckline revealed a tantalizing amount of her high young bosom and the bodice ended just below, defined by a dark blue velvet ribband tied in a bow in front with long streamers nearly to the hem. The sheathlike skirt hung straight as a column, clinging to and outlining a startling but gratifying length of thigh as she moved.

William was speechless, his mouth dry, his pulses accelerated. Even though all these things were the result of the charms revealed by the dress, his first coherent thought was that she should not be wearing such a gown. He glanced covertly, jealously, at the squire, but found him smiling at his wife and relaxed. Thank heaven there were no other gentlemen here tonight, he thought, for he did not think he could bear anyone ogling her.

They went in to dinner and for a time he was able to tell himself the evening was going well. He and the squire had a great many things to discuss and Liz a great many questions about his house, and Isabelle ate and sipped her wine and nodded and smiled agreeably. Not at him, however, he noticed; even though he sat directly across the table from her, he never quite succeeded in catching her eye. He became so distracted by this after a time that he lost the thread of the conversation several times.

Isabelle was very much aware of the effect her behavior was having on him and was not at all displeased. Suddenly, almost involuntarily, during a lull in the talk, she looked directly up at him and said sweetly, "And how is Mrs. Deene keeping?"

"Mrs. Deene?" he repeated in surprise.

"Yes. Is she enjoying her visit?"

"Why—I am sure I c-could not say," he stuttered in bewilderment.

"Oh, I made sure you had seen a great deal of her. Do you tell me Mrs. Symes has not invited you to dinner?"

William turned red and looked flustered and guilty, for indeed an invitation had reached him from Mrs. Symes just this morning before he set out, but in his eagerness to get to the Grange he had only glanced at it and tossed it aside.

"William," said his sister enigmatically, "I must advise you never to take up playing at cards."

Isabelle laughed, a light tinkling sound that seemed to go through William like shards of glass. "I see that she has invited you. Now you will be able to report to us on how Mrs. Deene fares."

Taking pity on her brother, Liz rose. "Shall we leave them to their wine, my dear?" Without waiting for an answer, she left the room and Isabelle followed demurely after.

"How close it is tonight," said Liz, moving across the drawing room to throw open the long French windows onto the terrace. "Quite stifling, in fact. I think we are due some weather soon."

"That would be very tiresome. What should we all do all day?" Isabelle joined Liz at the window and as she did so a sheet of lightning spread over the horizon, lighting up the undersides of the dark heavy clouds huddled there. They moved back into the room and sat talking until the men came in to join them. Then Liz moved to the pianoforte and began to play, and the squire went to stand beside her. Presently they began to sing, their voices blending pleasantly.

Isabelle sat listening while William took a seat opposite her and glowered at her with drawn brows. He was angry with her for her insinuating remarks, and could not hide it. At last he said bluntly, "Why did you speak in that way of Mrs. Deene?"

"Oh, was I disrepectful? If so, I beg your pardon."

"Why should you beg my pardon?"

"Well, I mean that I would not like to offend you in regard to her. I could see you were quite taken by her."

"She is a pleasant woman. Sets herself out to be nice to everyone," he said stiffly.

"Not like others you know, is that what you mean?" she said with dangerous sweetness.

"Yes, it is nice not to be at swords' points with some-one," he replied sharply.

"I am sure it must be. I wish you success, I am sure, though I have no doubts at all that you will win through with very little trouble."

"What on earth are you talking about?"

The conversation, begun almost in whispers in defer-ence to the singers, had now become clearly audible to them. They glanced meaningfully at one another and rose quietly to disappear onto the terrace, closing the doors softly behind them. Neither William nor Isabelle noticed their going.

"Why I thought we were speaking of Mrs. Deene—and you."

"There can be no reason for our names to be coupled in that way."

"No? Perhaps I was wrong, but it seemed very clear to everyone that you found her company agreeable. Why, you flirted with her quite prodigiously at dinner here that night."

"I? Flirt?" he said with awful dignity, which fled as he added childishly, "and what of you with what's his name—young Poole?"

"It was quite the other way around," she said grandly.

"Not noticeably," he snapped.

She jumped to her feet. "You—you are—insufferable! You have gone out of your way to be rude to me since the day I first set foot on that dreadful boat of yours!"

He rose, his brows ruler-straight in a frown, and said, "And you seem set on proving yourself a smug, spoiled child. I fear that little has changed. I will bid you good evening."

He stalked out of the room. Liz and the squire, hearing the door slam, came in from the terrace to find Isabelle alone, the color flaming in her cheeks, her fists clenched and trembling at her sides.

"Where is William?" asked Liz.

"He—he—" Isabelle swallowed convulsively and at-tempted to speak calmly. "I believe he has decided to go home. I will go to bed now, if you will excuse me. Good night."

She fled, leaving them to follow her into the hall where the butler told them that Captain Perronet was waiting in the drive for his horse to be brought around from the stables. They went out to him. He was pacing with quick angry steps up and down the gravel drive.

"Will, dear, surely you do not mean to ride back to-night. It is so late and might come on to rain before you reach home. I saw lightning before."

There came a rumbling of thunder now to strengthen her prediction, but he only said, "Nonsense. Won't rain for hours."

"Really, old fellow, might as well stay here. Your bed is always aired and waiting," said the squire.

"Thank you, but I will go home."

"Oh Will, what has happened?" asked Liz, putting her hand upon his arm.

"Nothing. We—disagreed."

"Over Mrs. Deene?"

"Yes."

The groom appeared leading William's mount and he swung himself up into the saddle, raised his hand in farewell, and rode off.

Liz laughed softly. "What the devil are you laughing about?" demanded her husband.

"They quarreled," she said happily.

"And that amuses you," he asked in amazement.

"Oh, darling, don't you see? It was a lover's quarrel."

"Lovers? They have never seemed loverlike to me."

"No. That is why it is a good thing, this quarrel. At last they are behaving like lovers."

"What are you up to, Lizzie?" he said suspiciously. "I thought this girl was recovering from a broken heart after being jilted."

She took his arm. "Come, my love, let us walk for a bit and I will explain it all to you."

In her room, Isabelle was ready for bed, but still paced angrily up and down the room, pulling a hairbrush roughly through her hair as she went, so keyed up with rage she could not begin to think of bed.

Oh, he is cold and cruel. I should never have believed he could be so—so mean and insulting, she fumed silently. He had no right to accuse me of flirting when he could not even have noticed had I been, he was so busy making up to that—that creature! And he does not even bother to deny it, telling me that she sets herself out to be pleasing. Is he so blind he cannot see she is setting her cap for him? Of course he is. All men are. When some woman like that begins flirting with them, they think it is their own irresistible charm that causes it, not the fact that they are available and good prospects for husbands.

Oh, the wretch, the monster of self-satisfaction! They deserve each other, and I wish them well. With that, she yanked her hairbrush through a tangle so ruthlessly it brought tears of pain to her eyes and she threw the brush across the room and herself across the bed and cried.

Somewhat relieved in her feelings, she rose at last to find a handkerchief, blow her nose, and mop her cheeks. She went to the window, threw up the sash, and leaned out. The night was still and tense with the looming threat of storm, and heavy with the scent of stock and roses.

After a time she thought quite suddenly, it was my own fault, of course. I should not have provoked him so. It was stupid and childish of me. It is not my business in any case if he chooses to prefer Mrs. Deene. He is right, she is a pleasant woman, and I certainly have no quarrel with her. The tears began again and she let them flow, melancholy setting in as the aftermath of so much passion.

I have too few friends to quarrel with any of them, she thought drearily. I must find a way to apologize when he comes next time. I cannot repay Liz's friendship and hospitality with rudeness to her brother.

Fifteen

The sun rose with seeming reluctance the next morning, shouldering its way at last past the angry-looking low-lying clouds, and glittering brassily. It was not in the least a tempting day and the squire predicted rain before nightfall. Isabelle, wan and quiet after a sleepless night of see-sawing wildly from repentance for her conduct to renewed rage at William's, crumbled a piece of toast and sipped at a cup of chocolate. She brightened up somewhat when the mail was brought in and she was handed a letter from her Aunt Nathaniel. She opened it eagerly.

My dearest niece,
  I take my pen in hand again after this long while to write some news I thought it better you hear from me. I was feared you might see the announcement in the papers and have a shock. I met Lady Bromley this morning in the stores and she was ever so condescending and asked after you just as though nothing had happened. I was of two minds about even acknowledging her, but I could not bring myself to be rude. Anyway, after a time she told me her nephew was now betrothed to Lady Caroline Bray! I was that surprised, I cannot tell you. That young woman looked as smart as she could stare and I should have thought her too wary to be trapped by the likes of that scoundrel. Well, well, the ways of the Creator are mysterious. Perhaps she will make him so miserable (for you must admit there was something disagreeable about her expression, for all she

was considered a beauty) he will be repaid for his wickedness. Anyway, my darling girl, I hope by this time my news will have no effect on you. Your last to me sounded cheerful enough, I must say, and to think of you learning to ride like that! How brave you are. I suppose you see dear Captain Perronet often. I must say we all miss him here. Your papa asked me to send you his love and his regards to the captain. He—your papa, that is—is saying as how he might not go back to Continent after all, he is liking England so well. Nathaniel is trying to persuade him to take over our place in Kent. A fine big property it is, with several farms, and our manager getting on in years and wanting to retire to live with his daughter in Brighton.

Oh yes, I have another bit of news. Good news this time. It seems Mr. Tuberville brought a friend of his to visit the Richmonds, some fellow he knew up at Oxford who is already a vicar with a living someplace in Northhamptonshire, and it looks like Miss Victoria has made a conquest. Mrs. Richmond is as happy as a puppy with two tails!

I will close now, dearest child, with every fond wish for your continued good health and happiness. My regards to dear Mrs. Claypool. Do write soon to your ever loving

Aunt Nathaniel

Isabelle sat for a moment staring absently ahead of her, her mind riveted upon the one item in the letter that held any interest for her. Victoria Richmond and a vicar.

"Is everything well with Mrs. Holland?" asked Liz.

"What—oh, yes, perfectly. Perhaps you may like to read her letter." She pushed the letter across the table to Liz and rose. "I think I will join the boys now."

"Don't go too far away, my dear. Ramsleigh says it is sure to rain before the day is out."

The air had a metallic quality and even at this early hour the heat was oppressive. The boys were affected by it, bickering in a desultory way for a time and then going into fits of hysterical giggles. Neither mood fit her own, which was morose.

So it is not to be Victoria Richmond, she brooded. All

those things she hinted at in London were only her imagination. Somehow this did not cheer her in the least, for it
only seemed to point more definitely to Mrs. Deene, especially after the sentiments he expressed about her last
night. Though how he could even consider such a person—
they were not in the least suited. Around and around the
subject she went, worrying at it like a dog with a bone, in
a dreary and totally unsatisfactory way. She tried hard to
put the entire business out of her mind but it persisted. At
last she rose from the bank and told the boys she must
have a good gallop and left them. It was past midday now
and the sun shone only fitfully through great cloud masses
rolling ponderously overhead, with more and more massed
and waiting their turn behind until after a time the clouds
conquered the sky completely and hung menacingly low.

She rode on unnoticing, not even aware of the sudden
gusts of wind now rising in the rush of wind created as she
rode. Quite suddenly and without any warning, a great
finger of lightning zigzagged down from the clouds to
touch a tree near the path where she rode. Beauty reared
back, screaming in terror, and turning, bolted off into the
trees.

Isabelle cried out and sawed frantically at the reins, but
Beauty had the bit in her teeth now and did not respond.
Isabelle bent low over her neck to avoid low branches, but
her hat was carried away by one, and then their continual
clawing at her hair caused it to tumble loose from its knot
and stream out behind her.

Great fat drops of rain pattered through the leaves,
slowly at first and then faster and heavier, gradually soak-
ing her riding dress. But the rain seemed to have a calming
effect on Beauty, whose pace slowed the least bit. Isabelle
unwisely raised her head to look about and a sharp crack
on the forehead knocked her senseless. She fell abruptly
out of the saddle and lay inert. Beauty went on a short way
but soon stopped and came ambling back. She nosed at the
body, then turned aside and began to crop at the grass
beneath the trees.

William's night and morning had been no more pleasant

than Isabelle's. He had slept little and risen to brood about the house, feeling cross and out of sorts. He had no idea how it was possible he could have actually quarreled with Isabelle, much less what they had been quarreling about really. He had not dreamed it was possible that he could ever say such unkind things to her, but she had goaded him into it in some way. How could she have said such things? What sort of bee had she in her bonnet about that confounded Deene woman? What the devil was she to do with anything?

He found Mrs. Symes's invitation to dine where he had carelessly tossed it the day before and read it again. He swore, crushing it in his hand. Now what was he to do about this? It was for tomorrow and it was rude of him not to have responded at once, but he felt he would rather do anything in the world than go. He sat down at last and dashed off a reply, saying he regretted that he was already engaged to dine with his sister, which was not quite a lie, for he certainly intended to dine there no matter what.

The oppressive weather set his nerves on edge and by midday he could no longer bear inaction. He strode off to the stables and ordered his horse saddled. I will go and apologize, he decided, and force her to talk to me. I will tell her again that I love her and she must give me a hearing at least.

He took note of the lowering clouds and suddenly felt a sense of unease and urgency. He dug in his heels and urged the horse on faster and faster. When he reached the Grange, it began to rain. He rode directly to the stables, where he found the boys just returned, in extremely high spirits after their race with the rain.

"Where is Miss Holland, Ram?" William asked, looking about.

"Oh, she will be with Mama by now. She left us an hour ago."

"Come on, then. Lets make a run for the house."

Once there, however, it took some time to establish that Isabelle was not there. Servants were scurrying about under Liz's direction, closing windows against the rain, and when William could finally claim her attention she looked at him distractedly.

"Isabelle? Why—she must be about someplace."

"Will you send someone to find her? I wish to speak to her," he said determinedly.

"Oh really, Will, do you not think—"

"No. I do not. I must do this my own way now, Liz."

Liz knew there was no point in debate at this juncture and sent a passing maid to Isabelle's room with the request that she step downstairs.

"Goodness, how it pours. But I suppose we could not expect the fine weather to go on forever," sighed Liz as she watched from a window. The maid returned to announce, "Miss is not in her room, madam."

"Well, look about, she must be here someplace," said Liz impatiently.

A more thorough search was in progress when the squire came in soaked and dripping.

"Ramsleigh!" shrieked his wife. "The floors!"

"Shall I wait outside, my dear?" he said pointedly.

She laughed. "No, of course not. Come along upstairs, darling, and let me help you out of those clothes before you catch your death."

As they went upstairs, he squelching and leaving a trail of water, William called out, "But what of Isabelle? Have you seen her, Ramsleigh?"

The squire turned. "Gone missing has she? Was she out in this?"

"She was certainly out earlier," said Liz.

"Then check the stables. See if her horse is back," said the squire, and turned to continue upstairs.

William stared for a moment, wondering why he had not thought of this sensible suggestion, then turned abruptly and rushed back into the rain. Beauty, of course, was not there when he reached the stables and he ran back to the house.

"Liz," he shouted from the hall. "Liz!"

"What on earth . . ." she called, leaning over the bannister above him.

"Her horse is not there," he announced.

"Oh, for heaven's sakes, Will, she is probably taking shelter from the rain somewhere. Here, Mrs Travers," she said as the housekeeper appeared in the hall below, "is Miss Holland in the house?"

"No, madam. Every room has been searched."

"Dear God," rasped William harshly.

"Now do not make a fuss, Will, she . . ." Liz began, but he didn't stay to hear her out. He dashed back to the stables, had one of the squire's horses saddled, and rode out. The rain beat down upon him as he turned this way and then that, searching for some sign of her passage. For what seemed frantic, endless eons of time his search was fruitless. He checked the stream bank where he knew the boys fished and rode up and down the stream finding no signs. Then he found a ride through the trees and followed that.

He peered from side to side through the sheets of rain as best he could as he galloped along, but finally became discouraged and decided he was wasting his time here. He pulled up and turned about, and it was then he saw a little way into the trees a broken branch and just beyond it another. He followed along and found another and his heart began to pound. She must have come this way.

Then he saw ahead a crumpled heap and recognized her by the long blond hair spread over the ground. He shouted and leaped from his horse while it was still in motion.

"Isabelle—dear God—Isabelle!" he cried, running forward to kneel beside her. She is dead, he thought in despair. He turned her over and stared horrified at the bloody gash across her forehead, the still, white face. Fearfully, he reached out and touched her neck just below the jaw and nearly sobbed aloud when he found a pulse weakly beating there. Tenderly, he lifted her and carried her to his horse. He stood helplessly for a moment, wondering how he was to get them both mounted. He disliked the idea of heaving her across like a bag of oats and leading the horse back. It would be so slow and take far too long for Isabelle. She needed attention immediately.

At last he laid her gently across the horse just in front of
the saddle, her head and legs dangling, then heaved himself into the saddle and lifted her again, turning her into
his arms to cradle against his chest. He clucked the horse
into motion, much too slow while they were in the trees.
In a moment he heard a whinny and turning saw Beauty
following docilely along behind.

Once out of the trees, he urged the horse into a brisker
pace and was soon trotting up the drive of the Grange. He
shouted as he approached the front door and continued to
shout until the door flew open and an astonished butler
came out a few steps. When he saw it was the captain
carrying young Miss, he turned back, calling out to the
maid to fetch the master and mistress at once, then hurried
down the steps to take the limp form the captain lowered
into his arms. He turned with his burden at once, but
before he had even reached the steps, William was beside
him.

"Here, I will take her now," he said harshly, taking
Isabelle from him. "Get someone to see to the horses."

Liz came flying down the stairs, Ramsleigh behind her,
just as William entered the hall. "Good God." she cried.
"What has happened? Is she—is she—"

"She is unconscious—where . . . ?"

"Straight up to her room, Will. I must get those wet
clothes off her at once. Ramsleigh, send someone for the
doctor on your fastest horse. Mrs. Travers, send up hot
water to clean the wound. And hot bricks. As many as
possible."

Thus deploying her forces as she went, she led William
into Isabelle's room and directed him to put her on the
chaise longue. Her abigail came hurrying into the room
and began at once to pull off Isabelle's boots while Liz
began on the buttons of her riding dress. William hovered
until she became aware of his presence.

"Go away, Will. You cannot remain here."

"But I—"

"Go away at once!" she ordered in a tone that brooked
no arguments. He left reluctantly to hover in the hall

outside, worrying the maids and Mrs. Travers as they bustled in and out of the room with pitchers of steaming water and hot bricks wrapped in flannel. They took little notice of him.

Inside, Isabelle was stripped and dried while Liz bathed the wound, which turned out to be not nearly so devastating as it looked. She was put into a bedgown and Liz and Mrs. Travers carried her to the waiting bed between them. Hot bricks were placed all about her.

"Will you not use the smelling salts, madam?" asked Mrs. Travers.

"No—no, I think it is best to do nothing until the doctor has seen her. A head injury—well, I think it is best to wait. You go down and wait at the door for him and show him up at once."

Mrs. Travers left the room and was immediately confronted by William. "What is happening? How is she?" he demanded desperately.

"She is the same, captain. We have put her to bed."

"Has she spoken?"

"No, sir," she said, and hurried away.

William turned and tapped softly at the door and in a moment Liz opened it to peer out at him.

"I must see her," he said urgently.

"Will, do go downstairs. There is nothing you can do now. She is still unconscious."

"I said I must see her, Liz, and I mean to," he said firmly, pushing past her into the room. He approached the bed and stood looking down at the still, dreadfully pale face with the red weal across the forehead. He did not speak, dared not even ask any of the questions he had prepared. At last he simply turned and left the room.

Liz followed him into the hall. "Will, dearest, she will be all right. Go and change out of those wet clothes before you take a chill and we have two invalids. Then go down and tell Ramsleigh to give you a brandy."

He plodded away down the hall to the room always kept ready for him and where he kept some clothes, still without speaking. Liz returned to the room to sit beside the bed until the doctor arrived. She was more worried than she would admit by Isabelle's continued unconsciousness. What should they do if the girl died? How could she ever face Mrs. Holland with such news? Worse still, what would become of Will?

She heard a soft sigh and saw Isabelle's eyelids flutter open briefly then close again. "Isabelle—Isabelle," breathed Liz thankfully.

"What—what . . . ?"

"You had a fall, dear, while you were out riding."

"Beauty . . . ?"

"She is safe and dry in the stables."

Isabelle said no more and seemed to lose consciousness again. Liz hurried to the door to send someone with the good news to Will and found herself face to face with him, still waiting there obstinately, though he had changed his clothes.

"Oh, Will," she cried, "she is all right! She spoke to me!"

He started forward eagerly. "No, no, dearest, she is—sleeping now, I think, you must—"

He only pushed past her into the room. He bent over the bed and studied Isabelle's face for a long moment. It seemed to him she was less lividly white than before. She even seemed to be smiling! He touched her cheek with one gentle finger, then turned and left the room. This time he did go downstairs. He could do with a brandy now.

Presently the doctor came and was taken up. He examined the wound and bandaged it, counted her pulse, and listened to her heart. Then from his pocket he took some smelling salts and waved them under her nose. Again the eyelids fluttered and she turned her head away from the stinging scent in her nose.

"There we are, miss. Feeling a bit groggy, I'll wager," he said encouragingly. She blinked hazily at him. "What is your name, child?"

"Isabelle—Holland," she said slowly.

"Do you know where you are?"

"My room—the Grange."

"You'll do," he declared. "She will be right as a trivet in no time, Mrs. Claypool. Bed for a few days, plenty of beef tea, and a glass of port at midday."

He went briskly away to take a glass of the squire's excellent brandy to fortify himself before the ride home.

Liz blew out all the candles but one, tucked the bedclothes securely around Isabelle, and bent to kiss her cheek. Poor darling, already asleep, she thought tenderly, and went out of the room. Mrs. Travers waited outside.

"Will she be wanting anything, madam?"

"I think not. She is asleep. If you would stay with her for the time, Mrs. Travers, in case she wakes. I will come up again presently." Liz then went downstairs to relieve her feelings by a good cry on her husband's shoulder.

Isabelle was not quite asleep, but she had no inclination to open her eyes. She was remembering a dream she had just had. She lay cradled in a man's arms, rocked by the motion of a horse, with rain falling in her face. The man was saying over and over in a soft crooning voice, "Isabelle, my darling, beloved Isabelle. It will be all right. You must be all right. Dearest, dearest girl, we'll soon be there." As she had sunk back into blackness the words followed her, finally echoing into nothingness.

Now, remembering them, her lips curled slightly at the corners as she tried to smile. She gave way to weariness again and as she sank gratefully into sleep, the words went with her.

She woke with a headache to find Liz beside her. "Liz."

"Yes, darling. I am here. How do you feel this morning?"

"I have the headache."

"I have no doubt you do," said Liz with a little laugh.

"What happened?"

"You fell, or were thrown from your horse."

"Oh." About five minutes later she said, "I think I remember now. It was the lightning. Beauty bolted into the trees. A branch struck me." She lifted a hand to her head and felt the bandage.

"It is a very slight cut, dear, nothing that will leave a scar," said Liz hastily.

"How did I—get home?"

"Will found you. He had come here just as the storm broke and when we could not find you, he rode out to search for you."

"Oh."

"I have some broth keeping hot for you. Will you be able to take some now? It would help your headache, I believe."

Isabelle agreed to try, and Liz raised her against the pillows, fetched the broth from a hob in the fireplace, and fed it to her slowly, a spoonful at a time. After it was gone, she brought a brush and began to gently tease the tangles from Isabelle's hair. When it lay shining over her shoulders, Liz pulled up the covers.

"Now, you are to sleep again and no more talking."

Isabelle's eyes were already closing and she slept again. When she woke she knew it was midday by the way the sun slanted into the room. Liz was there again with a glass of port.

"Doctor's orders, my dear. Just drink it down slowly and you shall have some more broth and perhaps a bit of toast."

When she had eaten, had her bed gown changed, and various other necessities attended to, Liz said, "Does your head still ache?"

"Only the least bit. Nothing to speak of really."

"Do you feel sleepy again?"

"Not very."

"Then, my dear, if you feel up to it, could you bear to see William for a moment? I fear if I do not allow him in soon, he will break the door down," she added laughing.

"Yes, yes—I—I must thank him."

Liz laughed again and crossed to admit her brother. He came in quickly, his eyes fixed upon Isabelle's face. She put out her hand to him and he took it in both his own.

"Liz says you found me and brought me home. I—I thank you very much."

He sat down in the chair Liz had left, not relinquishing

her hand. "Isabelle . . ." he began, but then seemed unable to find any further words to say.

They sat in silence for a moment before she shyly looked away from the intensity of his gaze. "It was raining most dreadfully," she said at last to break the silence. "You must have been soaked. I hope you will take no ill effects from it."

He brushed this aside as of no consequence and tightened his hold on her hand. She knew she should remove it, but it was so comforting, his hands were so warm. "Isabelle," he said at last, "are you all right now?"

"Only my head hurts a bit where it was struck, but not dreadfully as it did this morning."

"May I—oh, Isabelle, I must speak to you. I must tell you . . ." He stopped again.

"Yes?" she prompted.

"Dearest—dearest Isabelle," he began. They did not notice Liz leaving the room and closing the door softly behind her. "I hope I do not—I hope what I say will not be harmful to you in your condition, but I cannot bear to keep silent any longer."

"Then you must speak, by all means."

"I love you, Isabelle, as you must know. I have tried to be patient and give you time, as Liz said I must, but I cannot bear this quarreling between us. If you do not love me, I will wait and hope that you will change, but I cannot allow another day to pass without telling you my own feelings. When I found you out there and thought you dead, I cursed myself for not having spoken to you. I knew then this was all foolishness. I am not cut out for playing such games." She turned her head away and he said despairingly, "Is it no, then? No matter, do not turn away from me even so."

"I am not—not—a very worthy person for you, William," she whispered, still turned away.

"Not worthy? What do you mean? For God's sake, look at me, Isabelle, and tell me what you mean."

Slowly, she turned to face him. "I truly thought I loved him, William. It was not the title or—or anything. And once having given my heart, could I go back on my word when I learned—learned—I had made a mistake?''

"No—no, I suppose not, but—"

"I was ashamed to admit that I could have been so wrong in my judgment—so stupid. I should have told him I could not—go on with it, but I—oh it was so—"

"Isabelle, you were a young, inexperienced girl—" he began.

"Yes, I suppose that is just what I was, but I prided myself on not being that. I was so vain about it, thinking myself superior, so level-headed and shrewd. I thought I could plan my future in a most practical way and then allowed my head to be turned by the first handsome fortune hunter to cross my path, like some green girl from the country."

"It does not matter in the least now, my darling," he said with a tender smile.

But she had not finished her self-castigation and went on unheeding. She felt she must admit all her faults. "Then when I—when he learned I was not wealthy at all—he—he—oh, if only I had been honest, I could have saved myself from all the humiliation! I felt only that, William, do you see? I was not pining away with heartbreak, but because my pride had been hurt."

"Dearest, I do not care for all that if only you love me."

"But I am vain and proud and stupid and—"

". . . and beautiful and lovable and altogether adorably human," he finished. "Now I know the worst and am warned."

"Not the worst—there is more. I have also been . . ." Again she turned her head away.

"What, love?"

"Jealous," she whispered, "of—of Mrs. Deene and—even before that—of Victoria Richmond."

"But—but why should you . . ."

"I thought you . . ."

He sat in silence for a moment while the true implications of her words were borne in upon him. "Isabelle, look at me," he commanded, taking her chin and turning her face back to him. "Do you mean to say that even then, back in London, you—you cared enough for me to be jealous of Victoria Richmond?"

"I only realized it today—yesterday. I think I really knew before, but I was too ashamed to admit it to myself. It seemed so fickle, so light-minded, so—so—girlish! Not in the least the way I had always thought myself."

"Oh, dear heaven," he shouted, "you darling idiot! To have put me through all this misery—all these weeks. To have wasted all this time we could have had together."

"Yes, I know it is very bad of me. I told you I was not worthy," she said.

He moved to sit beside her on the bed and leaned over her. "Say it."

"Oh, William, I—"

"Say it, Isabelle," he repeated inexorably.

"I—love you, William," she whispered.

"Then I forgive you for the silly goose you have been," he declared, grinning down at her. They stared blissfully into each other's eyes until she said, somewhat complainingly, "Well, are you not ever going to kiss me, William?"

Her lips were still warm from the imprint of his kiss, but now Silvia knew there was nothing to protect her from the terror of Serpent Tree Hall. Not even love. Especially not love. . . .

DARK SPLENDOR

ANDREA PARNELL

Lovely young Silvia Bradstreet had come from London to Colonial America to be a bondservant on an isolated island estate off the Georgia coast. But a far different fate awaited her at the castle-like manor: a man whose lips moved like a hot flame over her flesh . . . whose relentless passion and incredible strength aroused feelings she could not control. And as a whirlpool of intrigue and violence sucked her into the depths of evil . . . flames of desire melted all her power to resist. . . .

Coming in September from Signet!